the only good thing
anyone has ever done

sandra newman

# the only good thing anyone has ever done

HarperCollins*Publishers*

HarperCollins books may be purchased for educational, business, or sales promotional use. For information, please write: Special Markets Department, HarperCollins Publishers Inc., 10 East 53rd Street, New York, NY 10022.

First published in Great Britain in 2002 by Chatto and Windus.

FIRST AMERICAN EDITION

*Designed by Sandra Newman and Peter Ward*

Printed on acid-free paper

Library of Congress Cataloging-in-Publication Data

Newman, Sandra
The only good thing anyone has ever done / Sandra Newman.—
1st American ed.
p. cm.
ISBN 0-06-051498-1
1. Inheritance and succession—Fiction. 2. Swindlers and swindling—Fiction.
3. Identity (Psychology)—Fiction. 4. Brothers and sisters—Fiction. 5. Adopted persons—Fiction. 6. Young women—Fiction. 7. California—Fiction. I. Title.

PS3614.E66 O5 2003
813'.6—dc21                    2002038737

03  04  05  06  07  WB/RRD  10  9  8  7  6  5  4  3  2  1

To Jeff

the only good thing
anyone has ever done

# "This Isn't My House and You Aren't My Parents"

★ ★ ★

1 My name is Chrysalis Moffat.

1.1 I was born in Peru.

1.2 When I was three, I was brought to the United States.

1.3 Here I was adopted by rich white people.

1.4 Insofar as that is possible, I became just like them.

2 I am brown, and my face looks like a South American mask because my parents were South American Indians.

2.1 My body, too, is foreshortened, plump; next to Anglos, I look rudimentary.

2.2 PC people make a point of saying I'm beautiful, even to my face.

3 Although I am so brown, I give an impression of whiteness.

3.1 People often remember me wearing white clothes when I was not wearing white clothes.

3.2 They also think my surname is White.

3.3 It's a supernatural phenomenon, I think.

4 My father gave me the name, Chrysalis.

4.1 He was a biochemist.

# Discuss

No one in my family is interesting or praiseworthy; only my father. Born in rural poverty to alcoholic parents, he worked his way through Berkeley, received his PhD and was expected to have a brilliant research career in microbiology. Instead of pursuing it, however, he volunteered for Vietnam. My father fought in Vietnam for four years.

Although he would refer to the evils of that war, this was more polite, I believe, than sincere. Nor did he seem – though this must surely have been the case – to have fallen in love with jungles, technicolor murder, freewheelingness – to love the smell of napalm in the morning. In all he did, he was rather the simple, honest man. He was, pre-eminently, a man who loved dogs.

He got down on the floor and rolled with dogs; he swung children around and around by the hands, playing "airplane." Mom and Dad were always laughing behind their bedroom door, when we were very small.

You got the sense that, when all else failed and the world had weakened utterly, succumbing to corruption and mean-spirited trivia, still there would be Father, taller than everyone else and irreducibly blond.

He looked like John Wayne.

5   On the drive to my Uncle Jerry's, we used to pass my father's work.
5.1   It was called BSI: Something Something Institute.
5.2   It had a chicken-wire fence and a checkpoint hut with an orange barrier.
5.3   No buildings were visible from the road, only set-piece maples.
5.4   Eddie and I would try to get the guard to wave.
5.5   Mom would sing out; "Hello, Bull Shit Incorporated!"

6   Early on, we realized there was something about Dad's work.
6.1   He was always going to Chile or Guatemala, conducting studies.
6.2   We couldn't know what he studied; that was a state secret.
6.3   The date of his return was likewise secret.
6.4   Where in Chile too.

# FATHER: ELEMENTARY

A soldierly, upright:
he strode, and grinned, and gave
manly firm handshakes.
A is for Astronaut, like them,
like many Army men, he was
B permanently boyish,
brash, bluff, broad-shouldered
like a B-movie hero.
Or,
just,
BIG.
Moving on to
C he was a cowboy.
A cracker born in Cody, Texas.
"Howdy, podner, I'm headin' out t'the corral," he'd go,
corny for us kids.
We'd cackle,
cry, capsize
curl up with glee
because he was never there.
Conspicuous by his absence.
"Comin' home real soon, chicken –"
D Now he's dead.

But these big heads that watch over our childish night
skies, a nightlight left on to the end of time in a darkened
bedroom;
indecipherable and throbbing
nauseous
headachey
with its lolling top-heavy heap of cheap significance.

# AT THE DINNER TABLE: 1977

Dad looks like John Wayne. He has grown his hair out of its familiar crewcut and dyed it black to stop the women in Peru asking him for autographs. People in Peru don't know John Wayne is old. Those movies are all brand new there.

Mom is laughing and laughing. Dad sits up with his hands folded. I think he looks very fair, like when Eddie and I fight and Dad makes us sit down in "court" and come to a "settlement." Next to me, Eddie is making faces because we haven't had dessert yet and he knows there's chocolate chip ice cream.

"I'd kill to have been there," Mom crows, "the ladies in their ponchos mobbing the shady operative – Señor Wayne! Señor Wayne!" Then she does my father, talking into his wristwatch; "Operation Kookamunga, abort!"

"Lannie," says Dad, "I am not a shady operative."

"Señor Wayne! I see all jour movies!"

"Lannie. Nobody's laughing."

"Laughing? It's an effing laugh riot!"

Mom starts coughing and finally looks in her lap, distracted. Eddie pipes up:

"Mom? Are we having ice cream? I can get it, I can reach."

"Just one minute, Eddie, honestly."

And cause it's the dinner table, Mom has her tequila glass to hand, to grab to her mouth and her head bucks

chucks it down hard

two-handed, one

palm spread over the glass bottom to shove the liquor home

and hold the dry glass for a moment, leaving it time to shine and be seen:

# — 2 —

## "This Isn't My House and You're Not My Children"

### ★ ★ ★

1    My mother was an art historian.
1.1  That's what she put on forms.
1.2  And she held a Master's in art history from Berkeley.

2    Really she was just rich.

3    It was family money.
3.1  Her father had made a killing in real estate.
3.2  Pictures of his suburban developments hung in the dining room when she was a child.
3.3  My mother used to think he built the houses himself.

4    Her family were rich people all day long.
4.1  They held their children as if they were vases; the dog was groomed by a company.
4.2  Salad fork for salad, full dress for breakfast.
4.3  They were, in these respects, profoundly, paranoiacally, arriviste.

5    My mother was just, common.
   • She was never persuaded to like shoes.
   • Her knees were skinned, somehow. From her clothes, you knew she had a dog.
   • She always looked as if she had just washed her face.

6    Girls who wore makeup were weak, according to my mother.

# STORY

When she turned eighteen, my mother's birthday present was a mansion. It was strategically chosen for its location on a dull stretch of California coast. Her father thought the town to be ripe for development. A gift, then, bought in my mother's name for tax reasons.

"But I can't even <u>live</u> in it," my mother squalled. "I'm going to college, <u>remember</u>?"

"It's an <u>investment</u>," said her father. "For your <u>future</u>."

They had the hackneyed screaming match, in which father laid down the law and daughter wept; mother fretted, saying patient reasonable things.

Around them were the beautiful acquisitions – like a jury. High ceilings and marble and even the placid air with its scent of autumnal roses; my mother fought bitterly, at that age, against their sway.

"I'm going to burn it down!" she screamed finally. "I'll invite you all over and burn it down!"

Her parents died in a car accident one year later.

She lived in that mansion for the rest of her life; Eddie and I grew up in it.

Her mother, Lily, who really was like a white funereal flower, and trembled, used to say that tomboys grew up to be the nicest big ladies.

Her father used to say, "Lannie's going to blow everything we've worked to save, you wait and see!"

1    After her parents' death, she moved into her mansion.

1.1  No one else lived there; there was no gardener, no maid. There was no furniture.

1.2  The derelict guest wing leaked, and moss grew, demarcating the parquet.

1.3  It was 35 rooms, two towers, a private beach, and a cultivated wood.

1.4  In the wood, she found a pointy-eared white mutt she called Remember.

1.5  They used to sleep together on the beach on summer nights.

2    Her brother Jerry got away with the bulk of the family fortune.

2.1  She hated him, she called him "King Jerry," she was implacable.

2.2  There were court cases all her life; she never forgot that money.

2.3  The rest of the family backed him because my mother rode a motorcycle.

2.4  She never forgave them either, though she attended polite family gatherings.

3    When she was at Berkeley, she rode two hours to get to class.

3.1  She was penniless.

3.2  She sold all the mansion's antique doors.

3.3  She had three million dollars tied up in a lawsuit, but wouldn't borrow in case the bank "stole" her house.

3.4  When the money came through, she bought three cars.

4    Her mattress on the floor was surrounded by cigarette butts.

4.1 She'd taped cardboard over the broken windows on the ground floor.

4.2 In the courtyard lawn, one of her boyfriends had dug his name.

4.3 "It brought tears to your eyes," my dad said, "Lannie was such a slob."

For a while, he was only one of many rotating boyfriends. Then he put his foot down. He turned up at her house one weekend, wearing a suit, to say, "Okay, Lannie. Now we're going to buy furniture and then you're going to marry me. I had about enough of this runaround."

He was standing on her cracked white step, in sunlight, bearing a sheaf of flowers. The engagement ring was hooked on the first joint of his pinky; a diamond solitaire she wouldn't like. His stance was easy, friendly. They knew each other well; and he wanted, badly, to put the flowers down and touch her face.

She said, "No!"
But he was right.
Then he was in Vietnam.
Then he was in Chile at a secret destination, conducting studies.
For the rest of her life, my mother always had a mutt who would follow her down, down our private beach and out of sight, on summer nights.

# BEGIN AGAIN

1   When my parents married, they were both 21.

1.1   They
   • smoked marijuana
   • drank
   • rode her motorbike down to Baja

1.2   When there was no party on the weekend, they threw one.

1.3   Wet hair; sun-tender skin; sand in the toe of a canvas shoe.

2   No one had seen anyone so much in love.

2.1   They had inside jokes. She rode him piggyback to bed.

2.2   Dad once broke a man's nose for calling her a slut.

3   He was doing his doctoral work.

4   She bought art and sold it to friends of the family.

5   There was always money; there were always friends; there were pre-booked tickets and dinner reservations.

5.1   "There was a little place with a patio where we used to have breakfast. I don't think I cared then if the whole world exploded."

5.2   "People were different then. You did what was expected of you, even if it was no fun. You didn't try to run the world."

*Mother sat beside the pool and Father swam. We were not yet born, and Mother sat in her wet bikini bottoms on the concrete, and green light swam in tiger stripes in mimicry of the tiger stripes that swam down Father's back in muscles as he swam;*

*it is water but it all comes to a point like the last note of a perfect rock anthem and*

*here you are kneeling on wet concrete with both hands thrust*
*down into the water as if you could catch something*
    *he goes off to his copters and jungles*
    *Sergeant Doctor Jonathan Moffat*
    *Jack, baby*
    *She used to call him John Wayne*
    *Sometimes when she gets into the car in the sun, for the minute*
*while she waits for the plastic's heat to mellow, she slackens and*
*breathes on a sudden note of sexual excitement, shuts her eyes*
*surprised*
    *and smiles*
    *as if she's pulling out of a supermarket parking lot in Canada*
    *as if he's really here*

Your head is bigger than my head
Your arms are bigger than my legs
Your hands are bigger than my breasts
You
got right
through me
man, so I
lost so much weight
I was so
    I don't know *(She put her knuckles to her mouth, she put*
*the phone receiver to her lips, the cold plastic and its holes*
    *a nozzle*
    *nuzzle the nozzle and*
    *cry*
    *baby*
    *Are you ever really coming home*


My father used to say, if he'd had any sense, he would
have stayed and protested against the war. We had no concept

what hell guys went through there. War is about death, he would say, always remember that. Death.

He liked to say these things because he was a decorated veteran. He said them at dinner to people who had not been to war.

"It's not something to envy," said my father. "Not at all."

He said when we were grown up, there would never be any wars again. That's what he was working for, and with God's help, they'd get it licked.

The manner of his death was a state secret. No personnel attended his funeral, and Mom was advised not to advertise it in the paper. They buried an empty coffin. We saw Mom in a dress for the first time.

After that, often in the mornings we would find an uneven trench dug in the sand of our private beach. Mother had been out there pacing, and drinking, all night. Although it wasn't his job, the gardener used to go down and clear the butts from this trench. He would even seem to try to fill it in again, shovelling with his boot tips. At such times, he looked sad in a private, Hispanic way, as if he realized that grief was something in the earth and it was vast and it would outlast him. As if Mexicans can cope with these things, are heavy enough and wise, although I know that's stupid.

# "You Can't Go Home Again And Chew Gum At The Same Time If You Won't Listen To Me"

★ ★ ★

1  My mother died of complications following liposuction surgery.

1.1  A mild heart attack; pneumonia; septicemia.

1.2  Long-term alcoholism was the root cause.

2  For a while, it seemed that charges would be brought against the surgeon, who was clearly negligent.

2.1  But I had to bring them, and I was, at that time, living under my bed.

3  I had a mental illness.

3.1  I visited psychiatrists and took medication.

3.2  At first, the diagnosis was endogenous depression, meaning one that is just in my nature.

3.3  With time, I was changed to a personality disorder.

3.4  Mine is a "vulnerable personality," also termed "inadequate."

4  The nitty-gritty of the complaint was, dread.

4.1  Everything I noticed hurt: the act of perception was like walking on a broken leg.

4.2  If a lame bug struggled in the pool, that was me all over.

4.3  Eating beer nuts was a mistake that could never be rectified.

- People didn't like me.
- I couldn't stop thinking.
- Furniture brought back memories.
- I felt best under my bed.

5  I came out for the funeral, invigorated by just plain sorrow.

5.1 I notified potential mourners, signed documents, signed checks.

5.2 Because she had nothing suitable, I lent Mom the dress in which she was cremated.

5.3 Everyone remarked on my good sense.


## 6. CONCRETE DETAIL

The dress was a blue velvet strapless with a zipper up the back. I'd only worn it once, to my Uncle Jerry's fiftieth, held on the rooftop restaurant of some hotel. Because it was white-tie-and-tails, my mother wouldn't go to that party. She said she could wear a bathing suit to the bank, for Christ's sake, and King Jerry could kiss her ass.

On me, the dress swept the floor, on Mom it was calf-length: we were similar in girth but she much longer. I cut off the ribbon as being too festive. After some soul-searching, I neglected to have it dry-cleaned.

I helped to dress her, at my own insistence. People love each other in flesh and blood – my then conviction. I told the funeral people: she is my flesh and blood.

They gave her to us in the hospital gown, fastened with a sloppy bow over no underwear. I'd never seen Mom naked before, and I kept thinking, this is what I'll look like when I'm fifty – even though my mother and I are not related, not the same race, and I was then going bald from eating nothing but Wonder Bread. I thought it over and over.

At the same time the lipoed thigh like a butchered seal. Curly peacock blue stitches sprouted from brackish gouges. Even when she was alive, it stank.

Mom looked wide-awake and pitifully frightened. Her

fingernails were bitten down to the quick. I kept wanting to take her hand and swear I wouldn't let them burn her.

I cried and cried. Whatever I thought, I cried. My mother's friend Marta, who was helping me, kept saying, "Let's just get this over with. Please, let's just get this over with."

I wouldn't go in for the cremation. I waited outside in the car with my ex-boyfriend Stewart. It was a big station wagon which smelled of dogs. We listened to a call-in radio show about garbage disposal, and Stewart smoked. I wanted to smoke, but couldn't, I was too anorexic. Smoking gave me the dry heaves.

On the radio show, they were discussing the comparative environmental effects of garbage incineration and landfill. Stew kept trying to catch my eye but I didn't feel like laughing at anything that afternoon.

While we waited, a flight of Canada geese went by, very high up in their imperfect V. I kept hoping someone would shoot one down but of course they just flew away. Then Marta was knocking on the car window with the jar in her hand. When I rolled the window down, she said, "Here's your mother."

The jar had the manufacturer's name stamped in the bottom. I gave it to Stewart and made him promise to throw it away. It's now in his cellar with his fishing tackle.

He told me he opened it once, and the zipper from my dress was still there, curled among the ashes. "It scared the shit out of me," he said. "I thought it was her spine."

7    So that's how it was when my mother was obliterated.
8    Leaving all her worldly goods to my brother Eddie.
9    Who was on a drinking spree: for a long time he could
     not be found.

## Initiating Event: "The Phone Rings"

It's 3:00 A.M., two weeks after the cremation. I'm lying on the floor of my mother's bedroom, clutching a stuffed rabbit. I'm still in the black linen dress I wore to the funeral. I have taken showers since, but with the black dress on. To dry, I sit in the bathroom on a towel for as long as it takes. I have all the free time in the world.

My nose is hot pink and my face chapped. There's crust in my eyes and, on my lips, scabs.

The bedroom is white and high-ceilinged. It's densely hung with contemporary art. There are up to three rows of frames on each wall, starting at knee level. Because my mother's oldest friend is a painter who works in No. 2 pencil, there's a lot of gray, and torn, grubby paper. Words are conspicuous:

SHIT VALENTINE

*bawl*

"MYSTERY MEAT"

My favorite piece is drawn with the gilt paper stars doled out in primary schools as congratulations. On unpainted canvas, they cluster and bulge, straying from the No. 2 pencil paths of constellations. Some stars are only half stuck, with their legs curling. Some obscenely mount their fellows. It's nasty, and it's genius; and when I think about it, I'm not in pain. I've been staring at the stars all day and night, this particular night.

and for two weeks long, I've been praying to my mother –

and to God to please kill me instead –

Mom can come back and burn me, in the same dress –

but Mom was an electrical charge in a hundred pounds of meat –

which never ever believed in God –

And I've thrown her clothes out on the lawn; and sketched dead families on the walls; and spent an hour carrying all the food in the kitchen to my room, where I've put it in a duffel bag, awaiting my decision on how to offer it in sacrifice –

and crying. That stuff. No point going into detail.

Two weeks of this. Lying on the braided Colonial rug, Mom's bedroom. Stuffed rabbit, ears damp from chewing.

3:00 A.M.

The phone rings.

I crawled to the answerphone, and when I heard Eddie's voice, I picked up hastily.

"Hello! Hello?"

"Oh! Yeah . . . Chrysa?"

"Is it Eddie?"

"I guess so. Isn't *that* fucking depressing."

Then right off Eddie told me his scheme to turn our home into an institute for spiritual development.

"You just need the premises, and we've got premises in spades. In. Spades. And then you, what, you could be channeling Moses with a garden hose. These assholes are desperate. Yeah, like cancer victims. Heal yourself through spiritual hose treatment, Moses of Sinai said 'It made my teeth whiter in just six weeks!' Oh no, it's the peppermint schnapps talking.

"I've got the guru already, you gotta love this guy. Can't not love. We're talking, people coming in their thousands, with their fucking thousands. Of thousands of dollars. I'm totally serious here, so just save the remarks, this is *happening.*"

"*Eddie.* Did you hear about Mom?"

"Yeah," he said and shut up.

Five minutes passed.

It was weird because he couldn't see me, all sticky with my pitiful rabbit. It made me tongue-tied, so I just listened to the fuzz on the line getting louder and softer; the traffic in the background. You could hear he was in a phone booth.

At last he added, "Sorry, I'm a little down tonight."

"It's . . . it's good to hear your voice." I hiccuped and pinched the rabbit hard. "Really."

"So what did I get? I mean, sorry I'm such a pig, but you know I never had the normal feelings a son blah blah for a mother. I thought when she died, I got all excited, I was sitting there with the Fed Ex, NOW I'm gonna get the feelings! Roll on, normal feelings! But nothing happened so I throw up my hands. I'm <u>fucked</u>. <u>Up</u>."

"You got everything."

"What? Everything. What everything?"

"Well . . . I don't think there's much money."

"NO. <u>That</u> can't happen. That shits the bed. How much not much?'

I was crying again now. I blubbered: "You got the house."

"Well, yeah, the house. I mean, you can hardly . . . that's something. But not much money, could you be, like, any fucking less specific? Oh. I'm being hard on you, without any justification. That's not my intention. So that's all <u>I've</u> got to say."

There was more fuzz. At last Eddie said, "I've got my guru with me."

There was more fuzz. Eddie said, "Is there any cheese in the house? I, like, I don't have a cheese <u>problem</u> any more but I still need lots of cheese. So if there isn't any cheese, we'll have to stop on the way."

"I don't know."

"Right! We'll stop. Don't need that . . . the cheese

scenario . . . okay, look, we're at the Taco Bell, we'll do the cheese thing, be at your side in fifteen minutes. Kapish?"

And he hung up.

It wasn't fifteen minutes but more like an hour before Eddie came. I had time to shower and change. I hid the rabbit in a clothes hamper. Then I stood in the courtyard for the longest time, expecting him.

I stood there for the longest time.

The moonlight reflected in the swimming pool was brighter than the actual moon. In its thin, chlorine light, everything looked like plastic. The masonry and plaster, tousled palms and ivy – and Remember III the mutt stood guard on the balcony, looking like a toy goat from a kid's farmyard set.

Odd articles were strewn about the lawn – by me in my earlier frenzies. Mom's pink bra hung from a fig tree. A child's blanket with a tiger's face woven into it was spread on the pebbled drive. I kept stepping on spoons and forks in my bare feet. For the first time, these things appeared to me not as damning evidence but as a lead-in to an anecdote about my endearing frailty. *I threw all this stuff off the balcony, I was so upset. Her bra ended up in a tree!*

It was so strange! So pretty and it sent chills –

I love Eddie desperately, I folded my hands and pressed them, I was rooted to the spot with joy.

At last I heard the tiny sound of the motor on our private drive. It rose and fell because the lane follows the coast and there are many bends and dips. When it came up full-throated, I pressed the button for the automatic gate and it parted to reveal Eddie's rinky-dink yellow Hyundai jigging toward me over the loose pebbles.

Parking, it shuddered and let out one long huff. Then both doors opened.

Eddie came first, stepping out onto the tiger blanket. He was barefoot, in one of his suits with the tie loosened and hanging down his back. It surprised me; I'd heard he wore suits now but I'd never actually seen one. When I was in grad school, all he ever wore were Hawaiian shirts.

He looked just the same. That surprised me too. It shouldn't but you know it does. Like, my God, the likeness is uncanny!

"Hi," said Eddie. "Look, I got to apologize, what I said on the phone. Not like I remember what I said, cause I'm really smashed so you gotta forgive me."

"Okay."

"Yeah . . . what do you care." He pulled out a pack of cigarettes, and then Ralph got out of the car.

And when Ralph got out of the car and I saw him for the first time, it all rushed to my head. If I was expecting a guru at all, it was some little Hindu gentleman with curious whiskers. A paunchy gnome in orange robes, the guru would fold his hands, saying wise, innocuous things about "the lotus."

Ralph had no shirt on.

## Description: Ralph

He's named Allan Michaelson. No one has ever called him by that name.

His mother was a gypsy fortune-teller. "Mistress Lola." No psychic powers whatsoever, real name Irene.

"Dave something Scottish" was his father, in his mother's words. "I was fifteen, love. I didn't write them things down."

He was born in Britain. He came to the U.S. at eighteen.

Once I asked him if his kind of British accent was Romany. He said no, in his case, "gypsy" just meant "trailer trash."

Once he spent a year in the Rockies, meditating, only coming to town to buy tinned meat, tea and gas for his pick-up. He ate wild mushrooms and burdock. He lived in a tent and meditated ten hours a day.

When I asked him what effect it had, he said, "None."

He was good-looking like an excellent statue of a homely man. He moved well, just that, but it gave him status in groups.

6'2", broad-shouldered, baritone, that disheartening litany. White Male Deluxe.

A nice guy who wiped his shoes, who said "Gesundheit."

Just walking around the car to Eddie's side, he made me stare, I didn't know what it was but

it made your throat hurt and your heart speed up, and you didn't understand what he said.

★ ★ ★

He said something to Eddie and put one hand on the Hyundai, turned and first laid eyes on me. Then his face changed and he went absolutely still.

"Chrysa, my guru," Eddie said, and lit his cigarette.

Ralph was absolutely fucking still.

"Hello," I said, which is the very hardest thing I've ever done.

"Hi," said Ralph, in this hoarse, carrying voice. Then he rubbed his eyes with one hand as if clearing an irksome misapprehension and turned to get his bearings.

The courtyard is overlooked by two stone towers, each with a belfry from which the bells have been removed. Between them runs the coastal wall. Each tower develops into a house: the main wing to the left, with its balconies and fancy ironwork railings; on the right the smaller guest wing, whose rooms, on the ground floor, are only separated from the pool by sliding doors. On fine nights you can sleep there with the walls open, breathing in the jasmine. The pool is Olympic-sized, with mosaic fish and mermaids worked into the tiles. There are palm trees and statues. None of this seemed to surprise Ralph. The pink bra in the tree, the many spoons – none of it.

He did stare at the keyhole doorway leading out onto the beach. It startles most people when they see it for the first time. Since we're on a cliff, all it shows is greenish, yawning distance. It takes a while to put together the rumble of the ocean and the hole, which seems to open onto the Void.

This Void impression colors a person's first appreciation of what the property must be worth.

Ralph seemed to ponder, looking up and down the high walls. At last he shook his head. "Jesus," he said, "is this all yours?"

Eddie and I looked at each other. In that moment we were actually brother and sister. To anyone else, that house is one magnificent piece of real estate. To us, it's, *oh, that's where you ate a snail when you were eight and Mom told you the snail was in hell.* And *remember doing Tarzan off the balcony with jumpropes?* All our lives, too, we have been escorting new friends into the real estate and watching their feelings toward us insidiously change.

Eddie raised his eyebrows and turned to follow Ralph's gaze. "Yeah . . ." he drawled, chewing on his cigarette. "Doesn't it make you sick, when you think of all the homeless people?"

★ ★ ★ ★ ★

## MY BROTHER EDDIE
### a.k.a. Rat Boy
### a.k.a. The Sleaze King
### and His Many Bad Deeds which were
### Not His Fault

★ ★ ★

Five foot seven
Dark hair & eyes
Skinny
Long nose
Overbite (great lost battles of orthodontia) therefore
Called Rat-boy when we were kids.

A sweet kid, a nice boy. Everybody's favorite. Not
actually the valedictorian but might have been. Not on any
sports team because of his epilepsy. Just petit mal: he stopped
fitting at twelve, but needed pills, and he couldn't drink or
smoke or take drugs.

But – the cheerleader girlfriend. The hottest, always, and
another in waiting. He had a pack of friends, and my friends
used to say to me, "That's your *brother?*" and mime fainting.

And straight "A"s straight through high school and the
4.0 GPA at Stanford. A Psych major. Psychology of Cult and
Subculture – his projected MA subject.

Called Rat-boy when we were grown up.
"Five foot seven inches of sheer depravity," his boast.
Dark eyes the kind that seem mascaraed, that are sex-ee.
Lean not skinny. *Lean, mean* from fucking, dancing,
amphetamine.

Long nose/overbite I could still see plainly but others thought my brother was a good-looking man. A womanizer. Heartbreaker. Gigolo (actually; for money, for real).

More ways of looking at it.

All his best friends were women. He'd pound on their doors at 3:00 A.M., lonely. Insist on sleeping in their arms for no reason. "No ulterior motives, Missy, swear to God." He'd cry real tears, just for "how I feel tonight, Jesus Christ."

Crying spent, he wants to fuck.

"Come on, you didn't believe my bullshit?"

"I'm just gonna lie here saying please. Please please please please . . . I'm just gonna lie here with this massive hard-on saying please."

"Yeah, I know I'm a scumbag, but you gotta admit I love you."

Called the Sleaze King, then.

– By choice. He has a name tag made up, like the kind checkout girls wear. Pins to the buttonhole of his Armani suit, and forgets. The patient dry-cleaner keeps pinning it back on.

– independently, so often it was uncanny. "Who is that guy? He's like the total Sleaze King." "That's your brother? We used to call him the Sleaze King."

Eddie

- always needed a haircut
- bragged he owned no underpants
- wore that Armani suit ten days in a row
- slept in it at night
- had lice twice as a grown man

Police cars slowed down to get a better look at Eddie.
Eddie was always held up at Customs.

"Okay, so we're living together for three months and
he tells me from now on he's going to try to live totally on
borrowed money. And he gets this little diary, the kind that
locks up with a little gold key, like for a thirteen-year-old
girl? Like with kittens on it, my, God. And every time he
borrows any money, he goes through this whole routine of
unlocking it and writing down the debt. So, it's like, mega
serious.

"Then finally the lock breaks? Like, I didn't break the
lock, it was just lying around broken so one day I look at it.
And you know, he wasn't keeping all those records so he
could pay people back, ever, he was adding them up. He
borrowed 7,000 dollars in that time, it was only like a couple
of months.

"So I confronted him. I mean, he wasn't paying me any
rent or bills or anything. And he says it would be lying if he
spent that money on groceries, cause people lent it on the
understanding it was for booze and drugs. Well, I didn't throw
him out then, but I got really, really close."

Or, a pattern:
He comes home with her Saturday night. He leaves
Monday morning.
Monday evening, his suits are hanging in the closet
when she comes home from work.
"Didn't we talk about this? I swear to God we had this
total talk . . ."
"Don't throw me out in the street, is all, cause that's the
one thing I know I wouldn't get over."
"Oh, did I mention I love you?"

When she comes home from work, she wakes him from an alcoholic stupor, every single day.

But he's fun; he takes her places she would never ever go; they end up drunk in Death Valley at 3:00 A.M., with Eddie chanting rap lyrics at the stars.

Out of nowhere, Eddie begins to do housework.

He has said nothing throughout dinner; pressed, he gives her a troubled frown and says, "I just realized, you're chaining me to the material, and I can't remain on your level any more."

Eddie stops doing housework.

He has said nothing throughout dinner; pressed, he snaps, "Look, I know you've got this great superstition about fidelity, but all that is, is two people agree to lie to each other, and you can't actually coerce me against my one last purity."

He's apologetic, follows her around the house as she dresses for work. "You're different and it frightens me. I think that's what it is, I'm scared I'll go and marry you or something catastrophic."

By nightfall, he knows he is gay.

"What we actually need is for you to have children."

"This is all a result of me not taking enough drugs."

"Oh, of course, you're <u>never</u> to blame. Have you noticed? Have you noticed that fucking refrain?"

His suits are in the closet, but he has not come home.

Spotted by a helpful friend later in the week, asleep on a patch of grass in the center of town, with a very drunk sixteen-year-old girl stroking his hair.

"But I never <u>said</u> I loved you."

His suits are not in the closet when she comes home.

My mother said he made her believe in demon possession.

But she loved him more than women love their children. She would drive a thousand miles in a night to see him, if he called.

He loved other women, all women, instead of Mom. Mom, he would say, "Okay, but she's a drunk. You know what I mean? Okay, but she's a drunk."

And they drank together, out on the private beach in wintertime, digging the shapes of their coats deep in cold sand, singing Roy Orbison tunes like one person, lonely and rich and lonely and rich.

And on a leather string, Eddie wears a tin medallion, engraved with a medical warning of an allergy to penicillin he does not have. And in his Valium depressions, he will take out a deck of cards and lay them down, one at a time, in front of him. He'll say, "I wasn't always like this, you know. I wasn't born this way. To tell you the truth, I've got good reason to believe I've had a curse laid on me."

And in the briefcase he is never seen without, there are three snapshots. Tucked away beneath the flattened Whopper wrappers and overdue bills, three photographs of a teenaged girl. She's wearing pink dungarees, smiling in the seedy Chinatown of some metropolis. She has a Roman nose, brown eyes and hair, buck teeth – a face uncannily like a dachshund's.

"That's my sister," Eddie says. "She went down in a drugs plane over Costa Rica. I don't like to talk about it."

But I'm his sister, his adopted but only sister, and the picture, naturally, is not of me. It's of some other girl who actually resembles him.

On the back of each snapshot is written, in pencil worn down to a purplish shade of white:

LOVE, DC.

　★ ★ ★

"Doesn't it make you sick, when you think of all the homeless people?" said Eddie, and everything began to go black. The bright pool in its landscaped arena went out. I fainted

and woke on the kitchen floor. Which is green marble. Than which there is nothing more cold. And hard.

My first impression was that I had fallen there, and a jolt of pain ran through my joints. Yet I had fallen in the grass and was unscathed. That kitchen door is just the nearest to the driveway, so they had carried me in here. Someone had thrown the tiger blanket over me – covering my face but leaving my legs exposed.

"Hello!" said Ralph, and to Eddie: "She's coming to."

"Well, let her go from for a minute, I'm telling this story." And to me: "Go from! Don't come to! Go from!"

"Tell the story, then," Ralph said. "But I'm not listening."

". . . yeah, so I got this idea if she'd just let me piss in her –"

"Oh, Christ . . ."

"IF SHE'D JUST LET ME piss in her . . ."

I fell still again, trying to breathe like a sleeping person though my heart was pounding. Ideally, they would finish talking and go off to bed, forgetting me completely on the kitchen floor. Then I could sneak to my bedroom in privacy. Certainly I wasn't going to sit up and make an effort to be sociable. If they'd wanted that, they shouldn't have dumped me on the floor. Or at least they could have crouched around me until I woke up. I couldn't have been out more than fifteen minutes.

Even if they didn't really want my company, they should

29

have made sure I was all right. For all they knew, I'd fallen into a coma. I might just let them think that. I would have to stay a long time on the floor, of course, but it was a point of honor, and if I had no honor, I was lost. Certainly I was not a worldly success. But I could show real pluck, when it was called for. Years of introspection had given me inner strength. I had always felt I would be splendid in a war.

I could smell spaghetti on the boil, and the sharper scent of tomato sauce. It was Ralph cooking. I would have known it was Ralph even if I couldn't tell from the footsteps, just because Eddie would *never be cooking*. So I felt I knew that about the guru: he *would be cooking*. Of course there are many possible interpretations.

The guru might consider menial tasks to be a form of worship. The guru might have come from a single-parent family. He might have difficulty sustaining a relationship, and thus have learned to cook his own simple fare. The guru might have pretensions as a gourmet. Without knowing whether the sauce came from a jar, however, I could not proceed on any of these hypotheses.

". . . so finally she let me do it, and I did it, it was surprisingly hard cause I kept getting hard again so it really was surprisingly hard, har har, okay? And I thought, I thought it would be like this epiphany, I had this image of touching bottom and then I'd be able to come up, like it would be the lowest point, but then I'm looking at her, I won't draw you a picture, but I'm looking at her and thinking, no. No way is that the lowest. Cause it's not like, I slaughtered her, and she's not a five-year-old boy, and way there are people out there lower than that."

"Near enough."

"And yet it wasn't near enough, or are you even fuck-ing listening? The point is, it wasn't near enough! And I, then

30

I'd just abused this poor woman, who was totally a really good friend before that, and afterward, she was just the girl I'd pissed in, I couldn't, I'd look at her and just think, oh my God, I pissed inside you. I did. And I'd had to lie to her to get her to do it, like it was some fantasy I'd had since I was eight years old and used to watch my sister tinkle and get off on it, sorry Chrysa."

There was a pause: I could feel them both looking at me, imagining me tinkling with my legs spread to show hairless genitals.

"I didn't even actually," Eddie said finally. "Unless Chrysa remembers it and I don't."

"I think we should get her to bed."

"Right!" Eddie said. "I'll get the feet!"

Then they both laughed for some reason for a long time. Possibly something side-splitting had happened when they carried me in from the lawn. If I asked Eddie later on, he was sure to be evasive: "Like, are you really sure you wanna know?" After long persuasion, he would tell me some crass lie – about my pubic hair. When I had squealed in humiliation, he would laugh at me again for having been gulled. Pressed, he would say he'd forgotten all about it, "really totally." It was so childish! I'd forgotten how cruel Eddie could be.

And in the midst of this I heard a chair scraping and someone – Ralph – came walking over. He said to Eddie, "Keep an eye on that pasta," and took me in his arms.

I don't want to say he lifted me like I was nothing, but I <u>was</u> nothing, I was 89 pounds. And he went off with me, the blanket still over my face so I was like a kid playing ghost, and fading behind us Eddie calling sniggering from his chair: "Where you going with my sister? Man! Come back here with my sister!"

Down the corridor and up the stairs. The balcony then

and the open night – through a thick woolen blanket, damp and secret with my own breath – and the feeling of riding, being given a ride plus that other thing of being in someone's arms. So being in someone's arms smelled of spacious jasmine far below and getting a ride smelled of close musty wool.

In the dark, I was trying to remember what his face looked like.

I pretended so hard to be unconscious. He could have thrown me in the swimming pool, I would have just sunk. He could have done anything –

No one had touched me in a long time.

And we came into my room, from the balcony entrance, which meant he had to pause a long time undoing the shutters and reach to tease open the top latch. He had to do all that with my dead weight cradled on one arm. Stepping into the room, he rocked me.

Then he switched on the light and pulled the blanket off my face.

I opened my eyes without thinking.

He didn't look at all the way I had imagined him.

I shut my eyes again tight.

And for a short while he stood there, hunched over me as if gut-shot, shuddering with silent laughter. When the fit had passed, he said, "You're not fooling anyone."

He carried me over to the bed and paused.

The mattress, of course, was bare. All the bedding was stuffed underneath, with my books and papers, my mobile phone, my portable stereo. So he had a dilemma. I began to brace myself to be thrown on the mattress, possibly – and I felt this in the tension of his arms – with force.

But at last he bent down and placed me gently on the floor. He even pulled the blanket again up over my chin.

Then he crouched down, extracted sheets and pillows, and began methodically to make my bed.

It took him some time, shaking out the crumpled linen, neatly tucking each sheet to. He even plumped the pillows. Then, when I was expecting him to come back and fetch me, he stood up, said, "Good night," and left without shutting the French doors.

# BOULDER SECTIONS

## Argument

*Eddie met Ralph in Boulder, Colorado, where they
were both then living, some ten days before the events described
above. Eddie had been visiting the home of a Tibetan drunk,
whom he was trying to recruit as a guru. The Tibetan, alarmed by
Eddie's manner (Eddie had taken a bunch of pills), ran out into
the street for help. Eddie gave chase. Ralph happened to be walking
by, and, hearing the scheme, decided to take the Tibetan's place.
Five days later, Ralph and Eddie drove to California, here to
inaugurate the Tibetan School of Miracles.*

## 19. Boulder: "Colorado Ceramic Arts"

The pottery's back door is open, releasing a vacant fluorescent light on the asphalt of the lot adjoining. In the white doorway, Ralph stands, a spooky figure because there is no radio playing and he is not smoking or even leaning and when Ralph isn't moving he is absolutely still – even his hands, even his lips. It's very dark tonight, starry but moonless, and now, at 1:00 A.M., the small-town air of Boulder has taken deeply. You only hear one car at a time, hear dogs bark and doors close.

He is tall with harsh, aquiline features; black hair chopped short; big, chapped, calloused hands. His frame is not athletic but workmanly, the brawny arms suggestive of use. His jeans are patched with drying clay. His hair and the stubble on his cheeks are grizzled with it.

Behind him the concrete floor has a kindred patina, clay gone hard in all the pores. The walls, too, are splattered. And, in ranks, on long, unfinished timber shelves, sit jugs, vases, plates; drying or bisque, in a few fundamental shades of brown and gray. Every day, Ralph produces many times his weight in pottery.

He's been in the shop since 7:00 A.M.: this is his usual work day. He drinks three liters of water in that time and sometimes bathes his head and upper torso under the cold faucet in the deep mud-streaked sink. The kilns' heat takes it out of him again.

Since, alongside the usual cute pots, Ralph is making works of deeply meant and particular art, there is an air of high stakes about him; integrity. Sorrow, too – how he's soiled with trying, and even the keen air of night does not cleanse him.

He also sells dope in the back of the shop to friends and

friends of friends. Their children are allowed to make clay ponies while the grownups puff. For these transactions, Ralph accepts food stamps.

## 19(b). "Colorado Ceramic Arts"

He has scars on his legs from abscesses where Nepalese leeches once were torn away roughly, leaving residue. He has had shows of his works in Los Angeles, Philadelphia and Liège, Belgium.

He speaks fluent Tibetan.

He speaks it because one of his stepfathers was Tibetan, and, as a boy, Ralph lived for years in the Nepalese Himalaya. This is where he first made ceramics: on a hand-turned wheel as a semi-runaway while his mother smoked heroin on Freak Street in Kathmandu. Although he won't talk about those years, they were the last important time of his life:

when something really happened.

- A white cat led him into the mountains to meet God.
- The rhododendrons bled down the valley and he knew something briefly.
- His sister carried him back in her arms.

When he came to, he was at a plastic table in a tea shop and she was playing goats and tigers, the local chess, with a waiter. At that time of year, there were no tourists in Pokhara.

So they could play goats and tigers all afternoon.

Nothing has happened to Ralph since that time.

Locking up the back, he passes through the workroom into the shop proper. Here everything is immaculate, the cleanliness an intensified kind of silence. The glass shelves cast both shadows and reflections: as Ralph strides through, the room ripples.

It's like sunlight on the surface of the ocean, seen by a swimmer grasping up for it; and Ralph is like that swimmer in his graceful, weary, practiced movements. As he leaves, and stretches up to draw the steel security door down over his incurious reflection, he's briefly aware that he's going home:

then again only of wind and a shape –

something like a locust, but round enough to hold water –

which might, in porcelain, impress him as capable of playing goats and tigers through the afternoon, while, at a neighboring table, its comatose, agape brother overlooks Lake Pokhara.

Shouldering his satchel, he begins to walk home.

## 21. Boulder: 109b Pine Street

The building has subsided and the basement flat appears compressed beneath the gabled upper stories. The lawn is brown. There's a bashed, discolored picket fence, and a rusty mailbox. The light is outdoor-artificial, streetlight light, giving the scene the queer stiffness of diorama.

Ralph comes walking down the sidewalk.

As he comes to 109b, its door flies open and a small, squarish figure hurries out. It's an Asian man wearing a bandana tied around his head like a sweatband. Spotting Ralph, he calls out and comes toward him. They meet at the gate.

"It – dangerous man, in my house," the man stammers. "He is crazy, please. I think for police . . ."

The man's breath stinks of beer. He staggers and, catching himself, makes a tiny, suppressed yelp.

In the open door, Ralph sees a shadow. It is maneuvering finely as if untying a diabolically complex knot. That motion, and the varying lights made as it blocks and bares the lightbulb behind, give the impression of a pitch-black creature with many limbs, among them tentacles.

Staid Ralph interprets the situation: *Drunks arguing.*

Then he looks back at the panicked man's boxy, Asian face, and goes absolutely still. He takes the man by both arms, just beneath the shoulder, steadies him, and frowns into his face.

In fluent Tibetan, Ralph says that it really makes him angry when drunken gooks jump at him out of the bushes. It makes him want to stick a knife in someone, in fact, and he might do that right now. Then he shoves the short man away from him with a slight, powerful movement of the wrists. He has used the English word for "gook."

The man stumbles back and forward again. He raises one hand as if to shield his eyes. His face changes, cleared and sobered by dismay.

He says, in Tibetan: "Oh, no. It's you."

Then the drunk, stocky in his Levis and floppy-collared lumberjack shirt, stoops, swings to the picket fence, and vomits painfully over the drab lawn.

# 18. "Colorado Ceramic Arts"

It's a pottery shop with associated workspace whose lease Ralph took over when his old friend and colleague Rita Perkins died. He has been in sole tenancy for five years. Before that were eight years when he worked with Rita, learning from her the fine points of glazes and stains, firing techniques and appliances – all the tech stuff they couldn't teach him in Bhaktapur.

1    He met Rita during the time of his long meditations.

1.1    In town to buy provisions, he happened to wander past her shop.

1.2    In the window were the usual eyesores made to please tourists:
- vases "in the shape of"
- gilt cupids
- pink vats the size of dog beds
- a bust of Reagan

1.3    Used to long stillness, Ralph stopped and looked at them for one and a half hours.

2    Finally Rita came out. "Something catch your eye?"

2.1    Ralph smiled. "It's just, I'm a potter."

2.2    She had heard it all before: "Well, get the hell away from my window. If there's one thing I will not tolerate, it's good taste."

3    She used to call herself "Rita Perkins, Frontier Lesbian."

3.1    Her girlfriends were a rabble of table dancers and Marines.

3.2    She had orange-dyed hair and cowboy jewelry.

3.3    On her vacations, she hunted deer.

4    They stood in front of the shop window silently a while. Because neither left, the mood was apologetic, though it was unclear who was sorry and for what. When Ralph finally looked over, Rita was smiling, her eyes wet from suppressed laughter.

And he asked if he could use her shower, which was a way he had then of getting to know people.

5    Once, when Rita was gone, he missed her.

5.1    He resented all the girls he hired to help out in the shop, after Rita's death.

## The Rita Years

1    In the Rita years, he slept in the workshop or the woods. In either case he used a sleeping bag with no mattress. He had clothes and tools. He had soap and ID cards. Beyond these essentials, Ralph eschewed "paraphernalia."

2    For a very long time, he was studying Tibetan Buddhism at the Naropa Institute. He brushed up his Tibetan and learned kindergarten Sanskrit. At night he meditated for two hours, minimum. The bulk of his wages he donated to Tibetan liberation groups. He ate plain white rice and never masturbated.

3    Finally he had lost his faith. There was no revelatory moment or incident, and, in some respects, he remained Tibetan Buddhist. He still assumed that OM was the sun and HUM the soil, into which the sun's rays descend to awake the dormant life. But he did not say OM or HUM anymore, and felt no anxiety, ever, on that account.

## Personal Information

1    Ralph couldn't stand love.

1.1  Its bottom line was: bars, restaurants and cinemas.

1.2  Although they pre-existed Earth, even stars were deemed "romantic."

1.3  "What are you thinking? What are you thinking? What are you thinking? What are you thinking?"

1.4  He always felt like taking a long walk after sex.

2    Friends came to him with their problems.

2.1  Friends could sit with Ralph for hours.

2.2  Friends passed the time as if it was cheap fuel.

2.3  Topics of perennial concern included:
- recent purchases
- places to get good Chinese
- how others have wronged me
- this guy made a bundle

2.4  Once a woman sat in Ralph's tent with a catalog of camping equipment, telling him aloud what each item cost.

3    He had lost touch with his family, once and for all.


## The Years Post-Rita

1    Shortly before Rita's death, Ralph saw her in the hospital.

1.1  In the course of the visit, he joked that "What are friends for?" was a hard question. People thought it was rhetorical; let them answer it.

1.2  She rose up on her elbows, haggard and fierce. Scarlet blotches appeared on her drained cheeks.

1.3    "You should have the cancer," she spat. "You're the walking dead."

2    He believed that people should be honest, generous and kind to each other. What they felt, during, made no difference. Personal attachment was tomfoolery. No one would miss you one second after they were dead. He wasn't sure if he had ever felt "lonely."

This much he knew, but others might know better. Therefore he resolved to experiment with normal living.

3    He began to spend evenings in a sports bar on Pearl Street. There he drank beer and watched ball games on wide-screen TV.

3.1    When he failed to show up at the bar, he felt guilty. Working all night was a secret vice.

3.2    He had a long-term thing with a Women's Studies professor who did not love him. They got stoned together and took her Labrador for walks.

3.3    He got an apartment.

The furnishings were bland and appropriate, the walls bare. Nothing caught the eye. Nothing got in. The solitude there was not just Ralph's but universal; and it was generous and unimpaired as skies must look to mountains. There Ralph began to create real art.

The new works were undecorated and white. Their shapes were sad revisions of the shapes he had once made on a hand-turned wheel in Bhaktapur as a boy. There were even some based on the elephant's-head coathook, a tourist bauble which he made ugly afresh, this time *not in collusion with the viewer*. All his new ceramics had this trademark unfriendly quality. They might be bowls, but not bowls from which to eat soup. They were bowls in which to float a single violet, only to find it has vanished overnight.

At this point, people started finding Ralph spooky.

He was known to sometimes carry a knife, which, to his easy-going, hippie associates, was creepy like carrying a hatchet or a chainsaw. He told stories that took place in a Florida state penitentiary. Every time he passed a policeman, he muttered. These details were unnervingly at variance with his tranquil persona. If Ralph were a character in a Hollywood film, it would be about werewolves.

He commissioned some vats and salable figurines, but most of the stock of Colorado Ceramic Arts Ralph fashioned himself. He also sold through shops in Denver and Taos, and via specialty catalogs. Despite this industry, however, Ralph had mounting debts, verging – at the time he met Eddie – on bankruptcy.

The competition undercut him, selling cheap, slip-cast ware. New fire regulations had entailed steep building expenses. Then there was a break-in, and he had to replace a lot of glass. At the best of times, he was not a natural salesman.

So when a friend came to offer him a cut-price supply of dope, Ralph leapt at the chance, hoping the deal would patch the gaps in his accounts, as marijuana sales often had in the past.

## Initiating Incident: "Business Opportunity"

The deal came with a story; that alone should have alerted Ralph. Jigme Dorje, a former Buddhist monk, now full-time drunkard, had made a friend at his last rehabilitation center. This friend was involved in selling grass flown in from Hawaii. The low price offered was contingent on Jigme's participation. Jigme had no money whatsoever, and needed a backer. So Ralph was informed by Valley Girl Jenny, an old acquaintance from his Tibetan scripture class.

Through all the easy-going exchanges that led up to the handing over of the money – the cryptic answerphone messages, whispers at the shop's till, the preliminary meeting with Jigme over cream-cheese bagels – Ralph felt a gut certainty that he was being ripped off. Yet, because he couldn't logically justify the certainty – and because he urgently needed the money – he went through it all as if hypnotized, even saying, when it transpired that the money had to be handed over *two days before* the drugs appeared:

"Never mind. I know I can trust you,"

in a voice not his own.

The money was still in the envelope from the bank. It felt chunky. Handing it to someone was like giving them something huge and unwieldy: a safe, for instance. When it was done, and Jigme had left, walking too fast, Ralph immediately began to sweat.

Long before the two days had passed, he was raging, all the more furious for having known all along.

## 22. 109b Pine Street

Jigme staggered back from his vomiting and half-fell against the worn picket fence. At that moment, Eddie appeared, bombing out of the lit doorway with his trademark briefcase swinging. Charging up to Jigme, he bared his teeth in frustration. He arrived at the sidewalk shouting "Gotcha!," pulled up and stopped a few inches from his quarry, hugging the briefcase to his chest in triumph.

Ralph said to Jigme in Tibetan, "Should I help you now?"

"Dude!" went Eddie, noticing Ralph. "Do you speak Chinese? I mean, translate for me, I totally beg you."

Ralph said, "Sure."

Eddie raised the briefcase to the heavens and kissed it in thanksgiving, then put it down at his feet and said: "Look, it's not like I'm fucking asking much, I'm not even asking, I'm begging people to take my cash, is that wrong? Am I a fucking criminal? Tell him."

Ralph said to Jigme, in Tibetan, "I don't care what problems you have, I need my money back."

"Right," said Eddie. "I want to start a guru business. I need, all I need, right, is someone to come and pretend to be the Great All-Knowing Monk from Fuckhead Monastery, like this little shit would be perfect. I'll buy the goddamn clothes, all right? And I don't care, he can say the Great Lord Gewgaw says he's got to eat the ripe flesh of virgins, okay, just don't tell me cause I got this crazy phobia of jail. Tell him."

Ralph said to Jigme, in Tibetan, "Three thousand plus three hundred for not cutting off your head. You think I'm some American, too scared to cut your head off?"

Jigme put his hands to his blanched cheeks and said, "No!" hoarsely.

Eddie went frantic: "Look! You little goddamn worm, I'm just about really sick of this. You think you're the first? I've been to see every piece of holistic shit in Colorado, and all I can say is, the basic child's principle of investment for return is fucking lost! Lost!" Then, to Ralph, "Look, are you even talking here, or is it Papa Brick Wall and Baby Brick Wall. Jesus."

Ralph said to Jigme in Tibetan, "Wednesday. Three thousand three hundred dollars. If this man was not here, I'd break your arms right now. Look." And from his satchel, he produced the aforementioned knife, unsheathing it in the same motion.

Eddie ducked and grabbed his briefcase, raising it shield-fashion. "Jesus Christ!" he said, "What the fuck is wrong with you?"

Jigme slouched against the fence as before, stroking the bandana down over his eyes as if to gentle them. Thus half-blinded, he said, in a hoarse, practiced whine, in English, "Tell them I am dead. Tell them my father is killed by Chinese and my mother has dead from hunger in Lhasa. Tell them I am one fat ghost with the soul for a woman. No one should be unhappy for me. I don't understand, they say to me. I need to drink more beer so I can sleep."

Then Ralph lost his temper. He screamed in English: "You were born in India! Your mother lives upstairs! I'm not one of your college fucking kids who thinks your ass is sacred!"

A passing car slowed, allowing its headlights to become a presence, a harsher mood in the scene. It went by and then came to a stop some yards down Pine Street, idling there as if pondering.

Ralph said to Eddie, collecting his shattered cool, "I don't know why you want this guy. You realize he's an alcoholic?"

Eddie shrugged, his eyes following the knife. "People are into Tibetans. Like, who am I?"

The car that had passed, a silver Mustang, now reversed and stopped again level with Ralph, Eddie and Jigme. The driver's door opened, and a small blonde woman leaned out. In the spot of brash carlight, her petite face was red. She screamed at Ralph, "What are you doing, still hassling him? Haven't you done enough? Aren't you satisfied?"

Ralph said in a cool, carrying voice, "Did you stop to give me my three thousand dollars?"

"I just don't get how you can be so incredibly greedy!" she screamed. "Can't you get it through your puny brain that Jigme's sick? Can't you comprehend that?"

Ralph grabbed Jigme by the knot of the bandana, as if it was a handle tied there for this purpose, and yelled, "Sick is nothing! This is dead! It's dead as of ten o'clock Wednesday if I don't get my money!" He shoved Jigme forward and let go, allowing the man to stagger forward blindly.

The woman leapt out of the car and ran to Jigme, pulling the bandana free of his head as if it were some vicious animal. She yelled at Ralph as she frogmarched Jigme to her car, "You're evil! You think you're some kind of gangster? You're just evil, you're evil!"

through which Ralph, in an auditorium boom: "Three thousand dollars, Jenny! Three thousand dollars!"

She wrestled Jigme into the back and jumped in the driver's seat, slamming each door so hard the Mustang shuddered. As she pulled out, Ralph turned to Eddie with a rueful smile, as if to say, see how they try my patience.

Eddie stared at him for some time. At last he bent to fetch his briefcase, shaking his head. "Thanks a million," he said. "You're a real friend, Jesus."

Ralph continued to smile.

"Yeah, just grin at me, I love it. I mean, you have to, you are obligated to at least buy me a drink, cause — just smile, great — cause, you know, I'm actually in shock, my mother just died? She's being fucking embalmed as we speak, and I'm not just saying that because you totally failed to help me when I asked you like a human being. It actually happens to be true this time, which is what really fucks me up." He looked back at Jigme's door and said wistfully, "It's like the boy that cried wolf. It's like the boy that cried fucking wolf."

"Well, I'm walking home," said Ralph. "You can come with me if you want a drink, but I've got to get back and change my clothes." He ticked one fingernail against a clay spot on his jeans.

"Yeah," Eddie shook his head, "What are you, a mud wrestler? Honest to God, I weep for America."

Ralph started walking then, and Eddie, after a pause to assert that he might just not, came hurriedly behind.

## 23. Boulder: 1203 13th Street

The walls are freshly painted white.

The wooden floor shines.

There is no:

- television
- stereo
- computer

There are no:

- rugs
- personal mementos
- pictures on the wall
- shelves

There is nothing on the glass coffee table.

On the beige canvas couch is one book, closed on a stiff leather bookmark; a dual-language edition of the *Bhagavad Gita*.

The windows smell of Windex and the bed of detergent. The kitchen appliances look brand new. The clock is right.

Going in, Ralph asks that Eddie remove his shoes and Eddie asks if Ralph is some kind of Maoist. Ralph goes to the kitchen.

Eddie sits right down on the gleaming floor and puts his briefcase on his knees and puts his head on his briefcase.

He calls out through his crossed arms, "Did you have a really happy childhood? Don't tell me. You just, obviously, you're the kind who, your parents loved each other and you had a fucking collie."

"Do you want a beer?"

"Yeah, try and shut me up. That's the best thing."

"Do you want a beer?"

"Of course I want a beer, but I'm trying to talk about why you can't hear what I've got to say. That's the point."

Now Eddie rears back and clicks his briefcase open. Rummaging among the papers, he pulls out:

- half a ham sandwich with a match embedded in the bread
- a plastic brontosaurus
- phone bills
- bedraggled bunny ears, à la Playboy
- pens, tickets
- one fuzzy die

then he just dumps it all out on the floor.

Papers, socks, envelopes, pennies, fly everywhere. A travel-sized Listerine bounces, hitting him in the face. A snapshot of a lanky young girl in pink dungarees, smiling in the seedy Chinatown of some metropolis, skates free, briefly takes off kite-fashion, swoops down, hoverfoils some yards over the smooth floor, and finally tips over onto its face just where Ralph is about to put his foot, on his way back from the kitchen with two cans of beer.

## 25. Colorado – California (Montara Beach)

1    Ralph left Boulder owing
  - two months' rent for his retail premises
  - 1,200 dollars plus for sales of merchandise held on sale-or-return
  - miscellaneous sums to the gas, electric, telephone companies
  - the printer of his brochures; the delivery guys; the plumber who installed his sink
  - etc. to the tune of ten grand roughly
1.1  It took two days, in the matchbox Hyundai, to move the remaining ceramics to a warehouse.
1.2  Eddie paid the storage people with a hot check.

2    Within five days of meeting they were on the road to California.
2.1  Through the New Mexican desert, Eddie talked, restlessly stroking the stick shift with one hand.
2.2  The shadow of a small cloud lay on the blacktop far ahead.
2.3  A lone hawk tipped in the sky.
2.4  "You gotta admit, it's genius," Eddie said to Ralph.
2.5  "This card isn't authorized," the pump attendant said to Eddie.

3    Somewhere in Nevada, the ridges had turned red. The sun bled, low and huge.
3.1  "You realize what I'll do to you if we get there and there's no mansion?"
3.2  Eddie drank just one beer, several times.
3.2  "No, it was a thump. It was a thump in the engine."
3.4  Ralph put the Econo-lodge on his American Express.
3.5  Ralph put the auto mechanic on his Visa.

4    Arriving at last by dead of night, they were greeted by a starved hag.

4.1  "You looked to me as if your beautiful fur had all been shaved."

4.2  "Chrysa, I'm your brother, okay? You look like shit."

4.3  Mine was the sky moon and theirs the bottom, swimming-pool moon, bright by unfair means. I wept savagely in the sky moon, come stalking in the open French doors. I would not approach that shipshape bed, made against me.

I sat in front of it on my haunches, dried out. When I touched the blanket, it was a moment of drama. I looked around with my arm stretched out, surprised that there was no sound. Only the trees outside said shh and shuffled, like children tiptoeing past their parents' open bedroom door.

I don't remember getting out of my clothes. I don't know how I got there. I only know I woke up on top of the bed, naked and hot in blinding sunlight.

Before he could stop himself, Ralph trod on the photo. Then he stepped back hastily and, gripping the beer cans under one arm, stooped to retrieve it. Hunkering there, he studied the picture. It showed a buck-toothed girl of thirteen or fourteen years old, with caterpillar eyebrows and a strong Roman nose – a face uncannily like a dachshund's.

It was a moment of no natural drama. A car alarm was going outside, and some passing kids were running through a Monty Python sketch in shrill, unconvincing accents. Eddie was on his knees, chewing the cellophane off a fresh pack of Dorals.

Ralph looked at the back of the picture, signed "Love, DC," shook his head and said, "Denise Cadwallader."

Eddie dropped the cigarettes, swearing, and gaped.

"No – no way, man. You mean you know Deesey?"

"Of course I know her," Ralph said. "She's my sister."

# WHAT HAPPENS

1.) Eddie is born and I'm adopted.

2.) Our father dies, somewhere, we are reliably informed.

3.) At 22, Eddie meets a woman named Denise in Cairo; she, mysterious, dark, and very beautiful like in the movies – Hitchcock, for instance – tells him some unbearable secret and loves him too briefly, vanishing at a crucial point.

4.) Our mother dies, leaving only Eddie untold wealth.

5.) Eddie meets a man named Ralph in Colorado, and something impresses Eddie, something unaccountable attaches him to Ralph, as happens to guys whose fathers were sufficiently absentee.

6.) With his untold wealth, Eddie sets up a spiritual institute, making Ralph a New Age guru.

7.) Like other enterprises of spoiled children, this one ends in madness, grief and debt.

8.) On an island off the coast of Peninsular Malaysia, raving and alone, my brother dies. Unaccountably, Denise phones me with the news.

9.) Ralph and I fly to Malaysia, where the answers await us on a damp beach whose waters sparkle too much, in flecks, like cartoon radiation.

## "You Can't Go Home Over My Dead Body Until You Wipe That Look Off Your Face"

★ ★ ★

1     At Berkeley, my PhD dissertation subject was Marlowe's *Dr. Faustus.*

1.1   It's the old wheeze:
- man learns dark secret
- flies too near sun
- crash
- straight to hell

1.2   Moral: Don't think too much.

1.3   I was engaged in a deconstructive analysis, as I tautologically expressed it.

2     Dr. Faustus was an actual person.

2.1   A native of Germany, he plied his trade in the rowdy public houses common in the first half of the sixteenth century.

2.2   Dr. Faustus lost his post as schoolmaster at Kreuznach through "the most dastardly lewdness with the boys."

2.3   "This wretch, taken prisoner at Batenburg on the Maas, was treated rather leniently by the chaplain, Dr. Johannes Dorstenius, because he promised the man, who was good but not shrewd, knowledge of various arts. Hence the chaplain kept drawing him wine, by which Faust was very much exhilarated, until the vessel was empty. When Faust learned this, and the chaplain told him that he was going to Grave that he might have his beard shaved, Faust promised him another unusual art by which his beard might be removed without the use of a razor, if he would provide more wine. When this condition was accepted, Faust told him to rub his beard vigorously with arsenic, but without any mention of its preparation. When the salve had been applied, there followed such an inflammation that not only the hair but also the skin and the flesh were burned off. The chaplain himself told me of this piece of villainy more than once with much indignation."

2.4   In short, the historical Faustus was a vicious quack.

3      The myth of the great magician came later, posthumous to the man Faust.

3.1    In the legend, Faust performed marvels, played tricks on popes and kings, learned the secret ways of stars and immortals.

3.2    Faust summoned Helen of Troy to be his lover, and with her had a son, Justus, born with the gift of prophecy.

3.3    "The devil has honestly kept the promise that he made to me, therefore I will honestly keep the pledge that I made and contracted with him," said Faust, facing an eternity of torture.

3.4    The yarn was embellished by Marlowe, Mann, Goethe.

## *Chronology*

**1991:** I am working on a deconstructive treatment of *Dr. Faustus.*

**1992:** I am working on a deconstructive treatment of *Dr. Faustus.*

**1993:** Although I have not visited the campus in a year, I am still working on a deconstructive treatment of *Dr. Faustus.*

**1994:** I am trying to summon the demon Mephistopheles, drawing chalk figures on my floor and chanting Latin backward.

**1995:** Even my psychiatrist does not realize that, crouched painfully under the bed, with a flashlight, after my mother has gone to sleep, I am working on a deconstructive treatment of *Dr. Faustus*.

**1996:** I keep the deconstructive treatment hidden in a pillowcase; before I go to sleep I place an envelope full of letters from "good" people over it, and paperweight the lot with a King James Bible. I have not dared open the pillowcase in six months.

**1997:** Now that I have finally destroyed all trace of my deconstructive treatment of *Dr. Faustus*, I do not understand why I feel unhappy.

**1998:** My mother dies of complications following liposuction surgery. Eddie comes home with Ralph and I faint. I wake up on top of the bed, naked and hot in blinding sunlight.

And, seeing the room from this unaccustomed angle, I remember my deconstructive treatment of *Dr. Faustus*. I haven't thought about it in a long time.

In my deconstructive treatment of *Dr. Faustus*, I consider the manner in which incredulity "writes" the discourse about the magus. I draw on sources from *The Golden Bough* to the Bhagwan Rajneesh. Only it never quite gels.

I think of some ways in which life might have been different, had it gelled.

I lie in bed for some time, just feeling sorry for myself and malingering. I dwell on the negatives. I am flabby, dank, unlovable. Staunch, exalted souls rot in the mines, in the rice paddies, in the exploiters' factories, while I fatten like a horrible insect.

I go back underneath the bed and days pass.

Sometimes Eddie and Ralph come in to check on me. They say "Hello?" experimentally – but when I don't respond, they tromp around doing whatever as if they're alone in the room. Every now and then, Eddie sits on the floor and talks to me. I mostly say "yes" and "no." Sometimes I think of whole sentences I might say, but they're all weasely ways of asking why he doesn't love me. Afterward I suffer agonies of humiliation, just thinking that I almost said these sentences.

I'm trying to hallucinate. The hallucination I choose is of a mass of starving children in the courtyard, calling to eat me. I consider this a potent, apt hallucination. I know it would piss my mother off no end.

I don't quite tell Eddie or Ralph I am hallucinating, though I drop strong hints.

I keep thinking I'm about to come out from under the bed. Then I think something else. For hours at a time I recall old *Happy Days* episodes, amazed that we all found Fonzie sexy. I remember unlikely fish from *The Undersea World of Jacques Cousteau*. Did I make up the giant crab? Johnny Carson backward is Nosrac Ynnhoj. What is Nosrac Ynnhoj? would be my prize-winning *Jeopardy* question.

"You're going to have to come out someday, Chrysa. You know? Cause I'll make you. I'll totally set it on fire or something. Not. Kidding."

## The Undersea World of Jacques Cousteau
## Dries Up and Blows Away

1   Ralph kneels down beside the bed and slides a plate of chili in to me, smearing the dust ruffle with poppy-red sauce.

2    I throw up violently into a plastic bucket. It's yellow; the handle's hooked behind my neck.

3    They're sitting on the bed over me having a discussion.

"The bed is the actual problem, cause we don't talk about this but Chrysa was actually raped in this bed but then Mom was too cheap to throw it out. So no fucking wonder."

"I don't think the bed is the problem."

"And yet, curiously enough, the bed is the problem, or else I don't know why you bother to just contradict me."

"I think the problem is self-pity."

4    Eddie hauls me out from under the bed by my ankle, yelling, "I'll throw you out, I'll fucking do it, you don't wise up fast."


### Parenthesis


(It's fun to slide on the floor. Then I'm revealed, a horrible result like a turtle pried out of its shell. I'm covered in some kind of juice, unlike other sweat. Eddie goes, "Oh, *Jesus*."

I cry, "Leave me alone! Leave me alone! Leave me alone!" I am sort of trying to curl up in a crash position, but also to sit up normally, so the effect is as if two kids are fighting for the controls.

"Okay, you need a fucking shower, I'm not kidding. Right? You look like shit. I'm your brother, okay? You look like shit. Do you ever think of eating?"

"Leave me alone!"

He mimics, in a high-pitched voice, "Leave me alone!

Leave me alone!" And then – "No. You gotta come do something for me."

*"You're just fucking cruel!"*

He crosses his arms. I catch my breath and everything is devastatingly clear. All the things I have to say to Eddie are simple and friendly. Then the next sob comes and I remember that he doesn't love me.

"Well, get up," he says. "I haven't got all day, personally."

"I can't," I snivel. For a moment it's true. I can't even get up, and there he is, tormenting me.

"I need you to come to Mom's office," he says, with labored sarcasm. "It's like, ten inches, do you think you can manage ten inches?"

But I say stubbornly, inspired: "I'll have to crawl."

"I don't care if you roll! Do umbrella steps!" Eddie wails. "I want you to type a *mailing list,*

FOR FUCK'S SAKE!"

I crawl to my mother's office. Eddie shuffles behind me, muttering, groaning with impatience. I can feel the swipe when he mimes kicking me in the ass. Sometimes I'm on all fours, making a good clip despite a fake limp in my left arm. Sometimes, depleted, I fall on my belly and can only make pitiful, beached-jellyfish motions. In my mind, at any moment he might crack and fall to his knees beside me, clasping me in his arms. If this miracle can be achieved, everything will instantly be healed and bright. Why don't you love me? Why don't you love me? my mind is booming.

At the same time I'm so furious I want to turn and bite his shins. So I'm a hypocrite, really, and I can feel I'm going to get nowhere.

Can't give up, though, I tell myself. A quitter never wins.

Eddie's understandably exasperated; but satisfied, too. I feel in my ritual donkey imitation I am actually carrying both of our loads. It's strange how, to an outsider, he would seem to be the powerful one.

Finally we arrive at Mom's office. By now we have arrived, too, at the point where people just rave, as if in fever, and the things they say are all deformed by heat. So as I grovel up to the PowerMac Mom got new just before she disintegrated and was no more, Eddie's barking, "Me and Ralph can't type, cause we're men. So you gotta at least type or else you go live in the garden with the other snails!"

"Oh, you can too type! You can type!"

"We can't type! We're men!"

"You can type!"

"NO! You're gonna type and fuck you!"

"I'll type but you have to admit that you can type first!"

"We can't type!"

Silence. I'm crouched on the gray carpet in my mother's office. The furniture is glass and stainless steel and black canvas. It's like sitting inside an expensive suitcase.

Eddie says, "I got the mailing lists over there. They need to go on labels."

I blurt: "But I'll need the computer on the floor."

Eddie winds up and slams his fist down on the glass computer desk. Both of us flinch, expecting it to shatter. But nothing happens. Then he says, "Look what you made me do."

I'm shouting, "Don't dare blame me!" as he stamps out of the room.

I sob for some time, and think about homelessness. Then I move the monitor and the keyboard down under the desk. I crawl to fetch the mailing lists. There are 48 pages of addresses, single-spaced. I feel safe, realizing it will take me a long time. As long as I have labels, Eddie won't throw me out.

From then on, every day I furtively crawl down the

corridor to my mother's office, where I sit under the desk typing labels and printing them out. When my eyes begin to hurt from the screen, I stick labels on envelopes. Once, when I look up at the door, Ralph's there. I duck my head, ashamed because I look like shit. He says, "How's things?" and when I look up again, he's gone. Later, in the doorway, I find a cheese sandwich, neat on a plate with a folded paper napkin.)

## End Parenthesis

5    Eddie lies on my floor drinking peppermint schnapps. It's late at night, I don't know how late. Through the dust ruffle he tells me how cool it's going to be once the center's really going. But he can't let me stay if I'm some loony crawling around the halls.

I'm his sister and he loves me and all. He likes me, anyway. He loves me. No, he likes me, no, he loves me. No, it's something else that doesn't start with an L.

So, instead of rotting in my own shit, why don't I just wake up and do his marketing stuff; I got that Master's after all, and what good's a Master's if all I want out of life's to rot under a bed? I gotta admit.

While he speaks, I'm trying to hallucinate. I've got the starving children massed out in the courtyard. I make them wail: *Hey, Chrysa, someday everyone's gone forever! Let usss eeeat you! Someday everyone's gone forever!*

And I tell him through the dust ruffle that I would be glad to do his marketing stuff; but what about the children? They're expecting me to feed them.

Eddie doesn't answer. Eddie doesn't answer. Soon I understand, and burn with embarrassment. I'm only pretending to hallucinate, to earn pity. Eddie saw through me. Now he's going to tell Ralph.

6    A coyote howled in the courtyard, everyone was out of the house and only a real coyote. Eddie was gone too. I prayed to God for Eddie to be downstairs although I knew he wasn't. Finally I just lay in the cool night dust slack-jawed and thought that the coyote must have brown fur and his pawpads would be rough and warm. They would feel to him like my bare feet do, on the poolside tiles.

He howled. I lay and hummed along quietly. Finally I guess he was all howled out.

7    I don't know exactly how long I malingered. It's easy to mistake a month for two weeks, and vice versa. It can't have been important to our ancestors to tell.

It seemed like one incredibly long bad day.

8    Then I crawled out from under the bed and stood up. I reeled there, wondering, how did that happen? I almost got back under

but didn't, and there I was.

Healed!

In the windows, the day was blue. The grass below shone. I felt pretty atrocious, but that seemed less important now. It occurred to me that if I never told anyone I was depressed, I could have a brilliant career, and no one any the wiser.

## Upright Considerations and Doubts:
## "WHERE CHILDREN COME FROM"

★ ★ ★

1    In the spring of '71, my father was conducting studies in Peru.

1.1   He and his colleagues shared an unfurnished hut, little more than a frame for mosquito netting.

1.2   Its backyard was virgin jungle.

1.3   Out front, the ramshackle village had been abandoned; it was a ghost town soon to be reabsorbed by forest.

1.4   All the men carried rifles.

STATE SECRETS:
- Who his colleagues were.
- What they were doing there.
- Why all the people had left the village.

2    One night, Dad was woken in his hammock by a series of rhythmic cries.

2.1   A novice in the Amazon, he lay for a long time matching the noise to imagined perils.
- improbably huge mosquito swarms
- japing guerrillas
- the voice of the anaconda, which a man hears only once

2.2   Finally he was fully awake. He crept out, snagging a rifle on the way.

3    He walked down the dead street.

3.1   It took him a while to find the noise: he kept scanning the black wall of jungle.

3.2   I was sitting in the middle of the road.

3.3 Filling my lungs and squalling. Filling my lungs and squalling.

4  I was tied by a string to my older brother's wrist: he was lying dead beside me, and the thing making me scream was a sizable vulture perched on his chest, flapping its wings aggressively to drive me away.

5  My father scared the vulture off and took me back to the minimal shack.

5.1 Since some of his colleagues were medical personnel, they were able to save my life: I was malnourished, wormy, tubercular.

5.2 I became a project mascot.

5.3 Then Dad took me home and adopted me.

STATE SECRETS:
- How my brother died.
- What peoples lived in that region.
- Was it Peru specifically or just a Peru-like country.
- What did Dad care.
- Are the other starving children still sitting in the street, in that Peru-like country, and why.

6  "The second I clapped eyes on you, something told me, that's my daughter."

6.1 "Your father is in love with his own legend, end of story."

6.2 I found a photo of myself, a bony tot among enormous leaves. I stand with one fist up, smiling. My head is shaved. Because the photo's black and white, it looks authentic.

6.3 Eddie: "What if Dad just got the maid pregnant?"

7  I've never been to Peru.

"I got a phone call from your father, saying he'd found you. He called you a maiden in distress. I was mostly worried, cause Eddie was very small, that you didn't have some contagious disease. I said that, and your father puffs himself all up and says, 'Lannie, that's ludicrous. This is a little girl, a little baby girl.'

"I was so. Pissed. Then he got home and it turns out he thought I said 'religious beliefs,' not 'contagious disease.' The phone connection was always terrible, you know.

"I didn't think anything about it, then. I mean, I thought it was terrific. I kept waiting, maybe he'd bring back more. My friend used to save me news clippings of Mia Farrow.

"We were just young then. You know. We thought the rules didn't apply to us."

## I Have Told My Friends in Confidence:

- I was dropped here from outer space.
- He blew away my whole tribe in a bio-warfare experiment.
- I'm just adopted, from an agency, and my parents are so lame they had to make up this fairy tale.

## I Have Believed:

- The story he told like gospel.
- I don't know what happened, anything but that dumb story.

## The One Sure Thing:

If Dad had got the maid pregnant, we would never have heard the end of it. It's just the sort of thing Mom loved to announce at dinner, on those rare occasions when Dad was at home.

I was first just cries in the night of jungle.

E  Eddie – epileptic. E is for Eddie like C is for me, and
   everything beginning with his letter eyes/eggs/envelopes
   are eloquent of once, of our

F  Frailty. A flimsy duo: I the foundling just, not fed, there
   was no food where I was from, Eddie got called
   fag
   by kids at school. Therefore afraid to seem feminine, of
   being

G  gay. "Get away from me, *girl meat*."
   He called me goon, too, and geek, though he was the
   one I loved/ I was the one he loved
   and I, when I grew up, was gonna

H  take him home. To outer space.
   "When you're better."


and his is only petit mal, a small evil, his long, long look
at what you cannot remember. Mom says his name, then we
say nothing. We girls wait where we happened to fetch up,
seized:
   and watch Eddie watching what the dead see.
   Sometimes his face twitches, though uninhabited

There are three cans of Coke on the concrete shoulder of the pool. They're friendly there: if I get scared I can drink Coke. I'm holding on to the ladder because I can only doggy-paddle still. Beside me, Eddie treads water. I don't want him to say Watch Me Do a Somersault but I know he's going to.

I don't want Mom to come out of the house.

But I'm still not scared yet.

**Watch me do a somersault,** says Eddie, and I turn my head toward him. He holds his nose and goes under with a big splash. I look away and when he comes up, I say it was pretty good.

Dad comes out of the lit open French doors, stalks to the pool and nose-dives, as fast as that. We usually would hooray.

When he comes up I call out in truthful instinctive longing, **Daddy.**

He says, **How's my sea horse?**

**I'm fine, Daddy,** I say. **Daddy, why did you go away that time?**

He says he was in Timbuktu hunting killer gorillas. The gorillas there are so fierce, they eat up Daddies there in two big bites. Chomp, womp!

We usually would jabber and ask.

I say **THAT'S NOT TRUE.** I'm scared.

Mom comes out of the house. She stomps to the concrete shoulder.

She's <u>messy</u>. Her slippered foot troubles the Coke can on the left. That's mine, she's going to kick it over.

"It's an accident," I mouth. It didn't happen yet, but I think as if it did.

Mom watches us like a bad ghost. Eddie starts to splash.

Mom says, **I want to know how I got painted as the villain of this piece,** trembling and evil.

We paddle way below her. I'm scared.

She kicks my Coke over into the pool as she turns to go back in the open lit French doors.

The Coke drains a shadow into the turquoise water.

Dad says, **This is getting out of hand.** He swims. He swims hard, disturbing the whole water.

When he's done I say to him, **Daddy, I'm sorry I said what I said about you saying something wrong.**

He says, **Let's just make believe you were quiet as a mouse. Can we do that? Let's all pretend we're quiet, quiet mice.**

# Easy in Hindsight

1   As teens, we realized Dad was a criminal against humanity.

1.1  Reading between the lines, we held him responsible for US policy in Latin America.

- Dad brought down Allende.
- Dad "disappeared" trade unionists.
- Behind a two-way mirror, Dad supervised tortures, commenting on pregnant women dying in awful pain.

1.2  "CIA plus biochemist," Eddie sniggered, "Sick or what?"

2   One night in an Italian restaurant, we cornered Mom.

2.1  "You can't keep hiding all your life," we chanted, "We deserve the truth."

2.2  Our mother began to cry in a way we had not seen.

2.3  Hands shaking, she scrubbed her face with a red cloth napkin.

2.4  It was the first time we'd realized she could grow old.

3   "I don't know. I don't know, I don't know. I don't know, all right? I just don't know."

4   The gypsy violinist gave our table a wide berth.

4   My brother, desperate, gripped his salad fork and threatened to kill her.

4.1  I said, "Please," in a whisper and then focused on the statue behind Mom's head.

- It was labelled "JVPITER."
- Its torso was crisply muscled.
- Its plaster eyes were all white.
- It had bare, albeit genteelly meager, genitalia.

4.2  "Eddie!" Mom wailed as he stamped to the exit. Then she turned to me, took a deep breath, and sneered, monstrous:

4.3 "Eat your food," said my broken mom. "At effing least."

5 We cleaned our plates, but declined the dessert menu.

5.1 As she lay her Mastercard in the salver, I piped up.

5.2 "You're not my mother. You're not my mother. Why couldn't Dad just leave me in the jungle to starve?"

5.3 It was my turn to cry.

6 "Don't make a scene, Chrysa. Who's your mother? Holy Mary? If you want to know, I wish he'd just left me in the jungle to starve, too. I don't know why I married that prick. I must have been crazy!"

6.1 She noticed JVPITER then. "Hello!" she said over her shoulder in surprise, and glanced at his wee equipment.

6.2 "Well! You can't live with 'em!" said my mother, and laughed like a mule.

7 Eddie was waiting for us by the car, still holding the salad fork.

7.1 This dinner flashes before me whenever anyone says the word "dysfunctional."

I got out from under and stood. I was all better. In the windows, the day was blue. How the grass glittered, rinsed and rinsed by heady sprinklers.

I hadn't stood up in so long, it was like swaying on high. It was like mounting a caparisoned elephant. I was grown up. I was tall.

And I thought that once upon a time, a little boy was separated from his elephant by the chicanery of the Raj, and some twenty years later, still a boy ungrown because of the draining lack of elephant, he was brought in state to Delhi and remounted on the animal, festooned for this occasion in ribbons and paint and gilded finery; he climbed up and was initially awkward and bobbled from side to side, but then the elephant took; the elephant became as it were magnetized and attracted the boy's whole frame with its alternative balance and they promenaded off toward the open jungle, shedding tinsel on the Ministry lawns.

Later that day, Ralph came up to see me. He opened the door without knocking, and when he saw me sitting up on the bed, all showered, in clean clothes, he stepped back.

"Sorry. I thought you were asleep."

I said, "That's okay."

He stood in the doorway, absolutely still. Finally I looked up and said bravely that I wanted to eat, but I didn't want to eat in my bedroom, but I wasn't sure I could make it down the stairs.

He smiled. "You can't win, then, can you?"

There was a fly in the room that kept buzzing as if it was really desperate. Ralph just shut the door and went away.

So I made it downstairs and found him in the kitchen

and he cooked me spaghetti with green spaghetti. Eddie had taken the chairs so we ate standing up.

And when I grew mawkish, hanging my head over the smeary plate,

Ralph said, "Cut it out."

And he told me the story of his ugly stepsister, who had two passports at fourteen and traveled the world lightly with a briefcase of towels and cash, and broke the bank once at the Yak and Yeti Hotel Casino, Kathmandu, playing cards stalwartly through the many power cuts.

# CAIRO SECTIONS

## Argument

*Eddie met the only woman he ever loved in Cairo,
when he was 22. He could never say what it was about her.
During their romance, she gave him three snapshots of herself
as a young girl. Although these photos did not resemble her,
he treasured them for the rest of his life.*

# 11. 1987: The Pyramids of Giza / The Sahara Desert

*Your sister Isis comes to you rejoicing for love of you.*
*You have placed her on your phallus and your seed issued in her*
*. . . the sky is pregnant of wine . . . may you ascend to the sky,*
*may the sky give birth to you like Orion . . .*

The Pyramid Texts (2025 BC)

## A

- The King's and Queen's chambers reeked of urine.
- They contained nothing but 100 years of graffiti.
- There are no taxis.
- There are no other tourists.
- He keeps looking in his guide book to find out why he came here.

## B

- Nagged by souvenir hawkers, Eddie strays into the desert.
- He hides himself between two tall dunes before it strikes him: This is the mother fucking Sahara.
- He's thrilled.
- His prick stirs, he notices once again his thirst.
- Over that dull crest, desert for 1,000 miles.
- I could die out here, he thinks to intensify the buzz.
- Then he shuts his eyes and walks blind into the sand

# Preface

★ ★ ★

At the age of 22, Eddie went on a trip around the world. It was a college graduation present from our Uncle Jerry. The ticket was: London – Cairo – Singapore – Melbourne – Tahiti – LA, with 7,000 dollars for expenses and side trips. Eddie expected to be gone for ten months.

Mother was unhinged with worry over Eddie's epilepsy. "One beer," she opined, "one joint, and – kablooey!" She cut out articles about American tourists taken hostage, highlighting victims with medical complaints in pink.

If Eddie tried to watch TV, she used the commercial breaks to scaremonger: the Zambian hospitals staffed by Nazis; how Ann's son became a cabbage; Third World-dumped medicines that caused "instant" cancer.

At the climax, Eddie would storm out, raving:

"Stick me in an incubator! Someday, I might get sick!"

1     Eddie called collect from London every night to tell Mom she smothered him.

1.1   Three postcards arrived the following week:

1.2   *Dear Mom,*
      *Got here without dying. This is just to let you know I decided to use my middle name from now on cause I suddenly realized, Eddie = Oedipus, which just freaks me out. Like, I can't believe I was so lucky to get away, now I see what's really happening. Anyway, this is the last time I'm writing, so if you want to think I'm dead, it's not my problem. – JACK*

1.3   *Chrysa,*
      *Here in London which SUCKS. They all look like fucking*

*walruses, I totally get that Beatles song. So I've got this Finnish chick now, Martina, she's like seventeen. She's like, she left her hometown because "the people were not sincere," so basically dumb chick. But that's why I'm not writing after this cause I can only write when I'm lonely, sorry. Tell Mom I'm trying to be cool but I can't deal with her right now. – JACK*

1.4   *Chrysa,*

*Getting the fuck out of Europe to Africa, I can't take it here. It's like everything's neutered with so-called "civilization." Like Martina ran off with some other Finnish asshole named Casper (honest to shit real name) cause he sleeps with both men and women because he's comfortable with his masculinity or some shit, which I don't have to leave California to hear this shit. Like friendly ghost jokes or what. So I'll write from Egypt if I don't suddenly have a fit and die. – JACK*

1.5   That was the last we heard.

## 10. Cairo International Airport / First Sight

The arrivals hall is a filthy bare hangar. It's 3:00 A.M.: he's groggy from sleeplessness and the flight. Around him, a thousand grubby Egyptians jostle. There is no single file; there are no ropes and no officials. The windows show only the anonymous airstrip.

The crowd shifts, gradually condensing until he accepts the pressure of flesh on all sides, the taste in the air of breath. The foreign stink elates him, he shuts his eyes to hear their language. This is fucking strange, he could be anywhere. For a moment he falls asleep on his feet and dreams that he's asleep on his feet in a crowd of tired Egyptians. They're in a bleak airport. There's an unexplained delay. *But I'm not really there,* he realizes in the dream –

and wakes in a crowd of tired Egyptians, dropping his briefcase. He mutters *Sorry,* bending to retrieve it, then lingers in his hunched posture, staring at the grime spirographed on the tiles. He's not really there. He can feel it, the lack of himself where it's numb. Which is maybe just tired, or maybe, the beginning of some creeping epileptic death where your brain fizzles out bit by bit. He stands up trying to remember how to think, and sees –

some shoulders away, in an unpeopled pocket like a clearing, a white girl. She has long dark hair and a wan Pre-Raphaelite face. Meeting his eye, she doesn't smile but lets the gaze be, factual with exhaustion. She wears a yellow Santa Cruz T-shirt, decorated with a sketch of palm trees. He wants to tell her Santa Cruz is fifteen minutes from his house. In the pale flash of desire he feels, Eddie returns to himself, immediate and hot.

His restored being is a restive dollop of who knows. Floating above it, Eddie pictures a trumpet: loopy, canary yellow. From the round bell grows a sheaf of grain: he knows in that instant that the plant is called *benelia*.

*There is a music you can only play on his, Eddie's, horn. When Eddie dies, the wholesome benelia bread will be no more. (He has a quick flash of a long file of disappointed pilgrims, come with their ailing children to eat of the benelia: alas, there is no hope for little Rosa's crippled leg – the pilgrims wail, and*

Then he's freed and barges greedily, fighting his way to the immigration post.

- Cairo rules.
- He thinks he will live here for the rest of his life.
- This place is totally all the answers to his problems.

And he winds up at the Hotel Raffles, where the arched windows have no glass but only fretwork shutters; slumps on the iron-framed bed, pulls out his airplane book, Martina's copy of *The Celestine Prophecy*, of which he'd said, "You're reading this garbage?" then borrowed it:

in the front, she's written her address in Finland.

Real linen sheets, a ceiling fan that wags in an eternal game of tag with flies

and in the morning he is up at six and drinking sugar-cane juice for breakfast from a fly-besieged stall

another taxi

to the pyramids of Giza

And he wades up a dune blind; skis down and falls. As he kneels in the sand, a shadow passes over him. He thinks of a massive, sun-blotting hawk, is startled,

opens his eyes

There she and the Sphinx are, and nothing else at all.

## 12. The Sphinx

### Neat

A girl in a Santa Cruz T-shirt; long dark hair tied back from a pale face; long legs. She has dark eyes, like his, and the same narrow jaw, the same quizzically peaked frown like a spaniel's. They might be brother and sister.

But she's beautiful.

It's unsettling to what degree the stranger is beautiful: in this dun, monotonous waste.

"Hello," she says. "I remember you from the airport. But why are you kneeling in the middle of the desert?"

The sun blinds him and he looks down at her abbreviated shadow, whose hair blows and waves banner-fashion on the sand.

"Yeah . . . I guess I'm having a kind of dehydration episode?"

"Oh." She waggles a can of Fanta before his eyes, crouches. "How neat. It's like . . . a terrible advert."

He takes the can and drinks. It's hot like tea.

Her T-shirt has wet patches at the armpits and in a blaze on her chest. She's older than he first thought – older than him. When he notices the yellow stains shadowing her index and middle fingers, the mark of a heavy smoker, he's gripped by a strange remorse, a tug so violent it gives him a déjà vu of early childhood, when it's okay to feel this strongly.

She says, "Now all your problems vanish."

## Kismet

She's named Denise, but she prefers to be called Deesey. She's from Britain, but has lived all over. Now she's "just" on holiday.

He tells her his name is Jack, and she cocks her head.

"Jack what?"

They are picking their way back toward the Pyramids, barefoot in deep, baking sand, and when he says "Moffat," she stops.

"Jack Moffat?" she queries, with that spaniel frown.

He takes a deep breath. He has been using his father's name. "Yeah, why?"

"I don't know. I think it sounds like someone famous." She shrugs, and continues walking thoughtfully as if trying to place the name.

She's staying at the same hotel; a coincidence. They agree that the showers are surprisingly clean. In an aside, she comments, "Well, Jack's staying at the Hotel Raffles!"

Then they go on in silence; it's understood they'll spend the day together.

And when they come out of the long slog of sand to the road, there is a taxi idling by the now open drinks stall. He says, on an impulse,

"Kismet."

She balks: "What do you mean?"

She has her sandals twined on one hand. They are spindly, chestnut leather; a bad match for her cheap cotton shorts. She stands pigeon-toed and her bare feet writhe with the heat of the road, her whole stance is this discomfort.

"Why don't you put your shoes on?" he says.

But she laughs, unfooled, and states: "He refused to tell her what Kismet means."

## Morphic Resonance

The taxi ride is taking a long time. The heat has silenced them, and they are each draped out of an open window, eyes shut in the speed breeze. In that darkness, in which the whole world is warm and blows in on you generously, dirty and maternal, Eddie has fallen in love. He has decided he has fallen in love. *Now that I've fallen in love,* and *How can I have fallen in love so fast,* and, proudly, *Love at first sight.*

And then out of the blue, out of the turbulent warm darkness, her voice pipes courteously: "Did you know that the Sphinx was once under water? It's older than the pyramids."

She has leaned her head against the frame of the car window. It shakes slightly with the bumps, that passivity making her look sleepy. She's smoking her third cigarette of the drive, poking the end out to let the wind strip the ash.

She's still beautiful. It's just, fucking relentless.

He says, "Did you know the first use of the Sphinx was as a four-star restaurant? They've found seating for a hundred on the lower level."

The joke surprises him as it comes. He remembers that he's funny, and sits back, relieved.

But she just smokes, shakes her head, deadpan:

"What's amazing is that someone told me that same thing about the Tower of Pisa last month. Do you know Rusty? Blond, American, with a sailboat?"

"No."

There is a long pause. She leans back again, shutting her eyes, and her passivity strikes Eddie now as indifference.

He says, "Maybe it's going around."

She says from behind her shut eyes, "It's morphic resonance."

"Morphic resonance?"

"Mmm."

"Well, tell me. Now I gotta know."

"It's some New Age mumbo jumbo about how every-thing is really one," she says, and her manner refers angrily to some third party, who has stubbornly adhered to morphic resonance, in the face of all her efforts to disprove it.

## Lucky

They've gone for fiteer, the local pastry-bottomed pizza, in a low-ceilinged cellar where the chef has to bend his knees to make room to toss the dough. Until the beer comes, neither of them speaks.

And he is so in love. And he is so in love. He is in love. Love at first sight.

The radio plays soggy *Ya Habibi* Arab pop. She puffs a Cleopatra cigarette in time. He keeps being drawn to watch the chef tossing pizza dough – but she isn't, doesn't glance, so he is shamed and tries to resist the cheap spectacle. Arriving with the beer, the waiter places paper doilies on the table to receive the glasses, and the fans' wind tugs them instantly; Eddie and Deesey have to pin them down until the glasses land.

Then the moisture roots them.

He remembers all these details, years later. The table tops were gray pretend marble. He was not hungry in a particular way that he would never not be hungry again, without her. When he turned his head, his sunburnt neck crinkled sensuously.

Years later, he does not remember: the frightening possibility of not really loving her, censored time and again. How he anticipated love's euphoria each time he was <u>going</u>

to look at her. How sometimes it took concentration and patience to pinpoint the detail of her that would yield the rush. He triggered it greedily, seeking to maximize it, like a man eating too many corn chips in search of the perfect one.

He had to make her love him back, at all costs.

He was about to drink beer for the first time, too ashamed to tell her why he shouldn't. Sitting in front of the full glass, he watched the foam subside with a superstitious thrill. His mind parroted *one beer, one joint, kablooey.*

"Well," she said, "to Kismet."

"To Kismet."

The glasses met in a graceless side-swipe that made him want to try again. That urge haunted him as he sipped with show relish. Somehow he had known ahead of time its gruff metallic taste.

She said:

"But do you know what Kismet means?"

Distracted by his sense of looming tipsiness, he bought time. "In what way? What it means."

"Just, do you know what it means?"

He took a deep swig. Going down, the liquid numbed his throat.

She said harshly, "I'm serious."

He smiled helplessly. Already the beer was turning him into a retard. His mind prattled, *recurrence, grand mal seizures, chthonic-clonic.*

"Look," she said, "I'm not meaning to be heavy, it's just something that happened to me recently, when we were in Australia."

"Who's we?"

"Just we. That doesn't matter. We were in Australia. And we had an Australian friend, a girl, Jessie. We were at her flat, drinking, and we started talking about all the poisonous spiders they have in Australia. And Jessie told us a story about a friend of hers, also named Jessie. This friend Jessie was with a few tourists, like us, in her flat, telling them about the dangerous spiders. And suddenly she got up and went to the middle of the carpet and said, My God, there's a funnel-web spider right there, and pointed. And the spider jumped up into the air and bit her on the end of her finger."

Eddie laughed. Deesey said, "Exactly."

"Exactly," he echoed.

"So she told us this, and we looked around the carpet then. And she got up, laughing, and began to prowl about, you know, hunting spiders. And then she said, My God, there is one, I don't believe it. And we yelled out, don't point at it for God's sakes, and she laughed and pointed at it to wind us up, and the spider leapt into the air and bit her on the end of her finger."

"We just ran and dialed the ambulance, and we were slicing her finger open and whatnot, <u>sucking</u> it, and they gave her a shot. But she was in hospital for a week."

"Jesus Christ."

"Well. The funnel-web spider."

She shook her head and then very definitely turned away, turned her frown on the pizza chef, tossing his eternal dough. Eddie followed her gaze and for some moments they sat mesmerized by that deft swoop and catch and stretch. At last the chef winked at them, without missing a beat, and Eddie said, "So. What do you make of that?"

"I was *hoping*," she said, "*you* might hazard a guess." She shot him a fleeting scowl of reproach.

In the joshing, affectionate tone meant to enforce warmth, Eddie said, "That's so totally unfair."

She winced as if he'd sworn at her. She said, "It's not that it's unfair. It's that I'm fucking desperate."

Stung, he blathered, "Well, I'm not just saying this to fuck you up, the spiders were in league? Cause I was reading in the *Washington Post* on the plane, they did a study at MIT and spiders are actually highly intelligent, like dolphins. They have a sophisticated language that's related to Basque, only much smaller. So that's a possibility at least, but otherwise, I really hope you don't hate me for saying this, but, for all I know, Kismet is just a Broadway musical."

"Point taken."

The pizza arrived then, ending it.

Over food, she mellowed and was again gracious.

As they got up to leave, he said, "I only know I'm lucky to be here with you, that's all I know."

She smiled and said softly, "That's not enough."

## 9. Perspective: Turkey (10 days previously)

1    Recently Denise had found the corpse of her murdered father.

1.1    In the fetal position in the hotel parking lot, Dad sprawled in his lost blood.

1.2    Seeing him, she hurried her step. It was 5:00 A.M.

2    She went down on her knees, and there was no one on this planet left who had ever claimed to love Denise; with this death, her beloved were dead, to the very last; with this, death had licked her plate clean.

2.1    She lay down in the grit and cradled, spoon-fashion like a wife:
  - a winter log, too wet for the fire
  - a thing numbingly, tangibly gone
  - Dad, made of cold

2.2    In my arms there is nothing left.

2.3    She didn't cry at the time.

2.4    In her turn she was found, and the police alerted.

3    When she arrived at the police station, there was the killer. A passerby had witnessed him throwing away a knife, his sleeve soaked red. He'd been arrested before the body was found. He was skinny, nondescript: a mugger who had never meant this. When he found out who Denise was, he held his cuffed hands out to her, sobbing and saying nothing.

4    The next morning, Deesey caught a flight to Cairo.

4.1    She left without making any funeral arrangements, simply ditching the corpse of her murdered father.

4.2    Nonetheless, sometimes during her romance with

Eddie, Deesey would drift off, imagining the Turkish morgue, the eventual trench or furnace.

4.3 Eddie had no idea of this at the time.

## Inevitable

on together in another cab to the medieval town,
Islamic Cairo, where
in a minaret of the Mosque of al-Muayyad
high above the pellmell in clean air
he kisses her
and she lets him cling and taste her tongue's gruff metal
stroke her bare, wet neck
they part to view
tiny on Cairo's roofs
chicken runs, laundry lines, heaps of refuse, sheep, men
working in the open
"This is very very uncool."

And what he most remembers is their walk through the
mosque of Al-Hakim. There was nothing about that mosque,
but it was dark, the incongruous chandeliers unlit, and they
walked there under the eye of some dour Shi'ia divine, never
daring even to touch hands, for eons, it was electrifying.
    And that night Eddie got drunk for the first time,
matching her beer for beer in legendary Groppi's, which has
faded in his memory to a single frame of white ice cream, in
two balls still stiff from the scoop
    and a fountain which may or may not have had water

# Facts for Tourists: The Mosque of Al-Hakim

1   Built in 1010 by the mad Caliph, Al-Hakim bi-Amr Allah.

1.1  When he was a boy, Al-Hakim's tutor nicknamed him "Lizard" for his off-putting grimaces and manners.

1.2  He was eleven when he took the throne.

1.3  That tutor was then murdered.

1.4  The mosque was once used as a prison for Crusaders.

2   One of Al-Hakim's generals dared come in on him unannounced.

2.1  The general had just returned from a victory; hence the rash gesture.

2.2  He found the Caliph standing over the corpse of a disemboweled boy.

2.3  The general was beheaded.

2.4  Salah al-Din stabled his horses in Al-Hakim's mosque.

3   Al-Hakim patrolled the city streets on his donkey, Moon.

3.1  He had a special hatred of dishonest merchants.

3.2  Anyone found cheating was sodomized on the spot, by a huge black servant accompanying Al-Hakim for this purpose.

3.3  Napoleon stored foodstuffs in Al-Hakim's mosque.

4   He hated dogs: he had all the dogs of Cairo slaughtered.

4.1  He hated women: for seven years, by his decree, they remained indoors.

4.2  To ensure this, a moratorium was declared on the manufacture of women's shoes.

4.3  Nasser opened a school for boys in Al-Hakim's mosque.

5   Finally, Al-Hakim proclaimed himself divine.

5.1 Three followers entered the Mosque of Amr at Friday prayers to substitute his name for that of Allah.

5.2 Enraged, the congregation murdered them on the spot.

5.3 Hakim had troops raze and loot the city in retaliation.

5.4 Soon thereafter, he vanished on a solitary jaunt with Moon.

5.5 His body was never found; one, at least, of his followers, saw in this proof of divinity, and went on to preach his worship in Syria.

5.6 This is the origin of the Druze sect.

5.7 Most recently, the mosque of Al-Hakim served as a madhouse.

## 13. Cairo: The Hotel Raffles

He wakes up swathed in damp linen, on an iron-framed bed, fully dressed and baking in the dim, kaleido-scopic light filtered through a fretwork shutter, in the Hotel Raffles.

He doesn't remember getting into bed. He doesn't know how he got here. Although his mouth is dry, he isn't hung over, and it takes him a while to recall the beer. Then he's seized by a dank presentiment.

*Kablooey.*

There's an unframed, speckled mirror on the wall he doesn't remember. His bags aren't where he left them. What's more, he's sure he recalls the bed being placed against the left wall. Now it's against the right wall, and though it makes no medical sense, he interprets this as a sign of returning epilepsy, some glitch of hemispheric differentiation which means he's thrown a seizure –

possibly grand mal –

in front of Her. Then blacked out and been carted here by paramedics.

No matter how many times he tells himself that didn't happen, he continues being chilled and mortified by that seizure. He needs a doctor. He never wants anyone to look at him again. Somehow he has to get back to California without ever leaving this room.

He rolls to look under the bed for his bags, and spots first his copy of *The Celestine Prophecy*, the purple cover looking fissured and beaten, the spine broken deeply. That's strange, too; it was pristine when he unpacked it. It's as if he staggered back here (or was dumped off his stretcher here), sat right up and read 200 pages at a sitting.

And the bags aren't there. Only his briefcase lies alone,

the emptiness around it made horribly apparent by the white-tiled floor.

Now he feels the meaty drumming of hangover in his skull. Poum poum, it harps on. He flashes on the phrase: *the last knockings.*

*Eddie baby,* he tells himself, *you can't just hang here upside down all day waiting for your head to pop. A, you got better things to do. B, what do I know from B? B is for blah blah fucking blah.*

He hangs there upside down.

She came back with him. For some unknown reason, she stayed up all night reading *The Celestine Prophecy* before ripping off his luggage.

Now she's gone.

His heart writhes.

He dives to yank the case out. Now he has to ensure his passport is there, his traveler's checks, his toothpaste, for Christ's sake, which at this moment if he's lost –

Cradling the briefcase in his lap, he works the tumblers feverishly. The combination's easy: his birthday, 11 06 68. But when he's got them lined up and pokes the catch, nothing. He re-aligns them, cursing the tickle of sweat that creeps down his brow. No, nothing. He tries 06 11 68, just in case: nothing nothing. And he's trying 11 06 68 for the third time, dripping with fear, when she walks in.

She looks as startled as he is. She's wearing a threadbare cotton bathrobe, carrying a plastic bag with a bar of soap in it, wet from the shower.

He says, "I'm just . . ." and shakes the briefcase. "I can't get it to open for me, I don't get it."

She says, "21 21 21."

"What? You changed the combination?"

She just frowns.

He begins to work the tumblers again, blushing now so

he's in all kinds of pain and heat and his fingers feel thick and tremble, and as he gets the numbers in their neat configurations at last, she says,

"What do you want in my briefcase?"

He freezes. Finally he says, "This is your briefcase?"

"Yes."

"The – you're reading *The Celestine Prophecy?*"

"Yes."

"It's crap."

"I know."

At that moment, from the mosque across the street, the call to prayer blares out, amplified to a rock-concert boom. Eddie busts out laughing. Leaning on the briefcase, out of breath, he belly-laughs, though it pounds up in his forehead. She is regarding him, very poised and unlaughing, with the air of someone politely hearing something out before objecting.

And as the din subsides, she's saying, "Why are you trying to open my briefcase? I don't understand."

He catches his breath and says, "I've got one just like this. I mean, I just assumed this was my room."

"Oh." She puts one hand to her throat and takes a deep breath. When she lets it out, she's smiling but wan. She says softly, "The old identical suitcases sketch."

He blurts, "I don't remember last night."

She shakes her head. "Look, *as* you've got the briefcase, would you mind fishing my towel out? I forgot it when I went to shower."

"It's in here?"

"Everything's in there," she says. "That's my home, you know."

He shoves the catch and the case opens to a sloppy assembly of clothes, on top of which, indeed, is a small hotel towel. And on top of that a photograph: a standard 8-by-10 glossy, loose in a clear plastic report folder.

It's the portrait of a handsome young Army officer, leaning against a palm trunk in bright, intrusive sunlight. The sky is bleached; the light settings must have been slightly out. Eddie knows it well; he has the same snap on his bedroom wall at home.

He looks up at her, trembling deeply in all his joints. It takes a long time before he trusts himself to speak.

"Why do you have a picture of my father in your brief-case?"

She ducks in an impulse of surprise, steps back. The seconds that pass then are painfully long, as if each has to fall a long distance. She is smiling a taut, unnatural smile. She says: "It came with the frame."

# Book Report: *The Celestine Prophecy*

In the book *The Celestine Prophecy*, an American man goes to Peru in search of a mysterious twelfth-century manuscript, unearthed there by archaeologists. It contains nine "inspirations" of such a revolutionary nature that the Peruvian government and church are bent on murder to suppress it. On his journey, knowledgeable strangers meet our hero and reveal to him, one by one, the inspirations of the Prophecies.

The first inspiration has to do with the meaning of coincidences. The new vision of the world predicted in the manuscript commences when people begin to take note of the coincidences in their lives. By becoming more aware, they create a situation in which these coincidences become more frequent.

The second inspiration is a rather loose New Age reinterpretation of history.

The third inspiration I forget.

And so on until we come to the one where you see vague auras around trees and you put the book down angrily, thinking Richard Bach was bad enough.

I read it in the Starbuck's café at Borders, spending untold cappuccino money in my mulish refusal to pay for a copy.

Eddie's and Deesey's copies are still in Egypt somewhere, probably with the dog-eared Jackie Collinses and *Red October*s in the "traveler's library" at Dahab, the Red Sea village where they split for good.

# "You Can't Go Home Again In My Room, I Have To Sleep There"

1 Ralph recognized me instantly, though he had never really seen me before.

1.1 When I was absent, he pictured me as very blonde.

1.2 He considered me a saving grace of the new job.

1.3 Later I imagined these to be the first pale sprouts of love.

2–4 The night he made me green spaghetti, Ralph kept touching me. He would brush against my shoulder, reaching to fetch a pot or spoon. Once, too, he moved me aside with his hand.

"Excuse me – excuse me – excuse me," Ralph said.

I wouldn't say it was all right for fear of sounding eager.

He was telling the story of his daredevil sister.

5 She and Ralph had not grown up together, but only met in Kathmandu when he was twelve and she was fourteen. Immediately she spirited young Ralph away to the Himalayas, stealing 10,000 dollars from her father for this purpose. The same winter, she eloped with a dashing con artist, who later bled to death in her arms, gunned down by shadowy villains. That brought her up to eighteen years old.

6 I would find my own con artist: I would go to those mountains.

6.1 I would brave enemy lines to deliver the needed ambulance.

6.2 I would strap myself to the crown of a sequoia, defying the lumber interests.

6.3 Time was running out: I was going to be 30.

7 When I was thinking this, I was convinced spitefully

Ralph was no more illuminated than a dishcloth (there was a dishcloth lying on the sink, looking very inanimate). It even occurred to me that I could trump his sister by becoming enlightened. This might be less of a wrench, I thought, given my fear of strangers.

8    Ralph talked for about ten minutes. Washing up the plates, he fell silent.

8.1  Then I muttered something like "Excuse me," and went to bed.

9    In bed, it occurred to me Ralph's stories might not be true.

9.1  He might be embroidering, to impress a girl.

9.2  Ralph-guru might have invented them for me as a test.

9.3  Responding with puerile envy, I'd revealed my inner meanness.

9.4  "*C'est la vie*," I said aloud, in a carefree sophisticate's alto,

## 10. BY THE WAY

to the Jackson Pollock hanging over my bed.

This Jackson Pollock was the real article, a big canvas in oils. Once it had been the centerpiece of our parlor. It was blue and black and grand beyond question, even the contractors liked it, we as children liked it. It was worth about 50,000 dollars, even then.

When Eddie was fourteen, he'd painted a mustache over the abstract streamers and blots. He used fingernail polish, then panicked and attempted to remove it with fingernail polish remover. We hid it under my bed: I was fourteen too and kept clutching my heart, saying, "Mom is so gonna slaughter you, or what?"

Well, that was 50,000 dollars down the drain.

Mom was initially crazy, as you would expect. She screamed and ran downstairs to get her tequila from the fridge. Then she ran back up with the bottle in her hand and stood there fiddling with the bottle cap, staring at the big gorgeous painting on the floor with its weird scrubbed central mustache.

At last she opened the tequila and handed the bottle cap to Eddie. She took a mighty swig and said, "*C'est la vie*, Jack!" in the voice above described.

## — A —

The next morning I walked upright to my mother's office, aiming to type mailing lists sitting up in a chair with the computer on the desk. Moving the monitor and keyboard, I was energized. I would soon be applying for editorial jobs and meeting new people. I would converse in bars, nibbling the free cheddar goldfish, which I happily pictured in their red plastic "baskets."

I'd dressed up – fresh jeans and a polo shirt. I had initially put on sandals, but I hadn't worn shoes in so long they felt like skates or unwieldy hooves. I'd had to take them off.

Now I sat down to work.

My thoughts took an unhelpful turn.

I began to speak to Ralph in my head.

*I will give you the con artist and the Himalayas,* I told him, *but the spaceship sounds like something that isn't true.*

# ALIEN SPACECRAFT SECTION

*Self-explanatory: only one*

# SYNOPSIS: Denise Aimee Cadwallader

1    The light comes down her face and then the shadow focuses.

1.1   She is five years old, standing on a highway alone.

1.2   It must be when they lived in California: this must be that desert.

1.3   Though it is slithering and skipping on the dull ground, Deesey knows the beacon has found her.

1.4   She can't move her feet.

2    When she was five years old, Denise was kidnapped by aliens.

2.1   The spaceship was a radiant and mobile lozenge.

2.2   When it zoomed her, she went so fast the stars tailed.

2.3   She fell into the creatures' overwhelming hearth of love.

2.4   Then her memory goes out.

3    In hypnosis as an adult, Deesey still remembered nothing.

3.1   She tends to the hypothesis that the aliens were a false recollection, a Freudian screen memory meant to shield her from the actual memory of her mother's death from cancer.

3.2   "It doesn't doesn't matter, is my absolute bottom line. It utterly has not been let to change my life."

## — B —

By the time Ralph appeared, I was lying on my side on the floor of my mother's office, playing with my toes. I let him come in: I just carried on. Brazen it out, I told myself; you are "taking a break from work as many another might."

For a long time he just stood there, casting his absolutely motionless shadow. Then he said in his cool carrying voice:

"This little piggy went to market."

I whispered indignantly: "I'm trying to grieve!"

to my and his surprise.

## — C —

Ralph said, "What?"

"I didn't say anything." Then I sat up blinking as if waked from sleep.

He had a grimy badminton racket in one hand. He came in and sat in my mother's chair that I was supposed to sit in if I had been able to do mailing lists. I instantly felt deflated: now my work day was ruined.

"If you're interested in stopping being miserable," Ralph said, "I wanted to say, I think there's a simple trick to it anyone can learn."

"Thank you very much, but I think I have to be miserable, for ethical reasons."

He said: "Bollocks."

This created a surprisingly pleasant atmosphere. We laughed. It occurred to me that now I would have a friend in the house. This was so novel and frightening I instantly thought very loudly, *Oh, don't be stupid, Chrysa! Of course you won't have any friends!*

He suggested: "Maybe I'll stop you suffering without asking your permission."

I said, "Oh, that would be nice. Thank you."

He displayed the badminton racket: "I found these yesterday, when I was looking for a hose."

"Oh, did you find the hose?" I said, feigning interest.

"No," he said in a bored voice. "Do you fancy a game? That's what I'm asking."

"Oh! Jesus Christ!" I said in total dismay.

We both laughed again, it was strange. I said, "Is this part of your cure?"

He boinged the racket against his knuckles enigmatically: "Perhaps."

Following him down to the garage to get the net, I came up with a flurry of reasons to play badminton. It was an assertion of will over my disorder, which would thereby be enfeebled. This might be another guru test of my worth. More endorphins had to be a good thing.

Also, if I was going to be eating spaghetti et cetera, I'd better exercise. In this phase of my life, I could be athletic. It was hard to see it leading anywhere, however: I was too old already to compete in the Olympic Games.

All the while of course I knew I couldn't play badminton. The idea was insane! He might as well have been taking me to defuse an atomic bomb! But I carried on, pluckily, daring the unknown. If I even played one volley, it went without saying that the order of things would change and I would be freed.

Ralph got the net and rackets so I only had to carry the birdies. We had just gotten the poles rooted in the lawn when the timed sprinkler system came on, and we had to relocate to an unsprinklering bit of lawn. There the turf wasn't as soft. Plus us being wet: by the time we had the net set up, I was shaking.

We took our positions. I held the birdie up.

A black chasm opened between me and that first motion. Toss the damn birdie! I was thinking. Toss the birdie!

But I waned and hugged the racket to my chest.

"I really don't feel good, I mean authentically," I said. "Maybe we could play later?"

"Oh, all right. Brilliant," Ralph said. "Off you go, then."

But we just stood there.

I have never so keenly wanted to be alone. The cold grass made my bare feet ache. It was like a horror movie. Ralph looked devastated.

At last he shook his head. "What about this, I'll take you out for dinner?"

"Oh!" I said politely. "That's a good idea. Thank you."

# THE WHOLE POINT

1     Men don't find me attractive.

1.1   This is not my neurotic imagining.

1.2   Men don't don't find me attractive.

2     Though they are small, the breasts look down.

2.1   "Where's your ass?" a boy once jeered. "Steamroller accident?"

2.2   A stocky pygmy, I shop in the children's section.

2.3   Like a child, I swell at the waist.

3     Round as a bowl, my face is still fat when I am thin.

3.1   The features are puny and lost in a plain of cheek.

3.2   Women tell me I have beautiful eyes.

4     I'm cute like a guinea pig.

4.1   Torrid sex doesn't spring to mind.

5     Among the Yanomamo, I might be a belle.

5.1   I would make anyone do, I was not proud, I slept with Heinrich.

5.2   Once, after watching the babe lifeguard pull his trunks up, tensing his ass to settle the testicles, I had to go hide in the ladies' room and cry.

5.3   I am not above blaming my unpopularity on racism.

We went to a Chinese restaurant in Cupertino. It was coyly named "Ping Pong," which I found disturbing, in such close proximity to badminton. I paranoiacally hunted through the menu for squash dishes.

We were seated comfortably in a velveteen booth, in semi-darkness. The table was high, so that I the runt was hidden up to the shoulders. A swift relief stole through my mind. Dinner might work.

I realized that, as long as I was looking at the menu, no one would expect me to speak. Therefore I pored doggedly, long after any normal person would have chosen a meal. Repeatedly I attempted to read the text, out of a sense of duty, but the very headings – "Seafood Dishes," "Chef Recommends" – blinded me with loathing. Seafood Dishes! As if it matters!

I could not, for the life of me, put the menu down.

Its pages were embellished with sketches of Chinese coolies bearing bucket-laden yokes. I felt it was bad taste to depict the poor in a menu. It seemed like gloating. Those coolies would have liked a few seafood dishes.

Of course I really was as good as starving. So these thoughts should have been had by the fat people at other tables, but that is the way of the world (I thought).

I peeked at Ralph, who was a large-sized person. He ate plenty. Yet was a guru. Conclusion: eating plenty is not at variance with goodness, though of course that can't be true. (I had eaten plenty before, and it was at variance with goodness.)

What's more, the idea of Ralph eating Egg Foo Yung – in any quantity – made him seem irretrievably unenlightened. Yet the sage must eat. Should he only eat lentils, locusts and wild honey? What if the sage is offered a Ding Dong by an innocent child, who would be desperately upset, should the sage refuse the Ding Dong? Dilemma.

"Have you decided?" Ralph suddenly asked.

I slapped the menu down. "Would you mind ordering for me?"

He burst out laughing. I had delivered the punch line to whatever he'd been thinking: probably he had known all along I wasn't choosing. I'm very transparent.

When he settled down, I confessed: "I don't like restaurants."

That struck him even funnier. He was actually handsome when he laughed, because of his beautiful teeth, though I later learned two were not his. Now he laughed and laughed, flashing his white teeth/dentures, until tears came out of his eyes. The great misfortune was that, watching him, I began to cry just at the very idea of tears coming out of eyes.

I thought: *Why is he so heartless to me?* Et cetera. Once I start crying, I can think of hundreds of reasons to cry. Furthermore, years of therapy have trained me to home in swiftly on the most harrowing possible cause for my distress.

"You're crying," Ralph noticed, still smirking with the tail end of his laugh.

I said in a chokey voice: "I just need . . . I don't know. I wish —"

Ralph's face went cold and he interrupted me: "You can't carry on like this if you're going to manage the institute."

We sat for a minute at loggerheads. I said, "But I couldn't manage it." I rubbed my eyes with the cloth napkin, shook it out, and spread it on my lap. Then Ralph got up and walked out of the restaurant.

# REASON TO CRY

all I retain
of my Peruvian prehistory is in
a bad dream in which,

an infant, I lie in dry earth in                                        I
between the inky-dirty feet
of an itty-bitty
Indian girl
immersed
and jay-blue in the jungle's jade and bladed light:        J
the dream jumps

it's jolly old
John Wayne
    jumping her, and
    in jabs jags fucks
    of his knife, kills                                       K
and fucks her till her head knock
    knocks
        loose,                                          L
        she lolls, licentiously
        gushing her last
        blood, this lewd
            marionette of                        M
            my-real-
            mother I try to save
            most
                nights                         N

and "Dad" a red gigantic interruption of my home,
triumphing

and rising, wipes
blood and down there.
The glade is still with dead people; the red man sings
and there are oranges on all the trees,
already peeled. They drip

## *The Interpretation of Nightmares*

1    The dream began when I was fifteen, long after my father's death.

1.1  I don't remember anything like this and it never happened.

1.2  In some versions, he sings "Ten Little Indians."

2    My first psychiatrist would not shut up about the dream.

2.1  My second psychiatrist suggested hypnosis.

2.2  My third psychiatrist and I agreed it was a red herring.

2.3  Privately, I brood about the fucking thing, all the time.

3    Mom and Dad lied to me.

3.1  Something unspeakable.

3.2  Dad is dead and I will never find out what.

3.3  If you want excuses not to live, that serves, but then again

★ ★ ★

Sitting in the velveteen booth of the Ping Pong, driven to this extreme of reminiscence to explain the gross crying that had so disgusted Ralph, it occurred to me that I was a fraud. I knew that never happened. I also once dreamed Eddie was a giant vampire bat, flapping about me tenaciously and taking bites from my head. As who doesn't? Wake up — it's just a bad dream!

It was equally likely that what sent me off the edge was working on my deconstructive treatment of *Dr. Faustus*. I had heard similar stories about other students of poststructural literary theory who lost their minds. Many of the initiators of poststructural theory went nuts too. Guy Saint-Lazare even leaped off the Eiffel Tower with all of his books in his arms.

Examining the actual contents of my crying, I found a quailing sludge emotion, with a foul insecticide taste. If it was a peanut, you would spit it out. Yet I was indulging this toxic goo, giving it its head and letting it dictate my actions. People had every good reason to despise me.

Initially I was inclined to be angry and damn the people and be gloriously in the wrong. But, by a vast incalculable effort, for which I held my breath and strained and strained, I overcame this and ran out of the Ping Pong, letting my cloth napkin flutter away behind me.

### Denouement

Ralph was standing on the sidewalk with his arms crossed. He turned on me as I came out. "So, are you going to manage the fucking institute?" he barked.

Then we both smiled. He uncrossed his arms.

And you know these tall men, when they get you out of doors on a spring evening, and you're in a docile frantic state, and you can smell flowers.

They stand over you looking warm. You'd tell them anything.

# DAHAB SECTIONS

## Argument

*Eddie and Denise travel to the Egyptian coastal village of Dahab, where they dally in the sun and sand. Love comes and is gone. Meeting a former colleague on the beach, Denise shares bad news. Her profession is explained: the lovers part.*

# Facts for Tourists: Dahab

A Bedouin village on the Red Sea coast, snug on the border of Israel, Dahab boasts deserted beaches and an unspoiled coral reef. There are no hotels: however, travelers can rent cabins from 'Sheikh Ali' (so the signs read, in honor of the Bedouin owner, though one deals exclusively with his local manager, Haisim). Not for the luxury-minded, the one-room cabins are furnished only with a hard bed and floored with gravel. The settlement has no electricity or plumbing. The outhouses have toilets made of stone, and all water, for flushing, washing, brushing teeth, has to be drawn from the well by hand. Bring your own toilet paper.

Beer, soft drinks and simple meals (usually a choice of meat pie or vegetable pie) can be purchased from The Fighting Kangaroo, an easy walk down the beach. It consists of an open-fronted shack, in which the oven is housed and stores kept. On the beach, industrial spools, probably originally for heavy cable, are turned on one flat end and half buried in sand to serve as tables. Chessboards are available, on payment of a small deposit. The restaurant is also run by Haisim, with his nephew, who in addition will hire snorkeling gear by the hour.

Though Cairene by birth, Haisim, as the name "Fighting Kangaroo" suggests, lived for many years in Australia. There he embarked on a scholarly career and was briefly married. He came to this remote place to complete his anthropology PhD on Bedouin culture. At The Fighting Kangaroo one may view a photo taken of him shortly before his departure from Melbourne. In it he's crewcut, clean-shaven and bespectacled, shyly holding up his going-away present, a silver pen set.

# 14. Cairo: Loose Ends

1    "No, I'm not claiming it <u>did</u> come with the frame, that
was a joke, I can be <u>really</u> unkind without meaning to be, but
– abjectly, sorry."

"Why, then?"

"Sheer utter not thinking."

"No, why do you have a picture of my father –"

2    He'd passed out in Groppi's drunk. Was manhandled
into a cab, and Deesey saw him back to the Raffles. Revived
long enough to climb the stairs, he claimed to have lost his
key, inveigled his way into her room, passed out again. They'd
shared a bed – "Chastely, don't worry."

3    "Your father was . . . he worked with my mother. I knew
him when I was a child. I guess I must carry his picture
because I don't have one of my mother. She died when I was
small."

"They worked together where?"

"I don't know."

"You don't –"

"I was small."

4    "The coincidences are simply flabbergasting," she
drawled.

– as if she'd said "flabbergasting" umpteen times in
similar circumstances, until it had become a joke with her
and her "crowd" –

- unflabbergasted
- killing the topic dead with that preposterous term

5    She would leave that day for Dahab. She told him, and
raised her eyebrows. His heart sped.

At last, finally, she said: "Come with?"

6    They travel there by overnight bus. The bus improbably plush, air-conditioned, roomy. TVs mounted in the ceiling screen silent football matches. The cabin lights are off and even small children sit muted, as if dumbstruck by the opulence.

Deesey and Eddie read their twin copies of *The Celestine Prophecy*. They sleep. Then in the morning there's the Sinai.

7    A cab for the last leg: they walk down to the sea.

Its hoarse wash grows and falls with no apparent connection to the business of waves, their gleaming sprawl over the sand, white jumble of breaking. Everything trembles in the headlong sun. The breeze adds its note, and its distinct dry cleanliness.

8    "That's that, Jack. One room or two?"

## Fucking

They are alone in their cabin for the first time. On the gravel, every step makes a harsh crush, strange indoors, so there's that self-consciousness added to the rest. She is crouched down over her briefcase, and he feels huge and conspicuous standing behind her. He feels discarded.

His erection tortures him. It's a gross assumption he can't disown. Yet if she didn't want it, what are they doing here?

She rises and he takes her in his arms and because he has so exhaustively imagined taking her in his arms and the polite stages leading to the mind-bending blissfest itself —

the real thing jars. She was going to resist and be cajoled, but doesn't — laughs, kisses him fervently, matter-of-factly strips and lies down. Her breasts have tiny pale nipples unlike any nipples he's seen before. The way she's twisted to watch him, her stomach's wrinkled up, and he realizes for the first time that, as you age, even your stomach goes to hell. How old is she? If she's like ten years older, does that make this sick?

It's so all wrong. He's very frightened.

The sheets have a coarse weave. They feel greasy, and his eye keeps being drawn to the small screen window, whose mesh has gaps warped in it, as if burly local insects force their way through at night. From a lying position, he wrestles off his shorts, and as she turns to embrace him, he realizes she's brought him here to kill him. The thing with Dad's photo — luring him to this backwater — unfinished CIA shit — roped in by the oldest trick in the book. Her eagerness makes sense now: somewhere in her dumped clothes she has a blade secreted. What's worse is that she's going to slash his throat at the moment of orgasm.

His prick's hard as a rock: can't back out now. Rolling on top of her, he shuts his eyes and surrenders himself to death.

## More fucking

That was fantastic. They do it two more times. The sun's going down and he nuzzles her tit and nuzzles her tit: his heart's sailing. She too languishes and sighs the same delighted noise that's like she read his mind. Like, how totally great is this?

He will have another hard-on soon.

## 15. Dahab: seven days, seven nights

1    She only had one change of clothes: K-mart-caliber shorts and T-shirt. Her ragged bathing suit had to be safety-pinned on.

1.1  When he said she was gorgeous, she said, "Plastic surgery."

1.2  She washed her hair with soap.

2    The bars of soap were hotel minis:
- Radisson, Istanbul
- Hotel Benot, Monte Carlo
- one in Chinese

2.1  She lit her cigarettes with bronze-tipped matches from the Ritz.

2.2  British Airways socks: Lufthansa pen: Flightbookers wallet.

3    "I don't have to work because . . . I inherited money."
"Really? Who from?"
"Relatives."

3.1  She'd never seen that movie. She didn't know the band. The name Henry Kissinger rang a bell, but.

3.2  When he talked about school days, she didn't.

4    "If I say you don't want to hear, I am not not not speaking just to hear the sound of my voice."

5    She was a high-class prostitute in flight from her sordid past.

5.1  Her affluent husband beat her; his agents were on her tail.

5.2  In the false bottom of her briefcase she ferried
- heroin
- uncut diamonds
- footage of rutting statesmen

5.3 She was a suburban housewife who wanted to appear mysterious.

6  The idea of making love to her never left him.

6.1 She was something held and naked and ecstatically pierced, even when she was sitting across from him munching pie.

6.2 Four times a night – they had welts, they scabbed.

6.3 It would never end. There was nothing else in life. Dark hair was food and God and the end of days. Skin hot with fresh tan was. Sweat was and her faint, infantine cries, her struggling.

7  In the mornings, Haisim treats everyone to tea. It's served in an open shelter on the beach. Weathered rugs make a floor: the kettle perches on a blackened iron stand over a twig fire. Tea leaves and mint leaves lie in Ziploc bags to one side. The guests from all the cabins share their provisions: bread, watery yogurt, an occasional prized tomato.

7.1 Every day The Fighting Kangaroo and its pie. Every day beer: Eddie, still afraid, enjoys the secret that he's risking his life for her. They swim, they sun themselves. Then there's the reef.

## 16. Paradise: what, ever after, Eddie pictures
## when you say "love"

The coral is a wilderness of psychedelic fronds and luminous moss. Fish, improbably bright and many, pass under the swimmers' bare stomachs. The fish are gorgeous and ingenious, like shoals of jewelry. Through the melee flutter huge rays, and the occasional fat eel dozes, draped in a cranny. The shadows of larger beasts speed over the bumpy coral, sometimes triggering a lightning scatter of small fry.

Eddie and Deesey chase each other up and down the phantasmagorical cliff. They catch in embraces that plummet through alarmed fish – lapse into darkening blue for a long-held breath – break in a flash of bubbles. She takes her snorkel out to kiss him, the taste of salt and sweet and beer mingled with an electrifying sense of drowning.

Staggering out again is an exile, the sun too frank and the air a loveless medium, a medium for golems, automatons, the dead

## Making Love

It's somewhere in there, about day five. Like always, they're in bed. She's reaching across him to knock the ash off her cigarette, and he sees the pale range of scars on the inside of her arm. He's never noticed it before, and his first instinct is that it's new, some rash she picked up from the reef. It takes a moment for the odd translucence, and the shapes, like mock-veins, to sink in fully. *Suicide*, he thinks, with a lightning flash of excitement. He has the smug sense of finding her out: this explains her. The immediacy makes him catch her wrist, rough.

"What's this?"

She twists her arm free, offended. "What?"

"The – it's scars, right?"

"Oh." She looks at her own arm, concentrating, as if called upon to explain some passage in a book. "Yes, old scars."

"Well, Jesus. But, were you trying to kill yourself?"

"Oh, no." She gives him a surprised, affronted look, her nostrils pinched. "No, it's a sort of bullet wound."

He catches his breath with an adrenal rush: bullet wounds. Before he speaks he has to think how to sound caring.

"God. How did you get shot? Who shot you?"

"A robbery," she says, and that's all she says. She looks at Eddie with the thing she's not saying in her eyes, then suddenly smiles – insolent. She turns her arm over, putting the scars away.

His heart speeds with the craving to force it out of her, he is actually breathing hard. In the back of his head, he calculates the nagging required, the bullying, threats. There is the sexual twinge when he visualizes pinning her down and –

She says, in a flat, commanding voice like a hypnotist's, "Don't press this."

135

Then he ducks to kiss her belly, wanting to call back the easy warmth. He doesn't know how this fright happened, he doesn't know how his delight has been so poisoned.

She strokes his head, crooning, "Oh, no, you don't want to hear, he didn't want to hear, Jack Moffat Junior didn't want to know anything about her. No, he didn't want to hear, no no no." When he looks up, she's smiling. She says, "I'm joking."

He thinks, clearly and very distinctly from the enveloping love miasma, You have insect feelings. He stops and investigates her cool eyes. Then his thoughts absolutely get loose and he goes crazy, *she can read his mind and when he's sleeping she will tie him up and shoot him just shoot him, it's a joke to her, but when she tries the magic horn will blow and the Benelia Lords will ride to his rescue, halloing on their dapper steeds and then the Insect Queen will sprout her real wings and buzz atrociously, but* Eddie gets a grip. Her eyes are simply brown. She has crossed her arms, hiding the scarred patches: vulnerable. He takes a very very deep breath and croons, in a deep handsome voice he feels rising from some omniscient Jack self, prior and great:

"I really want to know. I care about you. Actually, I think I love you." Tears come to his eyes and he feels triumph. It's true.

And, as he'd known it must, her *insect nature* vanishes. She looks hurt, takes a harsh breath, laughs nervously. "No," she says, "People don't say those things to me, you know."

He presses it, thrilled: "I love you. Don't laugh at me."

Her manner alters again and she kisses him on the lips. They shut their eyes into a shared long dark pang. When they separate, she takes his hand and vows, with a child's naive seriousness, trying hard to mean it: "Okay, Jack – I'll love you, too."

# 7. Perspective: Quito (12 years previously)

1     She is eighteen years old, sitting on a hotel bed alone.

1.1   Urban South America: the armed men in the streets and the bright blue mountains, pollution smelling like beasts in the wet heat.

1.2   In the next room, she hears him humming as he packs.

2     She stares at her chubby, mosquito-bitten arms. A blemish on her knee is clouded maroon; she can smell her sneakers.

2.1   "Oh, you'll be a heartbreaker someday," he would say. "Mark my words."

3     Her briefcase is open, empty, beside her. Although the nightstand drawer is shut, she can picture the unruly pile of dollars there, the chore waiting to be done.

Her shoulders move, frightened, when he opens the door.

He stands in the doorway, his face maneuvering. His hand reaches back again for the doorknob. Then he stops and grins as if he's just now seen her.

"Whoa, puddytat, we said no long faces."

She looks up as far as his open collar, his neck grained scarlet. A plain iron chain there bears a medical tag warning of an allergy to penicillin, and it seems now related to the stifling heat – as if both are components of a term of punishment.

"I could come with you," she offers. Her ankle fidgets.

"Well now. All's I can say, you sure don't know my wife."

He sits on the bed and takes her briefcase in his lap with studied tenderness, like the toy of a beloved child. She turns away sharply, squints out the window at the sky. A chalky line spreads there where a plane has gone.

She says, "We'll work, though, one last time tonight?"

4    She loved that man as teenagers do, too hard, to her cost.

4.1    But he was killed, in the usual way. The blood showing oily against the asphalt, the sirens making the sound of fearful distance: everything grows cold.

4.2    She lay in the grit and could not reach him. She was reaching in her sleep.

5    Her father came to the hospital.

5.1    In him, every gesture was begrudging, suspicious. He was like a tiny, vigilant crab.

5.2    He said, "<u>You've</u> had an adventure," in his dim, couched voice. Her face was bandaged, her jaw wired, she could not answer. She watched him shuffle off and whisper with the nurse.

5.3    "They'd have had you looking like King Kong, had I not come in the nick of time," he said ever after.

6    Then she went to work with him.
- It so happened he needed someone suddenly.
- It so happened his last assistant had died – been shot.
- It happened in a parking lot, the woman bled to death, it only lacked Denise to lie unconscious at her side.

Denise would not admit that was strange.

"You mean it's <u>not</u> a coincidence," Dad said to her shut face, laughing.

6.1    They lived and worked twelve years together in that same loveless, bickering vein.

7    When her father was killed, Denise felt a flicker of psychosis.

7.1    Who knows why things happen, everyone knows why some things happen.

7.2 She lay in the grit, in his blood, in the hotel parking lot. She cradled him spoon-fashion, like a wife.

8 Eddie would die, too, without learning the above facts.

# 17. Dahab: Day Eight

So they're sitting at a Fighting Kangaroo spool table, her checkmate of the afternoon spread on the chessboard between them. Empty cans lie on the stacked plates from lunch: somehow they haven't faced the task of clearing them away. It's late, and the sun wanes, gentle on the sea.

She's watching the queue of tourists at the restaurant shack, frowning as if their beer orders absorb her. Among the usual tanned beach kids is an older man, a myopic geek in unbecoming shorts. Paunchy and dead-white, he stoops and shambles miserably, looking as if he's stopped here on his lunch break from a software firm. Deesey is captivated, and does not turn or seem to register Eddie's sally:

"So, about this you and Dad scenario."

It's something he's brought up several times: it now has an air of playful ritual. Her previous non-answers have varied from the nondescript ("Perhaps they were office picnics, where I would have met him") to a detailed recollection of Jack Moffat visiting her childhood home ("It was when we lived in Arizona. I know he came to the house once, he brought us a lobster. He had it in a pail, I do remember, and I was awfully surprised the lobster was green. It had rubberbands around its paws, you know. I think I cried"). This particular episode haunts Eddie because it convinces him on a visceral level that Denise really knew Jack Moffat. His dad was exactly the kind of guy who brought you lobsters in a pail. The little girl would definitely cry and his dad would tell her he was going to set the lobster free in the ocean, or some bullshit, whatever it took. Then God knew what became of the lobster, something frightening.

Now he's not after answers, but just fishing for her

attention. The prod flops, however: she delivers a Deesey-esque non sequitur:

"Do you think we could leave?"

"Leave?" A chill blows through him.

"I mean, the <u>beach</u>." She smiles at him, sardonic.

"No . . . yeah, I mean, I thought you meant . . ."

"I didn't mean <u>town</u>." She adds, "I think I know that man, you see?"

"Which one?" He turns to look at the bar queue.

"No, don't. Don't stare."

"You were staring totally." He forces himself to look away. "A nerdy guy or a beachy guy?"

She laughs as if that's funny, and admits, "Nerdy."

"Wow. Is he, like, a goblin? He's after your liver?"

"Let's just say, one of those things where I'd rather not see someone."

He thinks about it for a minute, inspecting her expression. That per usual tells nothing. She's smiling and he almost smiles back, joins her conspiracy, when it hits him with a jolt: *the nerdy guy knows her. Ask the nerdy guy, the nerdy maybe-CIA guy knows all about her.*

He has what he's come to think of as a Benelia Moment, flashing on a spy-movie shoot-out at The Kangaroo. The CIA nerd doesn't take kindly to detection; draws a gun from his sandal holster. Dashing from spool to spool for cover, Eddie knocks Denise down, takes her bullet, and et cetera. He lets it subside.

"Why don't you want to see him?" he says, stalling.

"Oh, maybe we should just sit tight, after all."

"No, honestly, you got to at least tell me that. Or, I'm supposed to cover for you?"

"Oh, the hell with it."

"I mean, maybe I want to meet this gentleman."

"Yes," she says, all tight-lipped, "Yes, I do mean, hell with it." Then she stands up with such a brisk unequivocal anger Eddie reaches instinctively to stop her, but misses, and she waves and calls: "Michael!"

Eddie turns sharply, in time to see the pot-bellied geek stagger in the act of opening his beer. He peers first to either side, for other possible Michaels. Then he sees Denise. His face goes strange. He shakes his head and sets out at a precarious trot, making big bug eyes to show his wonderment.

Denise says to Eddie: "There: you get your wish."

Approaching, the geek smirks and holds his beer can up in a clumsy mock-toast. Deesey meets him and squires him back to the spool table, gushing: "I was just saying to my friend, what a coincidence. Of all the places."

Michael nods, squinting at the chessboard. "It's such a surprise."

His accent is Germanic: he is pasty and narrow-headed. His Las Vegas T-shirt is blotched with sweat. Although he frowns, there is an underlying blankness to his expression. He carries his body, too, with pointed awkwardness, like an embarrassing item entrusted to him by a stranger.

"This is Jack," says Deesey. Eddie gets up, but the geek just blinks at him in pained confusion and looks back at Deesey. She carries on, releasing Michael's arm with a coy shove: "Michael – I didn't know you took vacations."

"Of course I take vacations. But you're here. It's strange. Where's your father?"

"I don't know."

"You mean . . . you don't know?"

She shakes her head. There is a complicated moment in which she glances at Eddie and back at Michael, and her face changes more times than that. Then she says, "Dad's dead, Michael. He was killed."

"Oh, my God. No."

"We were playing in Istanbul," she adds, as if this follows logically. Then her face crumples and at last she begins to cry.

As soon as she does, Eddie feels the release of some spring in her, all this time tightly compressed. He reaches for her and she lets herself be taken, leans back, slack in his arms. She repeats: "He was killed."

"No. How can that happen?" Michael looks down at his feet, in such distress he squeezes his beer can in both hands. "Killed?"

"Oh . . . muggers, you know. Someone who saw he had a lot of cash. Just like . . ."

"He was always so paranoid. Yes."

"He was right." Then she begins to shake with laughter. "I was out, and of course I shouldn't have been out."

"Denise, sit down, sit –"

"Mmm, he used to say, will you be laughing when I'm dead, and I actually, I'm gutted, but – I don't know what's so funny."

Then Michael too begins to shake with laughter. His eyes remain stubbornly blank, as he jerks and barks, and the sum of this performance is one of such defenceless ugliness that Eddie is chilled. And he feels this somehow justifies him, is a last straw that permits the inapposite question, "Playing in Istanbul?"

Deesey catches her breath deeply. Michael too falls still and sniffs, looking quizzically at the chessboard. Deesey says, "We're blackjack players."

# HOW TO PLAY CASINO BLACKJACK FOR PROFIT

1     Blackjack is the game also known as 21 or Pontoon.

1.1   The aim is to get a hand whose sum is 21, or as near 21 as possible, without going over.

1.2   Each player is dealt two cards.

1.3   You may request as many supplementary cards as you wish.

1.4   However, if the hand goes over 21, you "bust" and lose.

1.5   Picture cards are counted as ten: aces are one or eleven, as the player chooses.

1.6   The combination of a ten card and an ace is called a blackjack and, in most casinos, pays off two to one.

2     In casinos, all the gamblers play against the croupier.

2.1   Croupiers play to predetermined rules.

2.2   This allows gamblers to devise strategies which take those rules into account.

2.3   (For techniques, refer to Appendix A, Pro Blackjack.)

2.4   A skillful player with a suitable bankroll earns in the region of 100,000 dollars a year.

3     All profitable systems are dependent on the ignorance of the casino staff.

3.1   Where law does not prohibit it, gaming clubs will bar skillful players.

3.2   Where law prohibits exclusion on the basis of skill, the casino can make the game unprofitable by various means.

## *Disguise and deceit*

4     To delay their exclusion, players ape the manners of foolish gamblers.

4.1 They crow about hunches: they agonize pitifully over choices which are actually predetermined.

4.2 "Picture!" they shout with the mob, and "Lucky seven!"

4.3 They have elaborate cover stories: play the oil tycoon, feign alcoholism, flaunt rabbit's feet.

4.4 Nonetheless, they must play and vary the bet exactly as prescribed, and sooner or later, the security guards swoop.

5 Once a pro has been spotted, his photo goes into a file.

5.1 In some places, all the casinos share information. Thus, by one exposure, the player burns out an entire region.

5.2 After some years of play, the pro must alter his appearance regularly: grow beards, wear hats and specs, dye hair.

5.3 Most of the excitement and the lore of blackjack derives from this amateurish spy routine.

## *The Life*

6 An average day:
Waking at noon, the player breakfasts at his cheap hotel. He (profession 90% male) then proceeds to the casino, where he plays cards all day. Lunch and dinner are in the casino restaurant. If there are other players in town, he may meet them after work to discuss blackjack. If not, he plays and plays, until he no longer trusts his judgment. Returning to his hotel, he soon falls asleep.

6.1 Dreams, in the main, center on blackjack.

7 Teams of players take all their meals together, and share rooms: saving on expenses is a crucial part of pro play.

7.1 When the casino finally bars the team, they exhibit hysterical glee.

7.2 In a mood of careless jollity, they fly to a new exotic city, where the identical routine begins *de novo*.

7.3 Casinos are open seven days a week.

8 It's a boring job with long hours.

8.1 Professional blackjack players curse and hate their profession.

8.2 "When are we going to be replaced with trained monkeys? Roll on, the trained monkeys!"

9 Still, when pro gamblers leave the game, they will be found:
- running racetrack betting schemes with computerized predictions
- playing video poker machines, to an exact system
- suing casinos which have illegally barred them

9.1 Denise had lived in this environment from age twelve.

# Chat

Michael stayed through the afternoon, reminiscing about the departed father, Peter Cadwallader, about old times and "powerful" games. Denise dried her eyes, warmed to the theme, became animated. Soon they were discussing the minutiae of blackjack: the spread in Avignon, the riffle in Perth.

"Well, ace depletion is obviously a fact, but it only means subtracting from the running count –"

"But this means no true count!"

"Not necessarily."

"Oh! I don't know where you play, to have counts like this!"

Eddie fetched beer. He cleared the chessboard and took it back to reclaim the deposit. He went for a walk unannounced, but no one asked where he'd been. Finally, he settled down to just, undergo suspense.

1   She would take him with her. They would roam the world, gambling.

2   Denise in Monte Carlo, Vegas, in hotel beds.

3   The roulette wheel spins, gorillas eye Eddie's stack of chips in impotent rage.

4   "You're a natural," Denise whispers, awed by his quick grasp.

5   He would scream, he would beg. She loved him, she had said so. He would hold her to that! She shouldn't have fucking lied!

6   When is this Frankenstein monster going to get the message? Hello! I want to talk to my girlfriend, alone!

At last he was emptied. He stared, undone, at the darkening surf.

At last Deesey too stared impartially at the darkening surf. Michael finished what he had to say about baccarat, fell still, yawned.

The sunset was purple and dull: The Fighting Kangaroo had closed its shutters. Above, the stars had come out boldly, avid in the absence of rival lights.

"I guess —" Denise said finally, and stood.

Michael sprang up after. "It is very good to see you."

She took his hand — then kept it for a moment, snagged. "Where are you headed?"

"Macau. Macau tomorrow!"

"No, but they changed the rules."

"Ah — the rules are back. Ronnie's playing there. The rules are back!"

"Well." She let his hand go. They said brief goodbyes. Michael shook Eddie's hand and walked off, poring over his steps in the sand.

Deesey turned to Eddie then, said, "I suppose."

And she scowled seeing Eddie's face.

And he was cold in his shorts, bereft and weak: as if he'd been opened.

All she could say was, "I'm sorry, you must have been bored to tears." She only had to touch him, but she turned to go. He followed her down the beach.

And they were walking, barefoot in firm sand. The occasional stretch of water ringed their toes, and they talked with estranged, parallel gazes out at the sea, as if what they missed were the few, far, sand-colored lights of Arabia, which rose and gave way with the floating waves.

## Release

"My father started playing when I was seven or there-abouts. I was at boarding school – not a happy time. Well, finally I coerced him into taking me for the summer, that was in Las Vegas and a bit in Korea. In Korea I started playing, you know, I was only thirteen but I was bigger than most of the croupiers. So, that's been more or less my life.

"It's not that I wouldn't have told you, I just have the habit of not. From playing so long, and we never know any-one and you mustn't trust anyone, and then you just do leave town. Finally. It's not conducive."

Eddie objected: "Bottom line, you're saying I was going to hit you over the head and steal your money? Thanks."

"No, in fact I don't even have my money on me. I'm just trying to explain to you, the one thing players never do tell anyone is that they are professional gamblers. It's really taboo, really. Plus I just did find my father dead, I am so awfully sorry."

She said, glib and hateful. And added, with the air of someone wrapping up a task: "I can see in your eyes that you find this exciting. Though it's hard for me to see, I know others do find it glamorous. And I would take you with me if I didn't know what it did to people."

"You don't know what I'd be like. I mean, what?"

"People become greedy. Stingy. Isolated. Really, it's not a normal life. I can't recommend it."

"Well, who ever said I wanted a normal life?"

She shrugged and carried on walking. Eddie stayed behind. Eddie let her walk away from him, let her carry on several meters along the beach. He was angry in a way that made him sure of getting his way. It was wrath, it was a power. His need was beyond any possible little wish of hers.

For an instant, he even pitied her: she didn't realize enough to be afraid.

Her slight back receded to an even beat, she didn't look back for him or slow, but what she didn't see was that he would do anything, sink to anything, anything for her. He had risked his life. That thought triggered it and he came on, shouting

## She Left with Michael the Following Day

"You think I'm really stupid, don't you? Don't you? Just say it. How bored you must have been, sitting with me day after day.

"You realize I have a lot of money? I don't know why I bring it up now, but I do know why, cause you never asked? Or what I'm doing here or anything about me? Or if I have a fatal fucking illness and I'm dying?

"The reason I say that, right, it comes to me, cause I do have a fatal illness. Like, not fatal instantly fatal, but maybe soon fatal. That's all. And you – it's just a creepy fucking feeling when, 'I love you, I love you' and, all the time, I could just die for all you bother.

"You know, I really thought I was falling in love with you, so that was sincere. But now I just wonder what you're doing with me at all. Cause it has to go both ways, I can't be a puppy dog for anyone. So if that's what you're about, I just feel sorry for you. I honestly just feel sorry for you.

"Are you just going to fucking stand there? Don't you have anything to say? You've got nothing to say to me? I'm begging you, okay. I'm begging you even just to say one thing and not just stand there looking at me like I don't mean shit to you, I don't mean shit –"

1    The morning she left, he found three identical snapshots of Denise as an ungainly kid, in a row on his briefcase.
1.1  Each was signed on the back "LOVE, DC."
1.2  "DC" might be "Deesey" in a cute shorthand.
1.3  Or the initials of "Denise Cadwallader."

2    She might have signed all three the night she left, in a ritual of thwarted passion.
2.1  She might have signed them all long before, when she got the prints, intending to hand them out as keepsakes.

3    Were some men walking around with four, five, six photographs of DC?
3.1  Or had the best pre-Eddie garnered only two?

4    She is ugly. On one arm she has a grimy band-aid. Her skin is blotchy and her dungarees don't fit. Looking directly at the camera lens, she grins, and her eyes gleam with big-time, shameless love.
4.1  This is the girl Eddie loves for the rest of his life.
4.2  Often he considered getting the photo printed in the *New York Times* with a plea for information on her whereabouts.

5    Though for years he boozed and smoked dope and took pills by the handful, some designed for cancer patients, some for our animal friends,
5.1  Eddie never had another epileptic seizure.

6    He never mentioned gambling to my mother or myself.
6.1  But he bought a deck of cards, standard Bicycle pack, and, in his cups, he sometimes dealt to himself, doing a basic high-low count in his head, as prescribed by Stanford Wong's classic tome *Professional Blackjack*.

## "You Can't Go Home Again Without Me, I Will Be Desolate"

### WE SELL/WE BUY
### (May–August '98)

1   Ralph sold Mom's art.
   - Via ceramics, he knew the rudiments of the trade, and got real money even for less favored artists.
   - Soon the house began to fill with blank walls.

2   I sold antiques.
   - I made a tent of blankets and went in there with the phone and a glass of straight vodka. Then I had to crawl out again for the phone book.
   - The guys at Half Moon Bay Antiques knew Mom of old. "Oh, how is Lannie?" they cried, happily reminded, and I told them she was doing super.
   - I sold furniture and jewelry. I sold an old computer and a dusty guitar. I sold my mother's Mustang to her cocaine dealer, Spiz, who had known me since I was a tot and called me "Crispy-lips." I found Eddie's watch beside the swimming pool and sold that.
   - I sold the doors Mom bought to replace the old antique doors she sold when her mother and father died.

3   It was Ralph's idea that we three should move to the guest wing. Since the kitchen was there, the practical advantages were plain. Also, we would then be sequestered from future residents.

He made a sketch of his plan and all I cared about was that Eddie was downstairs in the guest bedroom, while Ralph and I would have what was now a single huge upstairs room, once my father's weights room. He sketched in the partition and then drew a door in it, though without saying it was a door. I held my breath over, was it a door? But he didn't say. I was feverishly imagining.

3.1 In the fullness of time, a partition wall with a door was built.

3.2 The door locked on Ralph's side, not on my side: that was another long day in my head.

4    Eddie came to throw a fit.

We'd been raising cash on his assets, which was <u>stealing</u>. He stalked around Mom's office going, "This is all mine! Mine! Eddie's stuff! Do we have hearing people here? Hands up, the hearing people!"

This produced whimpering in me while Ralph stared out the window. Social dynamics in groups of three are of course notoriously awkward. Eddie wore down to a low, steady hum of martyrdom, and sat:

"Twist my fucking arm . . . right, twist my fucking arm. Pen!"

Ralph tossed him a pen. Eddie pulled a checkbook out of his jacket pocket, picked the pen up off the floor and wrote a check for 20,000 dollars in favor of the Tibetan School of Miracles. Tearing the check off, he held it out to Ralph, saying, "You realize if this kills me, that makes you guys murderers?"

"What are we supposed to do with that?" I said.

"Look under rocket scientist in the Yellow Pages," Eddie said, "Maybe someone there can tell you how to open a bank account. And this is out of the buckaroo's salary," he said, making a face at Ralph.

"No," said Ralph. "And we'll need more."

"More?" Eddie posed with both hands on his throat.

Then he let his throat go, and stood up with a villain's sneer: "Whatever. See you later, I gotta go pick up this stewardess."

5    I woke in the dark to decisive banging.

5.1    "Chrysalis, I've just turned the hot tap on, so you've got about five minutes before the bath overflows. See you downstairs."

5.2    I couldn't get out of bed. When I got out of bed, I couldn't face leaving the room. When I'd left the room, I couldn't concentrate on whether I wanted a bath or a shower. When I got in the shower, I just wanted to stand there forever, with my eyes shut, and I was going to tell Ralph all this at breakfast, to wear away his resolve.

5.3    You can only not care about your appearance if you have jeans, but all I had clean were dresses, so I had to care. I couldn't do that, either, and lay on the bed looking at the ceiling for a long time, like a jammed mechanism.

5.4    "That's how everyone feels in the morning, Chrysa. I feel that way right now."

5.5    Every morning just like this, for the rest of my life.

6    Ralph reproved me for forgoing popcorn when I really wanted popcorn.

6.1    "<u>You</u> look smart today," he said if I did not.

6.2    Meeting my remaining friends, he dubbed them "pain-loving ghouls" and told me everything they'd ever told me, was shit.

6.3    "It's good, clearing out this Unhappy Childhood Museum."

6.4    Once, when I had failed to greet the builders, Ralph introduced me to them as the maid.

7    We spent money and we placed orders and chose. We

signed for deliveries and instructed workmen. We opened an account.

Because I gave them money, people treated me with respect. I felt magically better. I combed my hair and cut my fingernails so they were all the same length. My voice was louder and when the waitress snubbed me, I considered the possibility that it was not a very good restaurant.

The house smelled of paint and all day you heard men shouting.

Then all the walls were white and some walls were gone and some were new; it seemed like overnight.

There were ten toilets, there were male and female shower rooms. There was an elongated dinner table, like a bowling alley on legs. We ordered 50 chairs because it was a round number. The upstairs bedrooms were packed with shoddy beds.

Ralph bought a Spartan mat to sleep on, thinner than even futons. It smelled like grass and was the only furniture in his room.

I put off moving into my new room for total eons. Then one day I came home to find my bedroom stripped. I crossed the courtyard to the guest wing with beating heart, irrationally certain they were giving me my walking papers.

But in the window of my new room I spied the Pollock, all blue and black and wallpaperlike at that distance. I went up the stairs and sat on my bed, which had been set against some random wall that felt lopsided. Through the partition I was not sure I heard Ralph. I thought I would never be able to sleep again.

8     Ralph spent 5,000 dollars on white clothes. They were near-Amish in their austere cut, and some just 'said' white, though they were beige or charcoal. Eddie took one look at

the brand name on the shopping bag and put his hand to his pocket as if wounded.

8.1   In them, Ralph looked iconic, like the right actor cast as Christ. When you saw him with a bag of Doritos, it jarred.

8.2   We made cracks –
(Eddie: "So what is it? A tennis cult?"
Me: "Now you can't roll on the grass anymore.")
– at which no one laughed and we sounded jealous.

9     We decided to hold lectures in "The Land of the Lost," once a conservatory Mom built in a brief fad for horticulture and orchid-rearing.

9.1   Brief history thereof:

**1974**       Extension ordered and blueprinted, estimated cost 40,000 dollars.

**1975**       Conservatory complete, 100,000 dollars and three contractors later. Novelty glass stars in roof, guests ooh, ahh.

**1976**       Plants in place. Excitement of heiress. Her domain: Remember-II-the-mutt / young children barred. José the gardener under strict orders, keep out. In main building, glossy gardening manuals proliferate.

**1977**       Dusty gardening manuals move to shelf. Plants return to natural state. Psychiatrically troubled daughter tries to save world in person of tropical conservatory species, feeds, waters in untutored way. Resulting jungle. "Land of the Lost" moniker inspired by children's TV series about young family stranded by time machine prang in Jurassic rainforest hell.

**1978**       Dad dies.

**1979** Plants die.

**1980** Stench from unfrequented glasshouse. José the gardener requests, gains admittance. Room cleared, ammonia smell. Solitary folding chair forgotten, left on bare expanse of tile. Chain w/padlock on door suggests folding chair as hostage in exquisite glass prison.

**– present** "Land of the Lost" nickname sticks.

9.2 On his last ever evening at home, my dad was standing with me in the dining room, looking through the glass sliding doors that led to the Land of the Lost. The dining room was intact then, a genteel room in the belabored style of the French eighteenth century. It even had ornate brass torchères, twice my height. There was a smell of beef cooking, it was a summer evening. Dad had one hand on my head as we peered into the dense jungle. Dimly through the plants and the leaded glass we could see a spidery magenta sunset, and in that light the various pots and trowels were invisible. Dad had just been told about my campaign to save the abandoned plants.

And he said, almost whispering, a just-between-us Dad ploy that made me squirm, irked, under his cajoling mitt –

"Tell me. You and Mom get along okay?"

I muttered, "Yes." But then, shrugging in that shirt-too-tight kid way, I said, "Sometimes I go and hide in there, when she's drinking."

He took his hand away from my head. "Is that so?"

I said, "Yes, she calls me names, so I go in the Land of the Lost till she . . . falls asleep."

"What kind of names?"

"I don't know. She doesn't like me." I didn't feel like

157

crying for some reason. He would tell me I was silly. Of course your mother likes you, your mother <u>loves</u> you. Sometimes Mommies say things they don't mean. So I blurted, risking all – "She keeps calling me the fat bat. Only, really cruelly. 'You fat bat.' " I looked at him and then quickly back at the jungle. I could maybe run in there now.

He crouched down to face me, eye to eye. Gripping my shoulders so I had to look at him, he said, "Listen up, bugaloo, how's about me and you go off together some time? That sound like fun?"

"We couldn't really go anywhere," I groaned, miserably yearning.

"Couldn't we? No? Couldn't we?"

Then we both turned, again drawn to stare into the hothouse, whose brutish foliage seemed to lean out over us, gloating –

and Dad said, muted, "Well, we couldn't go <u>there</u>."

|   | So he saw them too, the phantom |
|---|---|
| O | ocelots, orangutans, opulent Orinoco |
| P | parrots, smorgasbord of panthers, my |
|   | Peru pure and unpeopled |
|   | where I'm princess, all-powerful |
| Q | queen |
|   | of one too-quiet quarantine |
| R | for wrong children and remorse; |
|   | responsibilities |
| S | shed |

and when Dad died I hid there till nightfall, unsought, with each neglected hour more certain Mom would send me back to starve, vulture-torn, on my birthright's soiled rope

When I came out, there was Eddie in the kitchen.

He was pouring milk into a bowl of Count Chocula cereal, and when he saw me

he threw the milk carton on the floor

he knocked over the cereal bowl all over me

and said

he wouldn't be my friend anymore if I was going to be that selfish, disappearing,

and I said,

FINE.

# THE BIG DAY

From the belfry I can watch for cars pulling in. It's already ten to, and there are only three cars. I'm painstakingly groomed, and the dearth of cars is making me ugly again, it's infuriating. I imagine the gaffes Eddie's drafted-in ex-girlfriend, Lynn, is making as she greets and seats the too-sparse audience.

This is José's tower. The stone walls are unfinished, and heaped junk gives it a shed ambiance. Fishing tackle, paint tins, rakes and buckets lie in drifts. Photos of his son, Lorenzo, are glued to the stone walls, and a stack of empty Twinkie boxes betrays José's lifelong, ungardenerlike predilection.

Some weeks after my mother's death, Ralph and I were eating our 6:00 A.M. porridge when José appeared. He had two dogs in tow: his own springer spaniel, Libros; and Mom's pallid mongrel, third in the line of Remembers. By an invisible sleight of foot, José permitted Remember III to enter the kitchen while remaining outside with the gorgeous, albeit aged, Libros, who was really Champion Libros O'Shaughnessy, once Best of Group at the Malibu Dog Show. She had been called Libros by the son Lorenzo, whose dog she nominally was. Then a four-year-old, Lorenzo was puzzled at the task of naming his new puppy: his mother prompted, *What do you like best in all the world?* The now sixteen-year-old Lorenzo was recently accepted at Caltech to study astrophysics.

Ralph and I put down our spoons, rooting them in the porridge mass. We were sitting on packing crates, because we kept forgetting to ask Eddie about the chairs. Remember walked up to me matter-of-factly and sat at my feet, looking back toward José for further instructions. José stood with pretty Libros, embarrassed. At last he cleared his throat and lied,

"I took Remember for a couple weeks because your mother asked me, I should take her if you're very ill. I'm sorry I made you worry."

I had forgotten Remember. For the first time it occurred to me the name might be short for "Remember to Feed Me," as my mother too was absentminded and might remain so through many canine generations. This sort of thing was incomprehensible to José, who must have found the crying mutt and rescued her from my neglect. These things were beyond him: all he asked was that we should not acknowledge them. And though I needed to say that I would certainly have fed Remember, and I had been grieving and confused, I was not one to starve dogs, I said to honor his solicitude that my face be saved:

"Thank you very much. I was concerned."

He beamed with relief. Then he looked from me to Ralph to me as if he knew something. He sighed with paternal satisfaction, and Remember III stood up and did a circuit of the room, wagging maniacally in demonstration of José's joy.

I'd always liked to think José loved my mother from afar, in a hopeless, chivalrous way, which he certainly did not. I thought of this now, in my belfry vigil, recalling my fear that Mom would marry him while Dad was gone, and people would believe I was José's child. Of course I now would welcome this, though shrinking from the exemplary Lorenzo as a brother; probably, pettily, because he was obese.

There were still only five cars.

I finally collected myself and went down the circular staircase to the tall cylindrical room below. Ralph was there in his white clothes. An uncanny fine veil of light, falling from a mock arrow-slit above, made Ralph appear angelic, even though it passed him by to illuminate a rider mower. Eddie walked by the window, smoking a fat cigar. I had spotted him before, pacing around and around the tower, in a neatly pressed Armani suit, two sizes too big.

I whispered to Ralph: "Are you nervous?"

He shook his head. "Eddie gave me a Valium."

I looked at him to see, was he kidding, and he bent and kissed me.

He was so tall, it tipped my head back full to Dracula-victim posture. Then he held me against him. That shot me clean through, I caved in, I pealed for him.

He let me go and caught his breath deep as if it had affected him. I said before I could stop, "I can't believe this is happening." He touched my cheek, blinking, and walked out the door.

He crossed the yard with his same as ever unalloyed grace. I wanted to fuck him then and there in the grass.

I walked out the door and looked at Eddie as if Eddie knew. The fat cigar had gone out, looked rained-on and clownish. I said, "How are you?" and grinned like an imbecile.

"I'm so stoned," Eddie said, "I don't know how the fuck I am."

I said, "That's good . . . I don't think I can do this talk, though."

Eddie pointed at me with the cigar. "Do not even, I totally told you."

I said, "I'm just teasing."

For a few minutes we stood and stared at the main building. We couldn't see the Land of the Lost from there. Eddie said:

"You know, this is the wrong time, but I've been having these dreams where, Ralph can fly? Like, how unfair is that, when it's my dream, right? So in the dream I go and steal his white clothes, and I can fly, too, only I go out of control and crash into a plate glass window, and I'm lying there with the mannequins but they have real cunts. And it's like, I was not worthy."

I said, "I know. I have dreams too."

"Well, don't tell me."

"No, I'll just think it to myself."

"Thanks. I mean it."

Briefly, shyly, we smiled at each other like brother and sister.

In my dream, Ralph had bought a new dispensation. He had it home, and we were assembling it in a warehouse/garage. From time to time, Ralph would knock on it with a wrench and put his ear to the metal to admire its pure tone.

"What if it's a mower?" I feared in the dream.

Ralph put his hand out then in a distinctive palm-first gesture of forestalling, the <u>How!</u> mudra.

"Never mind," he said: "We have still paid good money."

It looked like five cars were it, and I sighed loudly by way of goodbye, setting out toward the new Tibetan School of Miracles sandwich board announcing the title of the first talk in the free introductory series: "Tibetan Wisdom: Lives After Death."

## Ralph crossing the courtyard, at the far end from the pool, where the olive trees are and the grass is careless with new daisies, thought:

1     There was something about me that was vanilla.

1.1   He would keep me safe, he could, it wasn't that mad.

1.2   If only kindness came in instant, if kindness even worked.

2     People are ingenious machines. You don't love them. The beloved is a graven image of what can be loved. How many times had someone made him a teddy bear, *but I love you but I love you.* Love took place between genitalia. This is what he knew, from his experience, to be true.

Sidestepping one of Remember's turds, Ralph looked up at a bent olive tree as if to say, *compadre.* He paused. He loved the tree and wondered why that seemed all right. Rita Perkins told him *horseshit, male horseshit. Boy thinks he's Jesus Christ, ain't even found the damn on switch.*

It all came back to Denise Cadwallader. The white cat had met them off the bus: they were teenagers, they weren't embarrassed to think it was a messenger. They'd followed it down a muddy path and up. It jogged along readily, with uncatlike stamina. They were still in Pokhara's equivalent of suburbs, still meeting people with burdens on the road. Then the cat leapt and Ralph knew. He had not anticipated knowing anything. He fell down. He could see the mountains but they were a clumsy drawing. Denise was a crude figurine. That sense of the world being the lack of something dogged him for years, and when it stopped dogging him, he felt unmoored.

3     How do you lie to these people? He passed down the corridor into the dining room. By staying close to the wall,

he kept out of sight of the open sliding door. Now he heard the audience, a discontented murmur. There must be enough people: otherwise they whispered. He remembered that he'd had a Valium but couldn't feel it. The tendency to hard-on had gone.

I came hurrying past, superstitiously avoiding his eye. I walked on and out into the Land of the Lost. He felt everything all over again. He understood how people gave up their souls for a moment's pleasure.

Listening to me begin the intro spiel, with a little nagging voice in his sub-brain reminding him what it cost me to do the intro spiel, keeping tabs on my unremarkable performance, which must seem to me like public humiliation, Ralph –

4    didn't grow up in a mansion. No one put Ralph through Stanford.
4.1  No one could tell him I didn't have my stash.
4.2  Once the deed's done, probably just a comfort fuck.
4.3  But. But the word but is just why things hurt

5    and

standing on the sidewalk that night outside the Ping Pong, driven spare by my opportunistic tears, he'd felt bitter and desperate; he'd smoked and watched traffic as if harshness was an antidote; been visited by the image of his mother, as she looked just before death, when her face was like a broken window; and he longed to see things grow and live, for a fucking change: and if he were God, he would rain on the forest, all night, just to make himself feel better.

At best, he could do the wrong thing well. He heard his cue and just walked in like people walk into rooms and everyone looks at them.

## "What Happens To You After You Die"

*See Appendix B.*

## "What Happens To You While You're Still Alive"

You sit on a folding chair in an empty conservatory. The floor is thin gravel, and because the sky is cloudy, it seems perverse to be under only glass, you feel exposed somehow: you think of lightning. A moment's trepidation, too, about the stars in the roof: if that means alien worship, you're out that door.

There's only like ten people here. The girl on the door said to "Enjoy the show," which you couldn't tell, was she kidding. Either way it doesn't inspire much confidence. This was Marie's idea. Shaping up to be like the Inner Angel people.

You're getting like an attitude. What you get put through for just wanting something more out of life. Makes you vulnerable. Inside, that tug of desperation, trying not to be excited, maybe *this is it*, and it's usually freaks and you want to shout *I'm not like you*.

A tiny little Mexican girl comes on to do the opening bit, though when she talks she doesn't have any kind of an accent. You're sizing her up for any signs of whatever this guy's supposed to do. She's well dressed, give her that. As she talks, her voice speeds up and she's looking at something behind you, you sense she can see the man himself waiting to come on. Her runaway happiness becomes infectious. You're kind of leaning forward waiting for her to make a joke so you can laugh. But she doesn't, it's kind of a tease, you sit back and shift your feet as if your shoes are too tight. It's that moment where you want to smoke.

You're bugged, too, wanting to peek back at the guy, but it's like whatever she can see is big and you should wait for the moment. She's so excited, this girl, you start to imagine some magnificent sadhu decked with psychedelic braids and amulets, in a welter of snakes. Then she sits down, the little Mexican girl abruptly goes and plonks in the front row, and, though she's wearing that expensive dress, she curls her legs up Indian style on the chair. Then she slips the shoes off and bends down to place each on the floor noiselessly. It's a kind of sweet performance cause she seems to think no one can see her.

The man himself comes down the rows of chairs and he's nothing like that. He's just like, some handsome guy. Because he's wearing pale clothes, he looks like the ghost of a movie star, and he has a way about him, but he's just some guy. When he gets to the front, he turns to look at you and falls entirely still.

While he speaks, he remains absolutely still.

He's telling you what's going to happen to you when you die.

Now, this is kind of weird because you're not even listening. It's stuff like, the green light and then you see the green Buddha. Now the blue light and you see the blue Buddha. All the time these lights, if you meditate on the nothingness in nothingness, you're liberated from the cycle of rebirth, which by the end you've had so many chances you can hardly see how anyone could <u>fail</u> to be liberated, even just by mistake. It goes on literally forever.

He's so still. Whenever he moves his hands, you stare as if they're something shocking produced by a magician. You start to imagine he actually hasn't <u>breathed</u>. Without meaning to, you find yourself holding still. You want him to spot you holding still and be impressed.

The voice is very deep and it's normal but it's not normal. It could be a hypnosis thing but not. Because the sky is overcast, he seems to shine against the gray glass and you don't know how long you've felt very calm, like you just couldn't feel forever, until you would think, I just can't, and you couldn't, and you were <u>dwindling</u>.

It's much too late, but you begin to listen. You strain to understand as if your life depended on it. You don't know why but you need what he says. Because he knows what happens to you after death. Because it's perfect. Because it inebriates you and

You believe him like a fool. You believe him like a fool.

Afterward the milling around.

The drafted-in ex, Lynn, signed a few people up for residential weekends.

She said, "Looking forward to <u>seeing</u> you again," in a repeating loop, her real job was cocktail bar hostess.

I stayed right in my seat until the last possible moment. No one talked to me thank God. They talked to Ralph but Ralph didn't seem to say a word. One guy was saying that he knew some friends of his would be <u>extremely</u> interested. People spoke emphatically and much louder, after, than they had before. Two particular women laughed in shrill spikes of sound that made me think of spear flowers. They were the ones with makeup on, which somehow seemed related.

Eddie was schmoozing an older woman, who later would become clear to us as <u>Kate Higgins</u> who deserved the name <u>Kate Higgins</u>. Then she was anybody. I even thought she better watch out and this whole fantasy where Eddie offered me her credit card and I was too noble.

We knew without surprise that it had been a success. In our three distinct ways of understanding that.

At last it was just Jasper (an artist friend of Mom's who was bowled over and just wanted to move in there and then), me and Ralph and Eddie. Jasper somehow got melded into "us" and we all four together knew it had been a success, in the distinct group way of understanding that.

We waited out Jasper, who finally left, backing out the door to keep looking at Ralph for the longest possible time. Then Eddie got out some cigarettes and we smoked and ground the butts out in the thin gravel. I went out first to make sure all the cars were gone. Then Ralph took off his shirt and we decided to take the Hyundai, because it seemed like the right car for these circumstances.

We drove to Pizza Hut. From the back seat I was looking at Ralph's bare shoulder. Out of nowhere, I said, "That woman —" and we began to laugh. We laughed, and shouted broken phrases, and laughed. The blue Buddha! That guy with the forked beard! Jasper's face!

In Pizza Hut we laughed, we drank a pitcher of margaritas. By the time we finished our pizza we actually felt happy.

"You guys," Eddie said, "Respect. But that was the funniest, single, thing. Like do not ever tell me you believe that shit, cause — my last illusion."

On the drive home we fall silent. The dusk hills pass under the car like brain waves: we part into our three distinct ways of not knowing what happens next. Parking, Eddie says something about having a coffee, but Ralph just says he's tired and then he's gone, up the stairs. Eddie and I shuffle by the door, staring around as if the place looks different. The night's sunk in: stars and quiet. I say tentatively, I'm tired.

"Whatever," says Eddie. There's him acting hurt.

I linger to appease him, say, "Well, it was. Wasn't it?"

"Yeah." He looks up, as if at the stars. "Maybe I'll go out again. Lynn's working."

I make a conscious decision to disregard the needs of others and say, "That's a good idea: see you in the morning."

He blanks me as I stumble off.

I get upstairs in a rush, to my room, then I just stand. I look at the partition door. I walk to the bed and back, noisily, so Ralph knows I'm there. I stand at the door again. Maybe he's already asleep.

It's possible when he drew the door in, in the plans, that he already thought.

He kissed me because it would lend an intriguing energy to my performance: that was the first and last time.

If I get undressed and lie in bed, he'll knock. If I begin to doze.

Even if that was the first and last time, I'll be all right. I'll be all right. I'll be all right.

I put my palm flat against the door, as if I could feel him through it and learn something. Then I coil my hand up and look at the fist. I'm going to knock, I'll get it over with, I'll know. I'll do it just because I would never do that kind of thing, it's a breakthrough, it indicates growth. I'll count to ten.

There is a knocking and I jump. I have to wait for it to come again to make sure, which door. But while I wait, Ralph says, "Yeah?"

It's his door to the outside, the one that leads onto the balcony. And I hear Eddie say, "Ralph, dude. Like, talk to me? Honest Navajo blood vow, five minutes."

I back off silently from the partition. The door opens, I hear Eddie saying, ". . . talk to you . . . is not the coke talking . . . her her her, it just came up . . . Chrysa listening? DON'T LISTEN."

Ralph says: "Four minutes remaining."
Eddie: "NO, MAN: WHISPER."

I guess they whispered. I felt my heart beating in a weedy, pitiful way. I got out of my clothes hurriedly as if Ralph might throw the door open. Then I put on a blue silk nightgown, all the while mentally accounting for me putting on a nightgown. I wasn't cold: I just felt vulnerable, after all that. Wearing a nightgown made me feel like a real manageress. I was trying to hone it so it would be honest, without giving any impression that I put on a nightgown for him. All the while he wasn't coming.

I got into bed and pulled the covers way over my head. It even occurred to me to go back under the bed so I would have to be <u>rescued</u> and Ralph would know why, and. Of course I couldn't ever, but I stubbornly refused to be pleased that I was cured. It was a <u>for what?</u> reaction, as if someone had dangled Ralph/carrot, and without my carrot I would rather be dysfunctionally insane.

My mind drifted over to my father and began to gently worry his memory. My mind appeared to me as Remember, tugging at my father's arm with her blunt muzzle open wide to fit his bulk. Dad was sitting in an easy chair, watching television, and he cosseted Remember, saying, "Hey, old girl, we got to roll with the punches."

My father kissed me deeply and I woke up in consternation.

There was a knocking at the door. I didn't wait to find out what door, I shrieked, "Come in!" pulling the sheets first up and then down, blind in a world of sheet.

When I had my face clear, my brother Eddie was standing there. He'd centered himself exactly on the bare patch of floor, so there was something apparition-esque in his placement. I told him I had just had a creepy dream. Then I looked at Ralph's door in shock and said, "What time – did I sleep for – how long –?"

"<u>Five minutes</u>," Eddie said towards Ralph's door with amplified unforgiveness. Then walked to my bedside:

"Look, your dream? I deeply care, but not now, cause Ralph's been giving me this story like my old girlfriend's from outer space. So I just need total nurturing, cause my being-nurtured thing has been subtracted from by that in a massive way, and I'm like needful? So, is that cool?"

"I was in the middle of something," I complained,

though I was lying in bed. It occurred to me he'd think I'd been masturbating and I struggled to sit up.

Eddie crossed his arms: "This. Is. Important."

He gave me an intense stare, somewhat marred by a peripheral cocaine sniffle. Standing so close, he activated my deep love for him. It was unfair but he's my brother and I feel untold loss of him, though I might wish this were not the case.

But then: as long as he was there I couldn't find out Ralph didn't want me.

"So what girlfriend do you mean?" I asked, beginning to feel stirrings of from-outer-spaceness in my memory.

Eddie said, "Oh, you know, some girl I met traveling."

The penny dropped. I said in worry, "Not Denise?"

Eddie jumped a mile and shouted, "Don't tell me you know her too!"

"No . . . no . . . Ralph had mentioned . . ."

"Oh, great. Bigmouth or what? You try to trust people." He sat down on the bed with a plump of I-give-up. Then he bent down and took his tennis shoes off, tying the laces together and setting them down on the bed beside him. Leaning back, he put one hand on my ankle, then felt around in the covers for a free patch, making a big deal of how uncomfortable it was. Finally he said, "Look, could I just get in? Cause, totally, brother and sister, and – look me in the eyes?"

I didn't look him in the eyes, but he said nonetheless, "Need."

I made an elaborate flapping gesture to imply his getting in was a matter of no concern or interest. It was funny how angry it made me. Had he not manipulated me into it, I would have been overjoyed to huddle in bed with Eddie.

He clambered over me triumphantly and slid in. Then he:

"But the point about what Ralph with his blah blah space monster cruelty that just upsets me till I'm ready to tear my head off with pliers and I don't know why you're even listening to this secondhand account of bull I totally ignored —"

## Argument

*The big light comes down her face, the shadow focuses. Denise Cadwallader falls into the creatures' overwhelming hearth of love. She is returned unharmed after no apparent lapse of time, but in the following months becomes disruptive at kindergarten. Upon the death of her mother, she is sent to a boarding school in Hampshire, where she is very unhappy.*

## 2. Santa Clara, California, 1965

1    She wakes sitting in the middle of the highway. There are no cars.

1.1    The Pontiac's tilted where it's parked with two wheels on the grass.

1.2    Mummy's still asleep. Mum's poorly.

2    When she tries to walk to the car, she falls down.

2.1    When she tries to walk to the car, she falls down.

2.2    If you lie on the highway, the yellow broken line steps up and up, teasing you into the hungry sky.

2.3    It was a white bean and she loved it. She tries to walk to the car.

3    When she wakes up again, she's balled up in a Mexican blanket on the car's back seat; they're driving. Bunny Betty's fallen on the floor and she can't reach. She begins to grizzle, and Mum says, "Deesey?"

Deesey quiets. After a little, she says, "Bunny Betty fell."

Mum says, "I'll get her when we stop, my treasure. I can't stop now, I don't feel well and it's late."

Deesey looks at Bunny Betty, lying ears down with her feet up on the hump. She tells her to sleep, and almost remembers something which makes her look up at the dark car window, its dull wedge of reflected light, but doesn't remember after all and shifts onto her back, humphing.

She says, "Mummy? Will you be poorly for a long time?"

Because Mum doesn't answer, she listens to the car groan. She says, "Mummy?" again.

Mum says, "I might be, Deesey. We have to be patient. Were you afraid when I was sleeping?"

"No."

"I won't sleep in the car ever again with you, I do promise."

Deesey kicks her feet loose from the blanket. She says, "If I don't be patient, won't the bean not come back?"

"What bean?"

"There was a bean, and you were asleep and it flew me, and you didn't know when you slept."

"Slept," her mother says. "I'm sorry, sweetheart, I don't feel well. Can you tell me about the bean tomorrow?"

"No. Tomorrow it's a secret."

"Well, I'll never know then, will I?"

Her mother takes the turn for their exit. Deesey gets up on her knees to watch as they pass the giant revolving ice-cream cone on Mr. Tasty's roof.

She doesn't think about the bean again for a long time.

## BUT

1    Suddenly, she's a brat.

1.1  Every night she must sleep with Mummy, then she must sleep on Mummy's floor, then she must sleep in the closet on the heaped linen.

1.2  "Cause, I throwed the cup, cause, but it went in the clock. Cause it's a bad cup and I was killing it."

1.3  Sometimes she won't come out of the road.

2    "Denise has trouble distinguishing fantasy from the truth."

2.1  "Discipline deficient."

2.2  "She is good at communicating with other children, but sometimes a bully."

2.3  "Please call me to arrange an informal meeting."

3    He is uniformly yellow and his eyes are glossy wet leaves, his mouth an X. The light shudders gently as if idling. Where the yellowperson steps, the floor dimples and briefly holds cloven prints. The wall's silver inconstant surface reflects a tot in pigtails, paralyzed with the mouth agape to show sparse teeth.

3.1  "Wake up, baby, you're having a bad dream. Deesey? Deesey, it's only a naughty dream."

4    Her mittens are safety-pinned to her coat, because she <u>will</u> lose them.

4.1  The fat pencils have to say "Barbie," and they must be pink.

4.2  She can write her name now in joined-up letters.

4.3  She is a loved child. My child is loved, no one has ever harmed her.

# SO

The office is furnished with beanbag chairs and red plastic kiddie tables. A teddy bear has a pink heart stitched to its chest. In one corner is a bulky desk, flanked by two office chairs, in which the child psychologist and Karen Cadwallader face each other. She is restless, has declined to take off her coat, scowls. One hand is at her rib cage, kneading in an habitual gesture, probing the spaced bones. She tells herself, *No one put a gun to your head, to come here.*

"Well, let's hear your ideas first, and then I'll give you my ideas." The child psychologist folds his hands.

Karen Cadwallader sighs. "I don't know that I have any ideas. She's very clever. That can be problematic."

"You're . . . British?"

"Yes. Yes, actually, I thought, we moved to America about the time this began. And of course her father is still in Britain."

"Why of course?"

"We work."

"And would you say . . . was that about the time you began to feel ill?"

"That's not connected. She doesn't know: work doesn't know. I haven't felt tempted to make it a mainspring of my life."

"You know, children notice much more than we realize."

Karen feels this escaping into some awful irrelevance. She wants to protest, she's six, she doesn't know mummies die. She can't know, she's six, don't make it worse than it is.

She says stiffly, "I didn't come here to talk about me."

For the remaining thirty minutes they discuss Karen Cadwallader's marriage, her early youth, her uterine cancer.

She never had much faith in the radiation treatments. They caught it early, she should have had a chance, but there's no right and wrong. She winds up with a phrase she's rehearsed tirelessly in her mental practice runs of finally telling Peter: "I can't take it so terribly seriously, the dying part. I'm a doctor myself, at the end of the day, it's rather old hat."

The psychologist waits her out. It's a probing silence that Karen physically opposes, squaring her shoulders in her now-baggy raincoat. When it is plain she will say nothing more, he rebuts gently: "Even doctors have feelings."

She catches her breath, feels idiotically that she's betrayed something. It's a feeling she recognizes from her occasional dreams about being kidnapped by the KGB, the truth serum dreams. In those she is lying strapped to a bed – naked, what else – and <u>she has already talked</u>. It's done beyond remedy: she is going to die in disgrace.

She summons up a flip, professional tone, fires back: "No, you see, I'm a <u>medical</u> doctor." And the time's up, she can frown apologetically at her watch –

and gather her things to go.

There's still time to get into her office at Bulwer-Sutton Industries if she takes the freeway.

She phones her husband from the office for privacy's sake: privacy meaning no Denise. It's a trade-off because office conversations are automatically recorded: theoretically someone combs these hours of tapes for suspicious exchanges. Since only senior staff have the clearances to listen to the tapes, however, and senior staff are far too busy to waste time in this fashion, Karen prefers to believe the tapes rot in a safe.

Peter answers on the first ring. He's per usual guarded, speaks rapidly to get it over with. She lets him rabbit on, hums to imply listening, dreads her turn. But when he has related the intricacies of his latest actuarial project, he winds up breathlessly, "This must be costing you."

In the ensuing silence, she grips the receiver with all her strength. Her face collapses into a rictus of grief. She knows she has yet again failed to tell him, that she will die before he learns she was ever ill, that this is all wrong: she is cruel.

Perhaps it's because she's in the office, but she's unhappily visited by the burly shade of Jack Moffat. It's a fantasy that's plagued her these six months.

Jack Moffat is her husband. It's him she comes to with her troubles.

In some versions of the fantasy, the Jack Moffat figure dissolves in a frenzy of activity: he is <u>fixing everything</u>. In some he just enfolds her in his arms. For this purpose, he is always wearing a voluminous coat, into which she disappears, gratefully, probably bloody fainting.

*Karen, you hardly know the man,* she tells herself, as if it were really anything to do with Jack, after all.

"I'll let you go," Peter says.

She blurts: "Darling, there's Denise."

"What? What about her?"

"Well, she's been upset, she's in trouble at school –"

"I don't know what you want me to do about it from 3,000 miles away."

She begins to speak but he breaks in:

"I am 3,000 miles away."

She begins to speak but he, angrily:

"Be fair."

She does not say, *Look, I am dying, you'll have to take her.* She does not say, *Be kind to me, for Christ's sake, I'm in pain.* She does not say, *I'm dying, I'm dying, I'm dying.*

She will not plead to be missed.

She says, "I won't keep you."

And then she gathers her things to go.

— to get home to pay the sitter: "Good night, Elaine, thanks ever so much!"

— to lean at the kitchen table drinking cold black coffee poured from the morning's pot, but she must

carry on after all regardless at the end of the day

— to change her clothes standing next to the washing machine, start the next load and take the stairs in three goes

count to ten and rest and count to ten and rest and

The damned mirror waits at the top.

"Careworn" is putting it mildly.

Someone loved that face once. Someone went down on one knee. He went into debt buying that crone a diamond ring. *Karen, my dear, it boggles the mind.*

## ONCE

1     It was always raining and it was always dusk.

1.1   It must be when we lived in London: this must be that grotty bedsit.

1.2   He had always already had one drink. In those days, people held hands.

1.3   "I'll remember this as the happiest time of my life."

2     It's real love plus my first real job.

2.1   Even the waiter has to hear her callow boast: "We work at the Hospital for Tropical Medicine."

2.2   You could say we worked: twenty hours at a stretch, and how you laughed at any damn thing, that exhausted, when you stood up your heart lost its footing. Every light swam.

2.3  "I bet he won't serve us now. Look at his face, he thinks *we have germs.*"

3    Two unbeautiful science graduates hold hands in a wet meadow. A cloud drifts across the sun, extinguishing its glamor. When the gloom is complete, the scientists walk away, as if satisfied by a job well done.

3.1  Then we lived together in the rainy darkness for ten years.


## TEN YEARS LATER THEN

4    In a Chinese restaurant in Monterey he whispers: "History."

4.1  She puts down her fork, startled from her food reveries.

4.2  "History, Karen. You have heard of it?"

4.3  He flags her with his new prop, his broadsheet news-papers even at the dinner table (her mother would forbid it, but oh, just please don't bring up <u>class</u>).

4.4  Yes, Peter, everybody knows Dad was a lorry driver, what else? Oh, you had to work while everything just <u>fell in my lap</u>.

4.5  She is almost crying. She pleads, crumbling a wonton: "Well, tell me about history, then. What's it all about?"

4.6  He looks at her with no love in his eyes, showing her the no love, in retaliation.

5    Tells her, slowly, with a viciousness, "It's about *conscience.*"

5.1  And he starts up, he leaves without his coat.

5.2  The *Washington Post* lies crumpled on his plate in all the grease.

5.3  A blotch spreads through the headline: KENNEDY PLEDGES TROOPS FOR INDOCHINA.

6    Alone on the bus, she held his coat in her lap.

"Some things are beyond me, do you understand? I can't judge."

"Oh, it's not for us to question why. Too right, Karen."

"You wouldn't even be saying this five years ago. You just . . . regurgitate."

"You weren't working on germ warfare five years ago."

"Non-lethal," she cries. "Oh, how you can not see."

"Well, I believe you, thousands wouldn't."

"But, that's what it is. That's what it is. I can hardly believe this fuss when all I would do, at worst, is give the Russians a bad cold."

"Oh, my God, Karen. I thought you were cynical. Not stupid. I never thought you were that stupid."

— but, after all, we were only standing in a Holiday Inn bathroom in dirty terry robes to have that historical exchange, and I was only this same homely swot, nobody: only five foot two! In fact, my bare feet were cold on the tiles and that distracted me from your important history, thinking I had best buy slippers. But I wanted to protest,

<u>I'm a good scientist. I'm just a good scientist.</u>

She said, "Let's just please just get dressed."

Deesey:

When you were born I didn't want to hold you. They'd washed you but you still smelled, and I thought, I can't do this. I'll have to get a nanny. You were too much like other newborn things, like the rabbits and baby mice, all the wet infants with their squashed faces we bred for experimental purposes. I don't know why things are born. I didn't make it so that things are born, for experimental purposes. But I wouldn't dare to be a mother to anything, I didn't realize but that's how it was, I wouldn't dare. Something about the sins of the fathers. I do realize no one wants to dissect you for medical science, I'm not crazy! But I couldn't hold you like a mother, I was nervous of touching you. Now I know how it was for that silly waiter; I have germs. Somehow I must have, I have germs. Now I'm so tired, I can't think what I mean I'm that tired.

She leans against the foul mirror, damning her awful sweat, the sickness, the tedious, tedious pain that she can't stop fearing. Tells herself, *Don't try to puzzle it out, you don't have that kind of mind.*

*You were a good scientist.*

*And then she gathers her things to go.*

*And you remember how they wheeled her down hospital corridors, Deesey, you envied her for being given a ride in bed. You ran behind as if you'd catch her, and she wouldn't die. You must save her but they're so fast. Your feet jarred you. And you remember double swinging doors which close to form a word, and this picture is what comes to mind when you think of death.*

And that picture of a very little girl, in a coat whose nautical buttons twinkle

in a big smelly new car, stopped on the highway in windy desert

Mum has pulled over to the breakdown lane just in time.

*Deesey be good I'm,* she says, struggles;
and falls asleep.

The little girl tugs Mum's limp arm. She announces,

"You wait here, Mum, I'll go call for the nambulance." When the child has opened the door, though, she just perches sobbing in the car's small light.

And the big light comes down her face. The shadow focuses.

"– so, he's telling me all this shit and I'm, whoa, dude, slow down. It's, you remember when Dad went away the first time and it was like, I got to ride in front? In the car? You ever remember things like that?"

Eddie was lying propped on an elbow, smoking menthol Dorals and flicking the ash into his tennis shoe. I was sitting up with my arms crossed over the frivolous nightgown. By then I had given up waiting for Eddie to leave and was tolerating his rant with listless stoicism.

I said, "Dad was never away the first time. He always went away."

"I don't care about fucking <u>fact</u>." Eddie bugged his eyes at me. "But you would never remember that cause you were so his pet."

I flinched. "Was I?"

"Jesus Christ! Were you. <u>Now it can be told</u>, Chrysa, there was some <u>untoward</u> too-pet element, which . . . Like, maybe that's why Mom never really liked you."

I said, "I wasn't in reality his pet."

Eddie snorted. "Dad was queer for you, Chrysa. Like, talking as a guy? Window-dressing shit to one side, a guy can form a deep romantic attachment for an oven-stuffer-roaster fucking chicken, given you dethaw it and it's got that, you know that neck hole? Guys are just a prick with attachments. Sorry."

"You're just trying to make something dramatic from . . . poor materials."

There was a silence. In the dark, you couldn't tell what so terribly impended. I had the familiar feeling that Eddie'd dismantled something in my chest.

He said, "Chrysa."

His hand groped over to my ankle and up my calf, to grip me solemnly on the swell of my new muscle. I started to cry. He continued:

"Chrysa, you got to learn to face stuff. It's a million years ago, already. Like, Columbus was President –"

"I don't want to talk about this right now."

"Mongolia was a world power – shit, are you crying? Oh, no. No, I made you cry? Come here." He shifted about ponderously to sit and hold his arms out.

He sat there with his arms out, waiting.

I was going to be manipulated into hugging him, and then my world would come to an end, my soul would go out, what he said would be true. I was still crying though the original feeling was gone. If I hugged him I could wipe my nose surreptitiously on his shoulder, dispensing with the looming need for a tissue. Perhaps the nose-wiping could redefine the annihilating hug, turning it into a light-minded prank. Crying jaggedly, I marveled at the power of toilet/snot humor, a universal of human experience: I thought of writing to Lévi-Strauss and suggesting it as a rival to the incest taboo, if Lévi-Strauss were still alive. I wondered if Lévi-Strauss, like Saint-Lazare, had lost his mind and cashed in his chips in a sly poststructural manner.

"Oh, fuck it," said Eddie, and let his arms fall. "Trying to reach out. Okay, listen, if I'm that transparent, I just need to know if Dad screwed you for my personal reasons, cause –"

"No."

"No?"

"No, he didn't. I was <u>ten</u>." The word <u>ten</u> came out in a little-kid falsetto, and I sobbed horribly behind it, snorting like a drain.

"Oh, man. No. I gotta hug you. Do not try to resist."

Eddie shuffled toward me on his knees. I held my arms

stiffly crossed over my stomach, to mime noncompliance. He got me roughly and crushed my face to his chest. He seemed very big and too much like a man, musky-smelling. As long as I stayed tense, my soul would not go out.

"Kiddo, kiddo. Kiddokiddo. Honestly, stop, I get this pain thing in the small of my back. An actual symptom."

"Oh, you don't care," my crying said / *I listened but it meant nothing to me.*

"Okay," said Eddie. "But – you do? You do?"

"I care. I care," my crying said / *while I triumphantly did not care.*

"Well, fantastic: care."

I stopped crying and was shivering feebly. He stroked the back of my head. You could tell he wasn't consciously stroking, it was just a reflex. I said on my own behalf, coldly, to try how it sounded:

"Okay, I don't. I don't care about you anymore."

He let me go so violently I seemed to bounce out of his arms.

I could hear him breathing rapidly. He said, "Turn on the light."

I turned on the light. He was sitting up, hugging his knees. The light felt chill where I'd sweated through the nightgown. The mussed bed shocked me. It looked as if we'd been energetically throwing the covers in the air.

Eddie said, "Okay, you can turn it off again now."

"No." I shrugged, brattish.

"Oh. Suit yourself." Then he sat there making frown after frown, as if preparing to make a difficult disclosure. I began to stare dully, out of focus, at his shoulder. The blue nightgown felt now like the costume my character wore in the "brother" scene.

"Chrysa," Eddie said, vehemently.

Despite myself, I met his eye. He went on, encouraged:

"I just, I thought, what would make it better, right? Is for us to sleep together. Cause, it's like, we're not even related. And – oh, don't. Don't –"

Without having intended to move, I found myself standing against the wall. I said, in that kid falsetto,

"<u>Very. Funny.</u>"

"No. Not very funny. Very serious. Really. I thought about this." He pointed to his head.

"<u>You thought about this.</u>"

He scrambled out of the bed, taking the top sheet with him. His tennis shoe tumbled to the floor, dispensing ash. I said,

"<u>Get out of my room.</u>"

He put his hands on his hips. "<u>No.</u>"

"You <u>better</u> get out this second."

"Not."

"Look, this isn't funny."

"Come on, lighten the fuck up."

"Will you get out of my room before I –"

He came toward me with his arms out like the Mummy. "Oooh – oooh – I'm gonna <u>touch</u> you! Oooh!"

"OUT! GET OUT!" I dodged, but he sidestepped and cornered me.

I was screaming OUT! while he danced, making tickling movements with his fingers. I started to laugh, helplessly, breathlessly, and say,

"Oh, come on, give me a break, Eddie, you got to be kidding me –"

And then he swooped and caught me in the corner, both of us laughing hysterically and he pulled me against him and I shouted –

The door flew open: it was Ralph.

Eddie and I jumped away from each other like naughty children.

Standing against the lit doorway, Ralph looked huge and dark. He said in a cool, carrying voice, "What are you doing?"

Eddie spoke up first. "Yeah, we were just, fooling around. Cause I was saying about the aliens coming down to save the Earth –"

Ralph said to me, "What's going on?"

I gasped: "Eddie wanted to fuck me."

Eddie and I glanced at each other. I couldn't help it, I smirked. It was mainly shame, but there was a crazed undertow of glee. I thought of announcing that the snake had tempted me, but when I looked at Ralph, it was chilling how untickled he was by our (I suddenly, conveniently believed) mere horseplay.

Ralph said, "Eddie?"

His voice described an arc from disgust to a kind of friendly amazement. He was prepared to hear it never crossed Eddie's mind to fuck his sister.

Eddie said, "Yeah."

Ralph stepped into the room. He said, "Maybe I should leave."

The horseplay scenario held for a long long moment, then I said,

"Don't leave. Don't leave me here with him. Jesus Christ!"

Ralph said, "Okay,"

and walked straight to Eddie. He put one hand on Eddie's shoulder and said down into his face, "I ought to kill you."

"Look, I'm going," Eddie said. "Cause, your thug deal, me no like."

"Go, then," said Ralph, not taking his hand from Eddie's shoulder.

"No, serious. The whole I-kill-you-motherfucker thing? I got one word for you, man. Cops."

Ralph took his hand off of Eddie's shoulder. I caught my breath.

Eddie said again, in a tight, smug voice, straightening up to enjoy Ralph's retreat: "Cops."

Ralph drew back slightly and punched Eddie in the head.

The fist carried Eddie's head back to the wall and pinned it there momentarily, then sprang free. Eddie staggered, shuffling and reaching out for nothing, then found the wall with his shoulderblades and slumped there.

Ralph said, "Say that again."

As if in reply, Eddie began to bleed. He bled in real time: you could see the trickle run from his nostril to his chin and drip. He began to say, "Man, that sucks, that just so sucks." He dabbed at his face with his knuckles and inspected the blood. "Asshole."

"I'm going to hit you again," Ralph said with absolute clammy hatred.

Eddie flinched and took a step to one side. Then he squared himself against the wall and said, "Fuck you."

I said, "Don't, this is so crazy."

Ralph looked at me in frozen unrecognition. Before turning back to Eddie and curling his arm back to gather the deep force of his whole body, punching again so Eddie's lip split over his tooth and needed two stitches, Ralph said to me:

"Aren't you going to cry?"

# LOLA SECTIONS

## Argument

*Ralph grows up in penury and neglect,
which inclines him throughout his life
to fits of uncontrollable rage.*

## Dave Something Scottish

"My mother's people, they were real gypsies, in caravans. And I had a gran, she'd take me out 'calling.' It were begging, really. Well, my dad found out about it, I got the belt. Him with his council flat and he weren't running his amusement arcade yet, but you could see where he was going. Begging weren't in it. But she let me keep my own money so I'd sneak off.

"So it was round hers and her mates you got the social. They were keeping a check on the kids, really, so we'd tell them a pack of lies. The social workers were all spies, weren't they? This one, Dave, he was good for a laugh, though.

"I'll never forget, he had this Ford Zephyr, with fins like that. I thought that was the coolest thing out. I was always pestering for a ride. I'm all of fifteen – trouble. So finally he crumbles and I'm there in the front seat, riding down through Sunderland with my hair combed out, all the great lady. Dave's yelling me to roll the window up but I weren't having it.

"And there as we're at the traffic light I see my dad just on the pavement, as near as you are to me now, with a face like thunder. You know, if I ever dared smile at a man I got wrong off him . . . well, we drove off, but me knowing. And I thought, might as well be hung for a sheep as a lamb and when we stopped I ran out and spent all my calling money on beer.

"That man, that social worker, he never knew what hit him. You don't want to get in the path of a gypsy lass who's had her first little whiff of freedom. I guess by the time my people were through, he wished he'd just gone to prison for me, they had every penny he ever earned until he just upped and pissed off back to Scotland. Or that's what I heard. I guess

I was busy having a baby and that so I didn't give him much thought. Anyhow, then they had me know I was on my own. Not that I broke my heart over them, not a chance. Over him or them. I never looked back."

## IRENE MICHAELSON
### *a.k.a. Gypsy Lola*
### *a.k.a. Seven Up*
### *and her ten years' borrowed time*

★ ★ ★

Five foot nothing
Brown eyes the kind that look black
Black hair.
Skinny, nothing to her
from speed, barbs, smack.
Irene for an Irish grandmother, dead when she was
born.
Rechristened Lola by the strip-club manager.

A stroppy cow: trouble. Off her trolley. Never in nick,
but that's nine parts luck. Spots/bad teeth embarrassed Ralph
but blokes were happy to shag her. A tart (for money, for real)
when money was tight: otherwise gave it free.

For that, "Seven Up." Untold toothbrushes in her bathroom. Which Paul? Which John? Which Tim? Which Alonzo?

"No, I do know two: with the Dexedrine script, and
with the Jag."

Loved men for their drugs: but not just. She'd ring at
3:00 A.M., blubbering: "Christ, love, even if you hate me from
my nonsense, I'd lay down my life for you, and all I need's
company."

Rebuffed, light another fag and dial the next number. In
a sighing aside to Ralph: "Never mind, pet: needs must."

And: "Men aren't half cunts, it has to be said."
And: "Do the washing up, love, Mummy's saying please."
And: "I <u>will</u> get married, when I'm 23, it's in my palm."

Lola did without
- hot food
- hot running water
- winter coat/umbrella/boots
- socks & underwear

so Ralph could do without them too. "I've got no bread in the house for my boy" her refrain, but gave her last penny, for the asking. "It's all about people, in the end. There's nothing else. It's about mates."

"So, my sister Irene's been on our settee eight months, that was August, little Ralph were only that old. Breast-feeding, but our Irene, she cannot sleep alone. You ask her. Any normal person, you or me, four people in a one bed flat, you couldn't get lonely if you tried. And Ralph were only by the settee, he hadn't got a crib. She'd put him in the carton from the telly. Our Staff used to leap in beside him, try as we might. We was terrified one night he'd poke her eye and that would be an end to him.

"Anyhow, my sister, she'd have a different one every night bedded down with her. All the blokes in the shops of the high street knew her, she'd be down there enticing them if she didn't have anything set up. Just turned sixteen, she was, though of course we all had to swear she were nineteen, and she has her dole to this day in the name of our cousin that was nineteen then.

"Well finally, eight months into this carry-on, ask her if you don't believe me, she come in one night wanting to sleep in the bed with James and me. Wouldn't take no. So we humor her, she'd got the spirit beaten out of us by then.

"But ten minutes, the three of us there, James switches on the light. He says, cool as that, 'I've never punched a woman in the mouth before, Irene.'

"Had her hand in his crotch, hadn't she?

"Well, she says - and remember I don't know what's going on – oh, she says, feathers all ruffled, Mandy wouldn't mind. By now, I've got a fair idea. I say, 'If that's what I think it is, I certainly do mind.'

"Irene chirps, like this: 'Well, you only have to say.'

"Then we tell her in no uncertain terms, out. And the wailing and weeping, oh, she can't go back, she's frightened. Of course, Ralphie hears it, and he joins right in. And Irene shrieking she'll have to cut her wrists, and next thing we know, she's punching herself. Punching herself all in the face. We were holding her down in the end, it took the two of us. Up half the night feeding her whiskey, and God knows we needed one ourself.

"She's passed out, finally, and James insists on going through her bag. Find out what the pills are, as if that's any help. But once he's got his mind made up, I let him fly. And what he finds is, no pills, but her address book. And what's mad about that is, Irene cannot read nor write. So she'd had them write out all their own numbers, and then I guess she had to have the next bloke read them back to her. But what really got James's goat was, underneath, often as not, she'd have them make a note. And it was one of two things, a sum of money which, you had to know, was what the man had paid her. Or else it was names of drugs, whatever he could get hold of, or had on prescription. Had them write it out themselves! I tell you!

"Well, we didn't throw her out then, but we gave the

201

housing officer no peace. I spent every afternoon haranguing him, till she got her flat."

Then, when Ralph was seven-plus years, a pattern:

She arrives home with armloads of groceries, jabbering a mile a minute. Ralph falls asleep to Mum scrubbing the skirting boards.

"There's going to be some changes, look at this place. Pigs, they are, pigs. Never again."

Wakes up to: "Jesus, I've been a shite mother to you. Tell me you don't blame me, Ralph. But don't lie."

As he leaves for school, she's lying on the carpet by the gas fire with one eye shut, chain-smoking spliffs.

When he comes home, she's still there, sleeping, with a naked man.

"Ralphie, oh, love! Come here and kiss me. Alonzo, wake up, you waster, and say hello to my pride and joy."

"Stick the kettle on for us, Ralphie, we're that knackered."

"Ralphie, have we got them ravioli, still? Be an angel —"

He falls asleep to John, Paul, Tim and Alonzo, drinking Tennants to The Kinks blaring in the front room.

The fag ash goes on the floor. The ravioli dries with the fork stuck in the open tin. Drunk and ranting, Paul pisses himself in the bathtub. John vomits in every room.

He comes home to them and falls asleep to them and wakes up to them. They change and change about, but never all leave. The women scare Ralph more because they want to touch him. Mum says

Ralphie!

Ralphie!

Ralphie!

The weekends, she has to go out to do her tarot. Then

she storms through them, swearing, in a bra and towel, trying to find the other shoe.

"I want you lot out when I get back, I've had enough!" she squeals to general desultory laughter.

Ralph comes home, the flat's empty. A thread of smoke still dangles, spreading lazily in one corner. He gets a box of Frosties, sits in front of the telly. The stink rouses him, he opens all the windows. Finds a long dog end on the settee, lights it listening out for Mum.

As he stubs it out, she arrives home with stacks of groceries, jabbering a mile a minute.

She'd say Ralph made her think again about changelings. "He never missed a day at that school, it ain't my side." And

"He takes care of me, not the other way around. Couldn't do without my best mate."

But she didn't love him like mums love children. One of their family rules was, Ralph never to touch her, first.

He loved Mum, just Mum. To Mandy, he would say, "She's not like other people, cause she's psychic. Mum needs to be treated special."

And they cuddled together under a blanket for warmth when the gas had been cut off, eking out the last tin of baked beans between them, lonely and poor and lonely and poor.

And when Ralph was ten, she had a kidney infection. Then it was "gastric folds," she couldn't keep food down, woke in sweating agonies. In and out of hospital, Ralph held the fort at home. The longest was the detox, where she lasted two weeks and arrived home at 6:00 A.M., cursing them fascist nurses; barefoot, ebullient, with unnaturally pale, pinned-out eyes.

And as that dismal year winds down, she learns the word "can't." She can't keep it together like she used, she can't see anyone, she can't be doing with them wankers, now Ralph can read the post.

"I can't do cold turkey, but I can't carry on, so Jim downstairs will give us one pill every day. Cause me, I can't do willpower, I'd scoff the lot."

And when she'd whittled it down to two milligrams oral methadone, tactically imbibed just before she'd have to leave the house, and even Mandy took notice and began to come by with cakes every now and then, and Lola's skin knitted up, her face was face-shaped once more and you could see she was a striking woman

## The ticket out

1    Thick and thin, Lola kept her tarot pitch at Portobello.
2    One day she told Peter Cadwallader's fortune.

1    He said he was a card player himself: flirting.
2    She'd had their cheek for a lifetime. Parried: "That's sixpence," curt.

1    But he could find nothing smaller than a pound note in his wallet,
2    which was as fat as the Collected Works of Shakespeare, if all old Will wrote were fifty-pound notes.

1    "I had him hooked that quick. Two weeks' time! No worries. Course, it wasn't me like you see me now.

2    "Well, I thought it would be a bit of dosh for us for a change. I thought, you'd have a father, everyone was always giving me grief, you without a dad.

3    "I did love him, though. Who knows what makes you feel things? He's like a horrible dried-up lizard, isn't he? Peter. Well, they say love is blind, don't they? I'm the living proof. I loved that horror like the last man on earth."

## 26. Montara Beach, California:

## One Hour Earlier / Eddie Knocking on Ralph's door,

## unwelcome

"... honest Navajo blood vow, five minutes, this is only cause I had to talk to you for hours, and it is not the coke talking, it's the same old her her her again, it just came up, is Chrysa listening? DON'T LISTEN."

"Four minutes remaining."

"NO, MAN: WHISPER."

Eddie turned and closed the door gingerly behind him, wincing at the noise the knob made.

"Say it, then, what?"

Eddie whispered:

"*Wow. You got some mean chair prejudice. Too good for furniture or what? That is fucked up.*"

Ralph sat on the floor, demonstratively. Eddie narrowed his eyes at the sleeping mat, then sighed and sat, wincing at the cold parquet.

"*Listen,*" Eddie pointed at his head: "*This shit is percolating. Denise Cadwallader?*"

Ralph whispered, "*What about Denise?*"

Eddie said, "We can stop whispering now," aloud.

Ralph looked away. "This is doing my head in."

"Are you okay, man?"

"No. No."

"That was a fucking Valium I gave you, cause, it could be anything, I'm not really Joe Organized?"

Ralph put one hand to his head and pressed, as if he had to hold his head on manually. That seemed to help, but he also had to say:

"About Denise, I can't tell you anything."

"Should I be getting you a glass of fucking water, cause I'm totally a veteran of the glass-of-water thing."

"I can't tell you anything, I said before."

Then Eddie rearranged himself, meaning business. "No way," he said. He pointed at the ceiling. "What are you under?"

Ralph sniffed, scratched his chin, looked at his knuckles introspectively – as if there had been a lull in the conversation. There was a pillow-feather caught in the hair on his wrist, and he was fishing it out, idly, when Eddie barked:

"MY ROOF."

"That's laughable," Ralph said, courteous, surprised. "If that's a threat?"

"NO, cause you're fucking holding out on me, shitbag, and here I'm like succoring you in my own home?"

"I haven't seen Denise since I was twelve. I don't know what you think I can tell you."

"Phone number. Mailing address. Cause <u>you know where she is</u>."

"No." Ralph sighed.

"I got about a million dollars. What do you got?"

"That won't work with me."

Eddie sat back. Spotting one of Ralph's shoes by his hand, he picked it up and put it in his lap. He pulled the laces out industriously, left-right, left-right, complaining, "I get like, I feel alone here. I'm like a ghost that no one sees."

"Never threaten me."

"Yeah, only now you're telling <u>me</u> what to do, so I could say the same thing to you." Eddie threw the shoe down and shoved the laces in his jeans pocket.

"Why did you ask me here?" said Ralph.

They both looked at the venetian blinds. There was a

ten-minute silence in which they both thought of the reasons Eddie had brought Ralph to California.

At the end of it, Eddie's face was beaded with sweat. He said, "Fuck you, dude. Just, fuck you."

Ralph said:

## *4.*

1   Ralph's mother had died of an overdose in Kathmandu

  - in a dirt parking lot, a roan mud around her thighs where the last vein used had bled for some time unstanched.

  - Ralph found her. He lifted her, to walk her back and forth like in the movies. It was easy she was that light. Then her legs would not unbend, she was the only cold thing on that summer day.

  - Peter Cadwallader was summoned to dispose of her: Irene had him on her flight documents as Next of Kin.

2   He brought his daughter

  - and at the airport, while Peter made the rote condoling remarks, Denise stood grinning. Her horsy face was sweet. She told Ralph, "Well, we've come to get you, finally."

  - He was wearing his old school uniform. Dipankar had cleaned and pressed it, but it looked chapped where the moths had been. The jacket cut him in the armpits, outgrown. "I can't leave," Ralph said. "I've got a job here. It isn't only Mum, why I'm here."

  - "Of course we're not going to make Ralph do anything he doesn't want to do." Peter cleared his throat.

  - Denise looked at her father with a minutely composed scorn. She held it on him like a flashlight, exposing him, for a count of three, then wearily:

3   "You don't have to come, Peter."

3.1   She was polite the day she went with Ralph to the pottery.

3.2   Meeting her, the boss looked at Ralph reproachfully –

as if, up to now, Ralph had concealed the fact that he was English.

4      Within three days it was out of control, Denise overwhelmed any other thing in his life.

4.1    The cakes she brought him, the gifts of bundled rupees. Though she hardly spoke, she kept him up all night, he would sit beside her watching her foot dig thoughtfully in the street grit. When she said, "Oh, dear, this is fate," his head spun, he was mortally afraid and joyous.

4.2    Under her sway, he stole 10,000 dollars from Peter's briefcase.

4.3    They fled to Pokhara, a ten-hour bus ride to the high Himalaya.

5      (On the way, standing in a sweaty knot of travelers, whose bags and livestock shifted noisily underfoot, Denise confessed to Ralph that she'd been stolen by aliens; since when, <u>she was very very lucky</u> – she bore down on <u>lucky</u> ironically, but wouldn't clarify, just repeating: <u>very lucky</u> –
and changed the subject, subdued:
"I am sorry about your mum."
She looked through the massed people then, the other travelers dim with their patience, at the brown huge slopes jiggling in the windows. Tears welled in her eyes.
"Well, <u>you</u> didn't kill her," Ralph said, angry.)

6      Pokhara: a white cat stood at the roadside. As Ralph and Deesey disembarked, the cat meowed vehemently.

6.1    "Oh! I see: we follow the <u>cat</u> now."

6.2    An hour later, it had become serious. The road led up. Their feet ached from the ride, they were dizzy. If they stopped, the cat hissed and crouched.

6.3  Ralph suddenly guessed. The cat leapt up and vanished into the sky's jagged hem. He leapt after.

6.4  The mountains swam in the deeps of the earth. Rhododendrons poured and grew. The clouds and their mother lakes entered the powerful stone, the grass drank them with its heels. Oceans swayed in the waist of the grass. This knowing was participation in its seamless play. It was a gladdened, headlong, adamantine life.

6.5  Ralph saw himself stagger, a wet scrap below and Denise wheeled and saw him pass.

6.6  He woke in a dusty tea shop, remembering that he'd forgotten –

6.7  He couldn't stop crying in front of her.

6.8  In a frenzy, he gave all the money away. The beggar children swarmed round. They screamed to alert their friends. Denise came out and helped him: she couldn't stop laughing. She cried, throwing money: "Hooray! Hooray! Free for all!"

★ ★ ★

"Jesus H. Christ!" said Eddie. "No. That's too far! Didn't they just tear you limb from limb and eat the flesh?"

"No, people in Nepal are surprisingly polite."

"I gotta say, you didn't tell me, when I employed you for the guru service, actually you hid from me you'd had this God thing."

Ralph frowned then and shifted: "What would it take –"

They both stopped dead. The mood became cautious.

Eddie finally:

"Yeah, dude, I'm hurt, though, you can't tell I care."

Ralph got to his feet. He said quietly, "I think I'm in love with your sister."

"Excuse me? Cause . . . cause, sorry, I'm back with the space invasion topic. Nix on the . . . Japanese game-show topics."

"No . . . I thought I should talk to you –"

"Not funny." Eddie scrambled to his feet.

Ralph repeated, "I'm in love with your sister."

"NO. No, I'm in love with your sister. Keep it straight! Or is this some tit-for-tat vengeance deal I do not want?"

"No," said Ralph. He shook his head. "Look, forget it."

"No – my sister? You go ahead, fuck her, what do I care. Only, take my advice and use a condom. Cause, thing about Chrysa is, she was a major slut? Before the crack-up thing, she slept with anything. Men, women, plague rats, spores, dead bodies. Shit, I even fucked her a couple times."

"Okay, I think I've had enough."

"In fact, that was her who gave me crabs, the second time? Big as mice, you could hear them! So . . . I can't believe how you totally just mind-fucked me. And I noticed you didn't tell me what I need to know, so."

Eddie's mobile phone began to ring. He blinked in surprise, swatting at it under his jacket. Fumbling it out, he poked buttons at random. "Shit. It never did <u>that</u> before."

"Can you take that outside, please?"

"Look, man!" Eddie shook the phone at Ralph. "This baby's ornamental. It can't <u>ring</u>!"

"Out. Please."

"Just, help me, where's the OFF?"

"Out."

"Off!"

"Eddie, don't make me —"

## "You Can't Go Home Again
## On Your Own Two Feet"

Ralph sprang back from the heartfelt punch, flexing his hurt knuckles. He looked at me and I was saying something frightened. Eddie was against the wall: small, befuddled, bleeding. "I'll leave you to it," Ralph said, scorning us, but didn't move.

Our hearts were pounding. We were breathing so emotionally it was like speech.

And Ralph left.

Eddie stanched his bleeding wound with one of my clean socks, while I called an ambulance on his mobile. I said that it was an emergency, but I could tell the receptionist could tell it wasn't. When I hung up, Eddie muttered, "Nice try."

We tiptoed past Ralph's room and out to wait by the untidy gravel drive.

We stared at the moon as if the ambulance would come from there.

From time to time we waved our arms over our heads, to idly retrigger the burglar light. Then we could see the Hyundai's tracks in the gravel where we'd come back from Pizza Hut, when we were still friends.

I was tongue-tied and cold.

Eddie whispered:

"No, I'm so not violent, but I'll come back with a sledgehammer. I'll come back with Spiz.

"I mean, I'm trying to be a friend to the guy, give him some break, and he attacks me? Physically? Cause tell me, what did I do? What did I do to him?

"This is the last thing I'm saying: throw him out now. Cause after that, I'm actually in fear of my life."

When the ambulance came, he told the paramedics he'd walked into a door, and we all had a good laugh. Then I stood in the courtyard waving as they drove off. I heard them start the siren as they hit the main road.

## Back in the Bedroom: A Tenacious Burro

They were gone! They were gone! I ran up to my room and sprawled groaning on the bed, stretching to rest my bare toes on the Jackson Pollock. For a long time, I pretended Ralph was going to come in and do all the talking for me. God! I didn't want to say a damn word!

"I have to think this over," I lied to myself –

and thought about that time I'd had to crawl to my mother's office, with Eddie mock-kicking me from behind. How I'd been like a mighty pack donkey, carrying the whole family's stinking baggage. I saw myself shuffling down an infinite hallway, with doors at regular intervals, behind which solitary family members watched TV.

Suddenly the scene changed: the donkey alter ego shambled through an antiseptic tundra. From the far blank quarters, Ralph's voice rumbled, formlessly threatening. The plucky burro soldiered on, butting the fierce wind, hell-bent on the great Unloading Bay of the Arctic Sea.

Scene cuts to icebound Unloading Bay, a glittering harbor overlooked by dark glaciers. Kicking away from the snowy beach, the donkey skates off over the sea. It passes a dining-room table leg, lodged diagonally in the ice. It lingers dolefully to sniff at a discarded sandal. It trots on, gamely skidding, toward its rendezvous.

At noon, a figure comes striding from the glassy horizon: a shadow man, his features indistinct with sadness. The burro balks, affrighted.

"Don't throw me out," the figure pleads: "I'm Good Ralph."

The donkey bows its shaggy head low to the ice, quivering like a virgin bride. The shadow man stoops to untie its burden –

I mouthed to myself: "This is sheer procrastination. Get up! Get up! Nobody's listening!"

I got up and walked over to the partition door, feeling tearful already, when it opened by itself.

# WE HAVE SEX FINALLY

★ ★ ★

Ralph looked <u>so pleased</u> to see me. He put his arms out. "God, Chrysa . . ."

His face was in full color and detail: he looked completely different from what I had pictured. I had to consider he might be Bad Ralph.

I let him hold me, just, to see what he had to say. He sighed and nuzzled my hair as if he needed comfort. And murmured:

"Is Eddie gone?"

Although I knew in my stomach it was base treachery, and I had a sexual agenda, and I mustn't, I admitted that Eddie was gone.

Then Ralph began to stroke me. His hand went all the way down my back. I was all choked up, I unconsentingly yelped but

"I love you, do you know I love you?" Ralph actually said.

I burned from these mere words and had no choice.

# A Battle Between the Forces of Good and Evil

1  We were grappling on the floor. He groaned and I said Jesus Christ. The weight of his body on me, its warm intent. Then the clothes –

2  We had to stand up again to walk to his bed.

2.1  Then I realized what we were doing.

3  Because there was only that paltry near-futon, I felt exposed. It made our embrace seem like an experimental procedure, from which all extraneous variables had been removed. A parallel Ralph/Chrysa coupled elsewhere in an identical chamber, and a science team would study our comparative success. The second couple were the control group, in which Ralph had not just bashed in my brother's face.

3.1  Ralph would leave tomorrow morning, with some stammering excuse. I would smile and say I understood because you're not allowed to cower on the ground, screaming. It would be sunny and the windows would be happy blue. The birds would twitter cheerily and hop.

Once Ralph left I would get under the bed/*I would not get under the bed*/I would/*no, I would not*

I would cut off both my hands. I would bleed expressively, waving my grisly fountaining stumps like roach antennae.

3.2  You won't be able to do this thing on a basis of distrust.

4  Thinking – bad.

4.1  He was stroking me as if no one was there. There was something reverential in the way his big hands slowed to entirely feel me that made me want to cry. It occurred to me he really did want to have sex with me: he wasn't just trying to be nice. I couldn't really give that much credence, but I reminded myself how people say that men will fuck anything, and maybe I should just take that at face value.

5     "You aren't really into this." Pulling back from me slightly, he made me hold his hand.

I said, almost in time: "No – no fear of <u>that</u>."

Then I wanted to laugh intimately but Ralph didn't laugh. He stroked my brow in an interpreting way, caring what was wrong. I didn't care what was wrong with me, I wanted to shout, Oh, <u>do</u> it!

He said, "But, you're sure?"

(Well, once people started asking things like "But you're sure?" you can forget it. We would now sheepishly retreat into our clothes. We would have a cup of coffee or something else that people really do) but I rebelled against this certain knowledge, peeping:

"Oh, I'm really very sure."

– flamboyantly unsure, but he pretended to believe me –

We fucked like second nature, on the brink of terrified. We fucked like people in love.

Then I opened my eyes. His body was there like an amazing free gift. I was surprised to see it was still night.

"Chrysalis Moffat, Chrysalis Moffat," Ralph muttered, looking at me with a dumbfounded nothing.

Then he said: "Do you love me?"

I was disproportionately shocked. I said, "Oh – yes. Really. I mean, of course."

He said, stiff with embarrassment, "That's good."

I had to look away. It occurred to me that Ralph might

be vulnerable. Like anyone else, he longed for reassurance. His ego was fragile: he was scared.

Yet I felt this was cowardly sophistry, an extrapolation from *what I would feel.* This once, I should accept I didn't understand.

Ralph said, "Come here," we made love again, the trance resumed. Caressing and sighing, we fell into pampered heightened sleep. Once in the night I woke up and we were fucking again. Already I felt a strange, magnified health.

# WHAT HAPPENS NEXT

1    What Ralph and Eddie had in common was a woman named Denise.

1.1  To Ralph, she was a sister:
- elder
- step
- long-lost

1.2  To Eddie, she was the only woman he ever loved.

1.3  Thereby the two men were tied
    – as if cuffed together for the duration of some action-packed adventure comedy, in which they overcome their differences to grow as people.

2    In my home, they opened the "Tibetan School of Miracles."

3    I did the books.

3.1  I did the marketing.

3.2  I did the admin.

3.3  I did the rest, the donkey work nobody else would do.

3.4  On this diet, I became a new, formidable person.
- I spoke right up.
- The waiter knew me.
- I had good skin.

4    Ralph took to deceit like a duck to water.

4.1  Deceit spawned manipulation; manipulation bred threats; an atmosphere of fear and back-stabbing was the banal result.

4.2  His subjects claimed to be enlightened, and even cured of physical and mental ills by these means:
- Sheila Matthews's thyroid cancer went into remission.
- Jasper found a gallery to represent him.

- Arthur Clough's piles shrank; Jo "Moose" Minty got a boyfriend; Anna Rossi's internet laundry company sold for two million; Kate Higgins lost weight.

4.3 The failures had themselves to blame.

5 From Eddie's point of view it was a gross misunderstanding: he never meant it any more than his prior scheme to build a rival Sea World next to Sea World, undercutting Sea World's prices by 1%.

5.1 When it came true, he went back into his shell. With a bottle, with pills, with a hooker to snivel to, Eddie lay low.

5.2 The School succeeded over his dead body, until

6 some months into the enterprise, Ralph cracked up.

6.1 He stopped eating, washing, talking. Approached by well-wishers, he trembled like a maladapted dog.

6.2 He sat by the pool in red tiger-striped swimming trunks all day long, stoned out of his mind.

7 "Words to live by aren't true," Rita Perkins used to say.

7.1 The guests raged, robbed of their pitiable misconception.

7.2 Meanwhile, Eddie flew away away without goodbyes.

7.3 Denise had written a brisk note, inviting him to play blackjack.

## "I Am Not Getting to the Point If I Can't Take You With Me / Sentimental Drivel: As Good As It Gets?"

★ ★ ★

I woke in Ralph's arms. Up above, he was huffing in my hair, it was damp and warm. When he saw me wake, he held still, did his stillness thing, was like a big oak holding still to let the children climb.

"Good morning," he said, "Chrysalis Moffat."

"Oh, yes. This is really wonderful."

I shifted to touch his chest, finding his heartbeat. It was unequivocal and bass: he definitely was alive. Of course this was not a real concern. Aloud and more materially, I worried:

"Is sex a sin? I mean, to your sort of Buddhist?"

Ralph said, "Yes, we're going to hell."

"Okay, then: if you don't want to tell me." I peered up at him. To my gratified disquiet, his expression was doting. His pulse quickened under my palm.

He said, "You can see right through me, can't you?"

"Yes," I lied. "It's very handy."

Finally he took the first shower: I went down to make us coffee, putting on Ralph's white shirt. It was already 8:15:

### The Real World

at 9, I had the new accountant, Snake Johnson, coming to explain the tax-free religious status forms.

Nonetheless I scampered on the stairs, euphoric. I imagined leaping free of the steps to land, dead. Shot down by a duck hunter, at my life's dizzy apex! Oh, I didn't care what I looked like or anything! If Snake could <u>tell</u> and despised me, and called me "Ma'am," sarcastically (he was from Oklahoma, and said "Shoot!" and "Freaking –": I had reason to suppose Jesus Christ might be his personal savior)

I didn't care! I didn't care, today I didn't care!

I did the little jink outside to come back in the kitchen, round the lurid purple ornamental cabbage which was my size, if I were balled up *qua* cabbage, and usually the vegetable intimidated me, but not today – today, I dared and was invincible; plunged in the door

walking smack into a chair. My leg sang with a <u>bone</u> feeling.

Eddie was sitting in the other chair at the table, adding Kahlua to a bowl of Cream of Wheat. A stitch poked coquettishly over his fat lip, looking like the leg of a beetle he was taking his time in eating.

"<u>You</u> look like shit," he said. "Is Michaelson gone?"

## The Kitchen Scene

"You brought the chairs back," I said, sitting cautiously. I crossed my arms over the incriminating shirt.

Eddie snorted. "No way – Ralph the Furniture Fascist must of. Despite I drilled him, they're Oscar Person chairs, that sleazeball designer who had Mom in, like, Svengali obedience, she'd buy his fucking toe clippings?"

I sighed in a discouraging way, but Eddie nonetheless:

"The eggplant-shape dude with the sneaky unsounded farting? Maybe you didn't smell, I smelled. So total moral objection to the fart chairs . . ." His animation failed and he looked at me with the exhausted need of a man who's been awake all night in the waiting room of a busy Casualty unit with a hundred sick, short-fused Hispanics and their children. "So? Did you, like, just say he was gone and I'm too fucked up?"

I looked at him with a feigned query. Then I "realized."

"Oh! You want to know –"

"Yeah, you're kind of not telling me the psychopath's gone?"

"Oh, I don't know. I went to tell him . . . to leave."

Eddie's nostrils flared. He saw the shirt and saw the shirt again and it was awful for him:

"NO. NO. Tell me you didn't fuck him."

"Of course I didn't!" I said automatically, scandalized.

And Ralph walked in; immaculate, white-clad, bearing a tranquil, shampoo aura. He came straight to me, bent and kissed me on the head. Digging through my hair, he tickled my nape. I felt my mouth tug inexorably into a simper.

Then Ralph straightened up and said to Eddie, equably:

"I'm sorry I punched you. I lost my temper."

There was a pause. The sun beamed imbecilically in the

windows. Somewhere out of sight, a radio played "The Girl from Ipanema." The pause became extended; paralyzing; hypnoidal. Implicit in it, and in Ralph's cool stance, was:

If Eddie threw Ralph out now, I would leave with Ralph.

"Whatever." Eddie broke the spell: "Male bonding, right?"

"I thought it might not matter." Ralph smiled magnanimously.

Then he turned his back to both of us and stretched — arms spread luxuriously, back arched, stomach out, in an attitude of perfected satisfaction. Eddie stared at me with the sick glazed eyes of a man who has sold his birthright for a mess of pottage.

Then while Ralph went to the cupboard, found a new bricklike pack of espresso and snipped it gaspingly open with the appropriate kitchen scissors, all his movements economical and right,

Eddie and I fell into Pause Two, a disconsolation. A cloud thematically drifted across the sun. My heart crumbled and I thought, *Oh, of course it's no big deal. I've just betrayed my only trust, is all.* And then, as if it logically followed: *Now I get to kill myself, no one can fault me. I won't right this minute, but the coast is definitely clear, ethically, were I to. However, then I'd miss all the sex.* (I looked sneakily at Ralph, and felt pacified. There was no pressing need to act.)

I remembered inopportunely that Deleuze, of the poststructuralist double act Deleuze and Guattari, had killed himself, like Guy Saint-Lazare. Or was it Guattari? Because of their book *A Thousand Plateaus,* I imagined them leaping suicidally from buttes. I looked from Eddie to Ralph, feeling that one was like Deleuze and the other like Guatarri, and it was therefore crucial to know which died —

"Coffee?" said Ralph, personable and apt.

## Loose Ending: Irrelevant

The Oscar Person kitchen chairs, 5,000 dollars apiece, were monstrous cast-iron toadstools, backed with spikes long and splayed enough to skewer a head each, their seats each bearing three large butt-imprinting holes revealing hollow innards hinting at foul contents; in sober fact, food inevitably straying into said holes until the chair stank and must be upended, and its guts scrubbed, by a strong man, whose arm would lodge in a hole, requiring the attendance of the fire brigade.

## Upshot

The School began — as if we'd always meant it to happen.

# "You Can't Go Home Again
If You Have Never Been There Before"

## "Tibetan School of Miracles," August–Dec '98

For some months we had no live-in pupils. Then it was light work. On Sundays Ralph gave lectures: Tuesday night was meditation class.

The time would approach, making us crabby. Ralph put on those clothes. Eddie hovered, advising:

"You give them echinacea food, only with addictive drugs. That's the only way this thing is going to work."

"No, I'll bribe some small-time Rinpoche off the internet, cause the white-guy thing is going to sink us, promise."

"Yeah, it's doing okay <u>now</u> cause up to <u>now</u> you did my whole ideas."

Jasper always came early, offering to help. He would smile and try to catch Ralph's eye, red-faced. I always left setting up the tea and chairs to the last minute so that he'd look needed.

People came and we must greet them in delight. Lynn, Eddie's ex, got 40 bucks a pop for just greeting. Finally I learned how from watching her, although I always felt ashamed if anyone could see me.

Ralph hid until a pivotal moment, then came out with ponderous grace, like a float. He spoke very slowly, and when he made a point, the audience inhaled sharply. His face preserved a hawkish exaltation, even afterward, when he just shook hands.

Ralph left and the people left, freed. Eddie and I stood watching the taillights diminish, outside in the dark, as if hand in hand. Remember ran out barking at the last minute.

"Well, that's over."

Ralph came down again in gym shorts. We drove to the video store, to Taco Bell, we were belligerently average.

On those nights, Ralph was never interested in sex.

## *August*

In that initial period, we were a threesome, a gang.

1  We had long conversations about the way the School
would change people's lives for the better and become
a nationwide force. We sat up late in the kitchen drinking highballs and having these conversations. It was like
being fifteen.

2  "But you believe in God, right, Michaelson? Cause you
<u>saw</u> God, which is a dead giveaway. And Chrysalis is just
the kind of person who would, cause. But what about
me? Where do I fit in?"

3  We listened to the *Easy Rider* soundtrack over and over.
When "Born to Be Wild" came on in a store once, I felt
I belonged, I smiled at the grocer. Then I thought,
"When this is over, I'll never be able to listen to the
*Easy Rider* soundtrack again," and had to leave the store,
chilled, without my spaghetti squash.

4  Ralph toyed with my long hair, loving me. I loved
Ralph back, I took a few pills and loved Eddie. We lay
full-length in the summer grass, out of our minds:

5  Ralph and I were on our waking-up walk, round the
private wood. The birds chirped boldly, thinking they were
alone. The air felt alive, its early clarity a throbbing presence
like a bass note.

And I confided: "I woke up not in agony today." I
just said it with no qualification, as it came, made cocky by
possession of good news. I said it and listened joyously: it
really was the case.

Ralph said, "Why were <u>you</u>, <u>ever</u>, in agony?"

Finally I asked him what he meant. I was out of breath then, though I shouldn't have been.

And he said he could not think of <u>anyone</u> who deserved <u>agony</u> less than me.

We went on a while in silence, then he put out his hand. He waved it in front of me; I looked at him questioning; he had to say, "Go on," before I took it. We walked and walked. The trees shook and the bushes tugged at our legs like lonely children. When we skirted a clearing, the low sun flying sideways in strobes between the trees made our shadows blink on and off. I felt muscles in my legs, as if I was strong.

Ralph said, "Have you noticed your hair and my hair are so alike?"

(6    Different times are different.

Ralph and I became inseparable.

Our relations were beautiful, like a foal we held in common.

No one would be careless with the delicate foal.

We walked down halls and they became true halls.

Rooms we stood in, shone.

Then it was over.)

### *September*

We added a day of exercises on Saturday: that brought in 400 dollars a week. Though it started as a joke, Ralph's tape, *Buddha Management,* was picked up by a catalog and sold 140 copies. Vegan restaurants, aromatherapists, "green" butchers, bought advertising space in our brochure. The first, for-real, fat-ass donations came in.

Eddie spent it all and more. He bought a motorbike he

couldn't ride, he bought a bear skin. He bought cocaine, lap-dances, drinks for the house. He flew to Hawaii but returned the same night, complaining that it was "all muggy and fat chicks."

He bought a leather sofa, then didn't like it when it came: it was left in the yard, where it mildewed and sank to its knees. Then he failed to set it on fire, even some.

When I confronted him, he barked, "Yeah, I'm trying to have a good time. I don't know what you <u>expect</u> –"

## What you expect

and looked daggers.

We were in the Land of the Lost, alone, I can't remember why. The morning sun was too bright: it made the gravel colorful, like aquarium pebbles. Eddie put his hands on his hips, pissed. I spluttered, "No, I'm worried about you. It's real cry-for-help stuff, what you're doing, it's scary."

Eddie made the cool, mock-surprised face of Humphrey Bogart not falling for the bad guy's ploy. "Spending lots of money is killing me, not."

"But I never –"

"Not."

"No, I genuinely –"

"Not."

We stared at each other for an improbable length of time without speaking. The smug tension in Eddie's face relaxed. Then we were just looking.

He looked older.

"Well," he said finally, "got to go cry for help."

"Yeah," I said equally finally, "Have fun."

## October

The first residential weekend was sold out: thirty people came to stay in the house. When Jasper arrived with his suitcase, three hours early, it was like a pajama party. He tried on my new boots, we made a Bundt cake together with the wrong ingredients. But then the others came too:

## Meditation: on faith

The gravel has been raked, the chairs removed, the glass is blue with clean. It's sunset, and the Land of the Lost is dim under the massed sky. Everyone is whispering and expectant but me

(because I fret about the practicality of evening lectures. It's all very well the lighting rental's more than covered by the takings, but should something <u>break</u>. Heating this is bad enough but if we have to light it −)

Ralph walks in. I stand up automatically, handing him his notes. And for the first time, everyone stands up behind me. The cross-legged people twist to see, then anxiously, hurriedly, scramble to their feet. They stand extra-straight, to compensate for their tardiness.

Ralph stops in his tracks, deadpan. He surveys us and then looks at the glass stars overhead. As he raises his hand, the rain begins.

For a long held breath, no one moves, allowing for the washing sound and the changed air. Then Ralph makes a pressing-down gesture, and we sit.

Throughout the talk, there is a special restlessness in the audience. Something has been achieved.

Afterward, I overhear Matthias, the civil engineer who travels all the way from Sacramento:

". . . and everyone stood at the same time, that's what blows my mind. I mean, we knew."

"Of course," says Kate Higgins. "I just felt it. Didn't you?"

"I don't know," says earnest Matthias. "I don't know what happened. I just found myself on my feet."

Kate nods, "That's it. And that's why it <u>happened</u>."

"You mean the rain?" Matthias says, balking.

"Well, of course! Rain-making has been happening for thousands of years. Just look at the Apache – or that story in Brazil, did you read about that? It was in the *New York Times*."

Matthias looks at his feet, searching. Kate smiles, maternal toward his novice surprise. Finally she touches his shoulder and helps him out:

"Do you feel ashamed that you never stood up before?"

He looks at her, bewildered, then decides: "I guess . . . we're so out of the habit of respect . . . in the West."

"Oh!" says Kate. "That's so what I felt. I've just got to give you a hug for that –"

## You Can't Go Home

1   Name a Buddhist text, Ralph can recite it from memory.

1.1   He meditates, immobile, for five hours at a stretch.

1.2   There is no triviality in him, and he cannot be vulgar.

His
- fear
- sexual desire
- ill-temper
- self-pity

don't show. He has no problems: he never makes mistakes.

1.3   When he fixes the air-conditioning, there is superstitious awe.

2   He's amazed at the purity of Tom, Dick and Harry's auras.

2.1 Kate Higgins must be patient with others who lack her deep insight.

2.2 "I'm giving you the mantra my teacher gave me," Ralph tells the needy.

2.3 He tells me and Eddie:
"I think I do fairly well for a complete fake."
"Watch me awe this cunt realtor."
"I guess you two despise me."

3 Only those with a mantra are admitted to Tonglen meditation.

3.1 Tonglen graduates may progress to Higher Practice.

3.2 There are stages and titles: I'm an advanced-level meditation adept, but Tantric Healing is by invitation and I'm not invited. Embittered, I suggest we call them "guppies" and "dolphins," but Ralph doesn't laugh. I am to understand he has his reasons. And he

4 • got college-educated adults to believe chanting made them into good people
• improvised secret teachings, attributing them to a guru named after his mother's Nepalese drug dealer
• healed the sick with a silver wand, formerly a chopstick
• never laughed about it, was first condescending, then vengeful – like a lover too slavishly adored

5 But I was happy for the longest time.

## Another Point of View: Mine

1 I woke with the program of my morning duties, primed to get the porridge on, peel apples, ring the bell.

1.1 I was late. I must get around to those receipts. I'd have to skip the meditation again, I must see the printer. If Jenny couldn't help out with lunch, I was doomed.

1.2 So much for my early night.

2 • "Could you ask, Chrissie, cause I don't want to bother him?"
 • "So what do you two <u>talk</u> about, when you're alone?"
 • "When he said that, do you think Ralph meant I'm <u>always</u> stupid, or just <u>that</u> was stupid?"

2.1 Walking with me, people stood self-consciously erect, flaunting their fraternization with the A group.

3 I worked so hard, it must be doing good.

3.1 I practiced fortitude every time I spoke in public; humility in scrubbing floors. I asked nothing in return and I thrived.

3.2 That Christmas '98:

We had a Christmas tree, complete with lights and heaped gifts. Twenty people stayed and we cooked from scratch. Anything that smacked of rejoicing, we did. We drank punch, we mulled wine and sang. For the first time, Ralph spoke passionately, invoking brotherhood. People wept, and couldn't stop smiling. Strangers held hands. My and Ralph's love would boom and proliferate, sufficing all, all, all California would thank –

3.3 And he told us the story of his mother, the beautiful gypsy, who got into a Ford Zephyr once with a man when only a girl and loosed her braids as the wind began and never looked back

## Argument

*Peter Cadwallader and Irene "Lola" Michaelson
have an ill-advised romance:
its repercussions.*

# Reprise

"I had him hooked that quick. Two weeks' time! No worries. Course, it wasn't me like you see me now. And, I had my tricks. That's the Romany side. My gran could just walk up to a woman in the street and get her rings off her. It's sheer mesmerism, you have to see it to believe.

"Thing of it was, he couldn't marry us, yet, account of some bother with his daughter I weren't ever good enough to meet. So, but, he meant to all right, and we just went ahead and told everyone like we was. That was like the same thing, really: it's what people think. Only then Peter pulls that he's not coming to our reception do, he's got work. Well, that looks wonderful, doesn't it, the bridegroom not shown up to the reception? But, Mandy stood by me, she was our 'witness' to the wedding had there been one to witness. Oh, I can be harsh on her, but she was solid for me then.

"We had a lovely lovely do on the roof of her block, King's Cross, where you can see the gasworks. Real champagne and that for fifty, it was proper. We had heart-shaped balloons for it, Karen Ann and I killed ourselves blowing them up all that morning.

"Well, I thought it would be a bit of dosh for us for a change. I thought, you'd have a father, everyone was always giving me grief, you without a dad. Dosh, mainly. I was tired, pulling rabbits out of hats. I couldn't pull any more rabbits out of any more hats.

"I did love him, though. Who knows what makes you feel things? He's like a horrible dried-up lizard, isn't he? Peter. Well, they say love is blind, don't they? I'm the living proof. I loved that horror like the last man on earth."

## Romantic Elopement: Gambler

1 How Gypsy Lola learned to play blackjack, some.

1.1 Her new short hair and long skirts, worn with court shoes. She took her earrings out, and what it made her feel, in secret.

1.2 Before long they flew to their first and next and next casino,

1.3 and, through winning, were soon thrown out

1.4 to plane it, to coach it, to the next, to walk with luggage in the driving rain forever to
- another filthy hotel room, the same bugs
- the same casino pit, the players' ill-lit eyes moving to the left, left, towed by the march of cards
- the slot machines ding for seven hours, every cunt smokes
- a close-up of a drain toilet, Apotheke's their chemist, Spain you don't need any prescription and it's pennies

1.5 Each town came to its end.

1.6 They cashed their chips in.

## 2. SCENE

if he wanted nice they could have gone back when she said. She'd told him she was tired but he chose not to understand English. So, down to him if her play was no good.

He was at his table by the window, doing the chip tally.

On the ceiling the same beetle from the morning was still clinging, paddling with its one good leg. Watching it, her heart slipped away: she thought with a far-off, futile trembling: *No, I love you. You can't get shut of me like that. I love you, I can't help I'm thick.*

"Oh, Gawd's sake, forgive me, it's just one of them nights. Eating that spicy food, I've got it all in my bloodstream." She rolled over onto her back on the stiff made bed, smiled at his profile.

"Whatever's in your bloodstream, Irene, I don't think it's curry."

Her heart staggered like a drunkard then, his face went in and out.

She said, "Don't tell me what I've got."

Then the cash: the garish Malaysian ringits, gay like money made for children; the khaki, serious dollars. He dealt them into stacks with a croupier's brisk assurance, crossing the notes when he reached ten.

"I think we may as well face that what we had was a sexual infatuation, Irene, and now it's run its course, we see we're mismatched. I don't see any point in . . . dragging things out."

"Oh! Maybe someone had a sexual infatuation."

"That's the sort of thing I mean. Your jibes."

"Don't even know what a jibe is, when it's at home."

"So, why did you marry me, Irene? I think we may as well have it out in the open. I'm curious. If the sexual interest was so one-sided."

"I married you because I loved you and I love you still," she chanted, loud, to drown his evil out.

"I'm sorry. I must have the wrong impression. You're telling me there was no financial element whatsoever?"

Then she started crying, she couldn't take this one more time. She wailed, "Stop – killing – me! You're a fucking butcher! You're a butcher! I can't bear it!"

"Oh, the amateur dramatics. I'll leave you to it."

He'd got his briefcase open and was packing the cash away. Snapped it shut and turned the tumblers on the lock – to keep her paws out.

A faint tinkle of Musak came as the lift passed their floor. She shut her eyes again and fingered the 500 chip she'd stashed in her bra. Get up and go to the toilet soon: thank Christ she had that blue Valium.


## 3. PRE-INTIMATIONS OF BLUE VALIUM

That time she promised Ralph a bicycle, that Christmas. Then, of course, the money weren't there, how could it be? His face when he saw the book was all he was getting, and him squealing it were too easy, *I'm too old for this, this is for babies.* Well, poor dumb Mum wouldn't know. That did it, she had to go and pick a fight. Him sent to bed with a slap. Brung his dinner in to him, but he wouldn't eat, wouldn't much as look at her and her bawling finally and raging,

*You're like ice, you're cold-hearted, evil.*

Saying all that to a little boy. It was her was the evil one.

She'd say to him, she'd tell him, *you never do appreciate what you got till it's gone.* Cause now she'd hardly wait to get free and see her son. That's what it was for, she'd got to remember, Ralph would have his bike all right, and more –

From the far bright corner of her dreaming, Peter said, "Reenie . . ."

His voice gone syrupy: she heard the ice move in his drink.

She shifted to peer, rubbing the crying out of her nose.

He was beckoning with one hand, intent on something out the window:

"Come on, you can't miss this for a little tiff."

She crawled off the bed, rested her feet on the floor to get the blood in. Went to him reluctant, grimacing, though he didn't look.

From the mountaintop resort site, the Malay jungle flowed down in stages of green and shadow. A few soaring palm crowns were spotlit in the dusk's sidelong orange, and in the sky overhead stood two furry upright rainbows.

"So, do you really hate me all that much?"

He reached back and trailed his fingers over her buttock. A chill went through her. She would say no, but not just yet.

"Irene?"

"I'll be with you in a second, I just must use the toilet . . ."

He said, insinuating, gruff: "I'll be waiting."

## Romantic Elopement: Gambler

1    Just leaving Ralph there. Just, fucking off without him.

1.1    "It's only for a while, like a honeymoon, then I'll be right back for you. It does my nerves, Ralphie, leaving you like this, but if I'm longer than a week, you'll go to Mandy's, eh?"

1.2    Peter gave him three ten-pound notes in an envelope.

2    A heart-shaped white balloon stirs in one corner, bumping its head against the wall each time you open a door.

3    • The phone went dead.    • The lights went out.
        • The radiator stayed cold.    • If there was a knock,
                                                he held still.

3.1    He bought cornflakes and jammy dodgers. He bought cigarettes.

3.2    Every few days he went to the public toilet, where he patiently extracted yards of loo roll, stuffing it into a Happy Shopper bag to carry home.

4    A shriveled rag of pale rubber trails from the hard puckered ring where the balloon was tied.

4.1    Ralph turned eleven.

## 3. Princess Margaret House, Shoreditch, 1973

She wasn't like a fairy, she was something else. Her hair was like his, and she was short like a child but she was grown up. Her dress was made of some material that didn't exist. Sometimes she had paws. She came from Mum's bed.

He drew her over and over. The ones that were closest, he saved in his cigar box with the 8-ball marbles.

You said Montara to call her, and Cossie when she went away. You had to say it out loud, even if there were people there. To whisper was cheating.

At first she was always nice, but then she started saying evil things. Telling him things to do, which sometimes he couldn't. That was when he started nicking stuff, all cause Cossie Montara said if he didn't get the phone on, Mum would ring for help. Then, he'd never even get the phone call, and Mum would die.

Once he told her Cossie Forever Cossie, to get rid of her, but when he saw her again, he decided he didn't mean it. Plus, it was only his pretend, she couldn't really hurt him.

She was haunting the upper-story windows, all down Old Street, that day he walked home with Belinda Myers.

Belinda Myers was like his fucking monkey on his back. Her and her soppy notes she left in his schooldesk, the bottles of pop, Jaffa cakes screwed up in a paper napkin. All the girls in his year were daft like that. But he daren't tell Bel to piss off, cause she was the tenth floor of Princess Margaret House, and if she got the hump, she might start snooping. Then it would be parents, and then the social, and then Ralph would be fucked off to a home, where, he knew it from Uncle James, they was all nonces. So it meant, grit your teeth at old Belinda's jabber.

It was only ten minutes' walk from school, but Bel insisted on going some "special" way that made it longer. She kept going on about other boys who'd tried to kiss her. If it was Jimmy, that was a three sick, but Rico was a whole ten sick. Ten was like when the dog eats sick and sicks it up again, in your mouth.

When Ralph said she should keep clear of boys, then, Belinda asked if he was jealous.

As they turned off Old Street, Cossie Montara vanished from the plate glass of the Best Café and reappeared way overhead, watching Ralph from his thirteenth-story window of Princess Margaret House. She put a dark pawpad to the glass.

Then he was scared. He looked up and the sky was gray, it was like when you touch metal after it's rained. Belinda Myers was chewing her lip.

She said, "You fancy coming down the canal?"

He looked at her, she was winding her blond hair down around her satchel strap. For a second he thought about getting his fishing rod. He could give her one of his cigarettes, they'd go looking for half-empty beer cans on the canal boats. Maybe he would kiss her if she really wanted.

But he forced himself to say: "Can't. My mum's not well."

Bel wrinkled her nose: "Yeah? What's she got?"

"I don't know. She's ill."

"Is that why you sold your telly to Alan? Cause your mum's poor?"

"She isn't poor, she's ill."

"But, is it? Cause, my best mate, that's Ann, she's Alan's sister, and she said, you was nicking things for him, but then it was your telly from home. So she said she asked if you'd got a new telly, and you said it wasn't, it was someone else's that you'd nicked, but she thought it was never, and when she asked Alan later on, she was right."

"I think my mum's going to die," said Ralph.

He looked for Cossie Montara then, but she was gone. That meant mum was really finally dead, Peter'd killed her: why he took her to France, to get her where the cops and anyone wouldn't never find out. Mum wasn't coming back, it was like a sex killing.

Now it was his flat.

He frowned at the skimpy, half-hearted trees the council planted at the front, to make you think you were in fucking Surrey. He hoped they would wither. Then they'd have to dig them all out again, a waste of money.

Bel grabbed Ralph's collar and kissed him on the lips.

He shoved her away, staggering. When he wiped his mouth, he was fleetingly afraid she would see his hand was bleeding. Only it wasn't even bleeding, that was daft: he threw his satchel down and swore.

Belinda danced away a few steps and shouted, "That's because I'm sorry for you with your mum ill." She stopped with her feet wide apart and tossed her head; belligerent, overjoyed.

Ralph shouted, "I don't want you sorry for me."

Then Bel rocked back, all pop-eyed, and screamed, "Well, you're a cunt, and I don't care if your whole cunt family dies!"

Ralph crossed his arms. He said in a deep, definite voice, "Now you'll die instead."

The little girl ran away.

He waited her out of sight and took the steps up into Princess Margaret House.

Cossie Montara was waiting for him in the lift. He pressed 13 and leaned against the wall, breathing the piss smell in deep. Cossie Montara wanted to comfort him, but he

249

didn't need that. Even if Mum wasn't really dead, because he'd <u>known</u> she was, that made him grown up.

Only, when he got in the flat and walked into the cold smell of the front room – he lost his bottle.

The dark flat: like it was looking at him. It had <u>enmity</u>. He turned to Cossie Montara, but it was hard to pretend her when you were frightened. Carefully not looking left or right, he dashed to the mantel. He had two candles stuck already to the top of the gas fire, rooted in a swathe of scar-like wax. He lit a candle praying *Hail Mary*. Lit the other candle, crouched down to retrieve the neat parcel of the book.

Its faded wrapping paper was worn to silken fineness. The outlines of repeating Santas were eroded; the remaining strips of sellotape dark and brittle.

He lifted the book out carefully, muttering, "Just a second, Montara, just a second." When he had it placed, he shut his eyes and opened it at random. Then he put both hands down on the cool paper, chanted, "Cossie, cossie cossie," and looked down at the flickering page.

## Book Report: *On Beyond Zebra* by Dr. Seuss

As the book *On Beyond Zebra* commences, young Conrad Cornelius o'Donald o'Dell has just triumphantly mastered the alphabet. Poised ecstatically at the blackboard over his chalked Z, he exults over his mastery of all knowledge, A to Z.

His joy is immediately squashed by a high-handed pal, who sneers at the poor things spelled with the letters A–Z, crowing: "<u>My</u> alphabet starts where your alphabet ends!" This boastful squirt, the first-person narrator of *On Beyond Zebra*, then gives the wide-eyed Conrad a tour of the post-Z alphabet, each letter of which represents an uncanny beast, inhabiting its own uncanny, post-Z world.

Dr. Seuss cheats: the letters do not denote single, new phonemes, but syllables composed of existing English letters. For instance, the Umbus, a cow with 98 "faucets," starts with the "letter" <u>Um</u>. The character for <u>Um</u> is transparently an amalgam of U and M.

Although this would seem to have killed any mystery stone dead, nonetheless, as an eleven year old, Ralph used this book to intuit alternate worlds, in which fantastic "other" things were possible. So, from the Itchapods, mop-headed creatures that

> Race around back and forth, forth and back, through the air
> On a very high sidewalk between HERE and THERE

Ralph derived intermediate universes, limbos in which only intermediate things happened. What those things might be was impossible to know, while one remained in the mundane, pre-Z world. By any means necessary, Ralph was resolved to pass beyond Z and into those other realms where he belonged.

I read it in the Starbuck's café at Borders. The above quotes were copied longhand as I sipped my Frappucino. The quality of the drawings disappointed me: I hadn't remembered Seuss being such a terrible artist.

Ralph kept his copy until he was 21, when he abandoned his BA in Fine Art at London's Slade School to study Tibetan Buddhism in Colorado. Then it was among the possessions he discarded; the photos, the letters, the books, clothes, records, he carried to the bin unbagged, in valedictory mood, in token of his dedication to the ascetic life.

# Epilogue

1     Lola lived with Peter Cadwallader for nine months.

1.1   When they split for good, he gave her 10,000 dollars.

1.2   In their nine months, she'd stolen as much again.

1.3   She took it to Kathmandu. It was a fresh start.

2     In Nepal she met Pemba, the "stepfather" who taught Ralph Tibetan.

2.1   He ran a small pottery, catering for the tourist trade.

2.2   He never married Lola, nor were they romantically linked.

2.3   Pemba sold her heroin.

3     And Ralph is the prodigal mother's son who came off the plane at Kathmandu wearing a blue school uniform for want of other "good" clothes and didn't recognize his own mother, in her sari, with her face painted red and gold to celebrate because she did that, and she jumped up and down spotting him and waved her arms, but he just weakly smirked as if his face itself were bleary with London rain and said, "Hi, Mum," and then she grabbed him by both lapels.

# MONTARA SECTIONS

## Argument

- *Different times are different.*
- *Ralph lied until he meant it.*
- *Talking about the Dharma, his face grew predatory, bright.*
- *He had experiences we did not understand.*
- *He showered three times a day: he could only fuck me in the pitch dark.*
- *In his absence, I loved him as much as ever.*

# January

Sheila Matthews moved in first – a nice lady who wore blouses and was middle-aged at my same age. She slept alone in the main house for a week. During that brief span, we were girlfriends: I tried her favorite Ben & Jerry's flavor, and learned all about her married lover and his shilly-shallying.

Then Kate Higgins's rent was unfairly raised. She came "while she was looking" and wouldn't leave. "Of course I insist on paying what I would be paying," she proclaimed stridently, but paid nil.

Jo Minty moved in without asking. Eddie and I were in the kitchen when her lavender Bug pulled up in the dead of night. Eddie stood up from his chair and froze like a baleful specter – <u>knowing</u>. Bumbling, hasty, Jo unpacked her car pretending not to see us yards away in the big lit bay window. She was a very fat woman who wore a ribbon in her hair – her mishaps with her cumbersome suitcase moved me – but Eddie said dead-voiced:

"Charging motherfucking gazillions by the fucking week from now on, or I am <u>killing spree time</u>."

Jasper stayed on and off. Jasper played "friend of the family," giving insider information to the new hands. He came to me once with an idea about doing up the unused belfry as an apartment: "Needless to say I'd pay materials, and we could talk about how long I kept it, I'm very open." When I said NO, he said, "I'm not being funny, doll, but is it because I'm queer?" I said yes, it was exclusively because he was queer, and he told me many a true word was spoken in jest.

More people came and more. They brought their own beds, they brought their teenaged children. They brought camcorders. At least one brought lice.

"I tried to leave, but I was <u>stopped</u> – like this <u>wall</u>," announced Harry, the retired cop, with dazed self-congratulation. Others chipped in with like tales, competing. Arthur Clough quoted his inner child and turned raspberry red as he wept.

Then there were just untold strangers in the house.

## You Can't Go Home Again/You Can't Leave

1    We come home to them and fall asleep to them and wake up to them.

1.1    We can always hear them: in the walls, outside the window, seething overhead.

1.2    They seem to lie in wait. They are behind every door.

1.3    When they finally speak to us, it's like a bad dream coming true.

2    No one cleans their area.

2.1    We are compelled to have a lock fitted on the refrigerator.

2.2    An anonymous turd is found on the shower floor.

2.3    Some free spirit refuses to yield his sheets, every laundry day.

2.4
- "He said −" / "She said −"
- "But it all started when they −"
- "Either she leaves, or I leave."
- "Ralph, tell him."

2.5    We have to go over the ground rules, every fucking day.

3    The graffiti in the bathroom:
- "I WANT TO SUCK RALPH'S DICK";
- "You guys are a lot of asshole who think your holier than thou";
- a quarrel in several hands about the Buddhist stance on graffiti

258

4     The lawn yellows where the smokers gather.

4.1   Frito bags glitter in the shrubs.

4.2   José sighs on his rounds.


## Embarrassing cocoon

(4.3 Our "guests" cannot even say hello to José. They breeze past him, look through him; pain him a thousand times a day with their incivility. In their presence, his face becomes expressionless. He looks like a servant.

One day Eddie and I are in Mom's office, having our ritual bicker about what constitutes "embezzlement," when Anna Rossi bursts in. She's come to inform me that José is cutting flowers.

"I saw him, and I was going to ask, but he just walked away from me. I mean flowers, not pruning, it's definitely a bouquet."

I counter stiffly: "They're to bring home to his wife. He's always . . . it's fine."

"Yeah, I just wanted to check, because I know it's not exactly stealing, but. I don't know what you want to do, but I wouldn't let my gardener do that. It's just the principle. I know my − Chrysalis?"

− she peeps, surprised, because I'm brushing past her like an insulted woman.

On my way down the corridor I hear Eddie, in his element:

"No, that's where you're wrong, cause under California law, the flowers are actually the property of the gardener. Menendez versus Disneyland, 1978 −"

Following the sound of the rider mower, I find José in the lawn's upper corner, cruising the cherry orchard. He gazes up wistfully at one tree's crown, where a beard-like something flaps, something like Spanish moss, only squarish and too meager.

The something is a bag I threw off the balcony, along with the spoons, brassieres, what-have-you, in my frenzy after Mom's death. Every time I see it my mind runs a film of the gesture it made, coasting off on the wind with its stiff handles opening, jaw-like, as if to breathe in. I had really breathed in, sharply, and was unduly relieved when it caught in a tree without spilling. It was a boutique shopping bag made of special ventilated paper, like vacuum-cleaner bag paper. It said DISSOLUTE in scrawled letters on one side. It contained my dirty panties, from when I had my period after Mom's death and was too scared to drive to the drugstore for tampons. I threw it in rabid self-loathing, to <u>get rid</u>.

It lasted forever. It hung there, lasting and putting me to shame. The bag became gauzy, but stubbornly hung, out-lasting autumn's leaves. Passing it in company, I suffered torments, keeping myself from looking up.

One day Ralph called me out, upset, to see the <u>cocoon</u>. I followed, dismally knowing. On the way, he enlarged on the hygiene issue: José should cut it down, fast, before it hatched.

"Otherwise we'll have caterpillars," he predicted, with a phobic grimace. "They sting."

We arrived beneath the cherry tree. The bag no longer said DISSOLUTE, the DISSOLUTE had dissolved (I thought hysterically). It waggled up there like a big ass.

I argued:
- Caterpillars go in, moths come out.
- Caterpillars don't sting, and are meek vegetarians.
- Doesn't he know what Chrysalis means?

Ralph said, too angrily, "Don't be ridiculous."

That afternoon I wrote José a note requesting that he NOT remove such and such cocoon. Sealing it, I felt powerful: <u>my</u> gardener. I wrote V. URGENT on the back and smiled at the idea that I was too busy now to write VERY out in full.

The next day José came to the office smiling broadly. "Not a cocoon," he announced.

I said, "Oh, but could you still please leave it?"

He stood in the doorway for a moment, pondering. Then he left, wishing me a good day. I went out later to check the bag and found José there, mooning up at it: I had to pass briskly, pretending to call the dog.

Ever since, José has been uneasy about the dishonored cherry tree. Now, as I run after his rider mower, he is transfixed – I have to bellow and wave my arms. Then he cuts the motor deliberately and climbs down.

He has a single Twinkie in his shirt pocket, still in the cellophane, and he offers it to me, commenting that I'm hungry. I accept it and hold it with solicitude, like a helpless mouse entrusted to my care.

He says, "You wanted to ask something?"

"Oh, only, cause if these new people are bothering you? It's just, I know they're pretty irresponsible and rude, and we –"

"No, no." He smiles, hearing my distress. "They don't bother me."

I insist, carried away, "No: they must."

Stymied, José turns to scan the wintry, bald trees, looking for a way out of my intrusion. I turn, too, to the orchard, shaken.

It strikes me that I won't close the school down for José's sake. I'm here not to help but to extort forgiveness – from my gardener, whose job is, for all he knows, on the line.

Fleetingly I feel, like a flavor in my head, how it would be to be a Chrysalis who drove away the clients because they darkened an honest man's life.

And I recall how for years I avoided José, and met him with teenagery mumbles and hanging head. Feeling how he must scorn me, I resented him. To me, his flowerbeds epitomized dumb complacency.

These are my true, puerile colors. I look up at the shaming bag.

Then, turning to me formally, his dignity somehow making it a statement on behalf of all gardeners, José offers:

"It takes all kinds to make the world."

Startled, I press the Twinkie to my heart. He smiles at me, including me in his kind.

"Thank you very much," I say eventually, "for the cake.")

# A Representative Day/"You Can't Go Home Again if That's All You Care About"

6:00 A.M.    **Exercise #1 in the series "Cheating Logic"**
             **Three Impossible Things Before Breakfast**

No one may eat until Ralph begins to eat. The porridge waits, a vapid unsweetened gruel. It no longer steams. There is nothing to drink and the room is unheated. They have been given the small spoons.

Yet the eight chosen guests sit in frantic anticipation. They are squirming, too, because Ralph never ceases to examine them. His eyes pause on each in turn, inspecting. No one may speak until he speaks.

After ten minutes of this ordeal, in rapid-fire:

RALPH:        What lies behind the mind?
1ST GUEST:    Nothing?
RALPH:        Liar!
2ND GUEST:    The liar lies behind the mind.
RALPH:        Who's the liar?
3RD GUEST:    I am.
RALPH:        No, you are. Knock knock.
SEVERAL:      Who's there?
(Ralph picks up his spoon. Now they must eat in perfect silence.)

10:00 A.M.   **Exercise #4 in the series "Cheating Logic"**
             **Life's Work**

The sand must be moved one grain at a time. Ralph points at "the origin," then at "the destination." We have ten hours to complete "the task," he informs us, and climbs up on a rock to supervise. Silhouetted against the rising sun, he looks massive with patience.

We bend and tweezer one grain of sand between our fingertips. We walk along the beach and stop about where we think the destination is. And back and forth. Soon the footprints ringing the destination point make it look mounded. Soon our backs hurt and our fingertips grow numb.

As the day warms up, the beach seems changed. We speed up, sensing progress. How many grains can there be? How many grains per hour?

The temptation to cheat by taking more than one grain at a time becomes overwhelming. In conversation afterward, all of us confess to having, at some time, taken more than one grain. "And the guilt. You know, you let everyone down."

An hour and a half in, Ralph stands up and calls the job off. We stop reluctantly, feeling we could have made it. We wonder one last time what the point is. As we follow him back to the house, we're coming up with all the possible meanings of the grain of sand exercise.

| | |
|---|---|
| 12:00 | Squeaky wheels get oil. |
| 12:10 | Delinquent 5% ruin it for everyone. |
| 12:20 | Bad apples spoil bunch. |

1:00 P.M.    **Lunch**

During lunch, Jo Minty reads aloud from a description of the typical putrefaction of a cadaver. Since I wrote the description, it makes me self-conscious. I eat more than usual, cringing at the infelicitous phrases.

## 1:30 P.M.

Where the cherry blossom powders the fine green lawn, three beefy women from Illinois are very loud:

"This is my real family, my other family just got their claws out for me."

"No, yeah, I couldn't live without this, literally."

"This is, I've been looking for this my whole life."

"Do you guys wants to go in, by now? Because the meditation started already ten minutes."

"Oh, my poor butt."

"Janine!"

## 3:00 P.M.

First a faint hickory smell, then a white curl in the air. I decide I don't really have to meditate, given that we're fakes, and twist to stare at Eddie smoking in the back.

He's got a pink highlighter pen and a stack of *Playboys*. When he sees me looking, he audibly farts, and the people all around me stiffen with rage.

## 4:00 P.M.

For some time the guests have favored white clothes, *à la* Ralph. More wear white until the others appear as rebels. They adopt, too, an encephalitic languor in their movements, feeling their way to physical grace. Arthur Clough stands on the balcony for hours, almost absolutely still.

But today Matthias arrives in the same suit Ralph's wearing.

No one will speak to him. Jasper comes over especially to ask if I've noticed, with a catty squint. Finally Mat can't take it anymore, and leaves before supper, even though it means driving all the way back to Sacramento that night.

## 5:00 P.M.

I find Eddie sleeping on his outdoor leather sofa. Roused, he proves chatty and won't let my knee go until I swear not to leave. I sit fatalistically and say, "What's up?"
– when Jasper hurries toward us.

He's clutching a white kitten.

He found her in the bushes by Walgreen's drugstore, in a sack with two dead siblings, probably thrown from a moving car. She's jumpy, with an air of <u>damage</u>.

The idea that those were bad people colors the scene. We imagine the bad people. The meowing sack recurs in our talk.

Every time we look at the kitten, we see that she is dying. Finally I say so. Then we all pretend that we can't tell because we are not veterinarians.

"I'm going to give her to Ralph," says Jasper, elated. "He just asked me – inside – but I said I'd get her shots first."

"He asked you?" I say, mystified.

"He's going to name her <u>Ralph</u>," adds Jasper, proud.

Eddie says, "That's the worst thing I fucking ever heard."

## 6:00 P.M.

Over supper, I ask Ralph about the kitten. When I mention the resemblance to his Nepali cat, who led him to God, he says in all seriousness,

"This isn't the same one."

## 7:00 P.M.    Exercise #9 in the series "Alternative Sense" Pin the Tail on the Donkey

The seekers stagger in their blindfolds, paper tails hopefully extended, straining to activate their inner sight. Ralph looks on calmly, with real eyes.

I take no part in this refinement of sadism.

It's painful to watch, like beggars being made to grovel for a muddy penny. I think, he's trying to prove something – what jerks they are. He is making them caper for him, to fuel some grudge.

On this issue I finally confront him, while we are

## 8:30 P.M.    Driving to Dunkin' Donuts in civvies

and Ralph and I have an argument, which I find grueling. No matter how right I am, he won't admit I'm right.

I cry, in gross misery, "<u>You don't even think it's funny</u>."

Ralph laughs, belittling: "Anyone who can believe that Pin the Tail on the Donkey is a spiritual exercise, deserves what they get."

"But they're all <u>petrified</u> of you. They'd believe anything you said."

He returns my gaze coolly, unfooled. "That's just the point."

## 10:00 P.M.    Not to give the appearance of hypocrisy

Ralph and I don't sleep together anymore.

We still have sex – some nights – in my bed.

Afterward, he leaves to sleep alone in his room.

On lone sleepless nights with my Jackson Pollock, I

fantasize sleeping with Jackson Pollock, who would never faint-heartedly deny his mistress. In the fantasy, all the other artists jeer at him: "Jack! How can you want that weird midget chick? You, an artist, who prizes beauty?"

He grins, untroubled, and squeezes me at the waist.

"Kiss my ass," says Jackson Pollock.

**4:00 A.M.**

I woke to the sound of clashing below. Putting on a T-shirt, I set off downstairs thinking fuzzily from my dream, *It might be Ralph back from the replacers. I wonder what they gave him.*

The lights were on in the kitchen, and Eddie was sitting cross-legged on the floor, separating Oreos and setting the halves on a plate, cream-side up. The silverware drawer lay beside him, surrounded by silverware. As I came in, he turned his face up to me with his eyes shut. Then he opened them – maroon with bloodshot.

"Hi," I said. "You look pretty sick."

"Never try to take your contact lenses out when you're on speed and you haven't got any contact lenses in."

I sat on the floor too. I looked at his Oreos, jealous.

He said, "Yeah, I'm sleeping here, cause I can't sleep in my room anymore, but I couldn't sleep really cosily here so far, cause it's a kitchen and the floor. Only today I'm on speed. I don't know how that will affect it - do you want these Oreos?"

"No."

"Yeah, I thought you were vibing me out for them."

"No."

"Okay."

He shoved the plate around behind him. I instantly

regretted not taking them, if he wasn't going to eat them. Furthermore, it was probably a game he was playing with me: he almost certainly knew I still wanted them.

Then I wanted to laugh. I felt so affectionate it was festive.

I said, "I'm going to go and get some blankets."

"Whatever. I can sleep here alone. It's cool."

"No, I want to sleep here," I bleated, suddenly threatened.

"Yeah, sleep in the refrigerator, I'm the last person. But – you want to see why I'm on this speed?"

## 28. Montara Beach, California, April 1999

As ever, Eddie's room is knee-deep in mess. Every concave thing has become an ashtray. The clothes will now have to be thrown away.

The mattress has been shoved against one wall, slumped to an L as a makeshift sofa, and on the bared bedstead, empty Pepto-Bismol bottles are ranged like sentinels. Eddie needs one more to have one for each oak slat, and because I know my brother, I know he thinks of emptying that final Pepto-Bismol bottle as an achievement, which will mark a watershed in his life.

A lamp, set at a tilt on a bundle of towels, has burned a hole into its skewed shade, and sends a searchlight beam across the room at a battered audio cassette. It's a 90-minute Woolworth's brand, with orange stickers, labeled in felt-tip pen: *Soul — various*. It gives me a start because it's mine.

I taped it from my friend Dina's record collection, when I was fourteen. The selections are therefore slushy, and by no means all Soul. There are, for instance, three BeeGees tracks in a row, which made Side A unplayable, once I had matured in reason.

Eddie had borrowed it sixteen years ago, as a tool in his campaign to seduce his first girlfriend. He'd then refused to return it, because "You were stupid enough to lend me anything, in the first place." I step forward instinctively to retrieve it.

"NO, behind you, Chrysa. You're actually blind."

I turn around: there are ten-odd cartons stacked against the wall. They're pasted over with Federal Express stickers and stamped FRAGILE FRAGILE. For some reason I'd expected something like cartons, and nodded pompously as if it was old news.

"Ralph's stuff," Eddie said.

I balked: "Ralph's what stuff?"

"From Colorado. Cause we put his possessions and shit in storage. Only I paid the storage people, so it's my name on the account?"

"Oh, shit."

"Oh, yes."

"But, you mean, he doesn't know?"

Eddie smiles. Then for a few minutes we both laugh gaily, unconvincingly, like a brother and sister horsing around in a dishonest '50s movie.

Then I say, "Oh, God, I must be as sick as you."

"You're on my side now?"

I'm thinking about it when he suddenly ducks and grabs a whiskey bottle from his pile of laundry. He unscrews the cap and swigs, then gestures with it at the wall of cartons: "I'm just basically looking for an address of someone. So it's address books and letters and shit. If you want to –?"

I suddenly feel wide awake.

We begin to manhandle cartons down and rip tape away. Since Eddie simply empties them onto the pre-existing mess, I follow suit. It's mostly newspaper-clad ceramics, although there are appliances at random, books, and puzzling unRalphlike articles: a basketball, love beads, Donald Trump's *The Art of the Deal.* At first we hold these "finds" up and giggle, but we're quickly jaded. The taboo recedes, and we're just digging through someone's crap. It becomes work. Then it becomes hard work. At last it is becoming "the kind of thing I really hate," when Eddie says,

"Yeah, if this fucks up, I get to drink myself to death."

He continues delving in his carton. Finding a baseball cap, he puts it on and looks at me. He shrugs at the expression on my face, says, "Chicago Cubs, why?" and goes back to digging.

"Don't you hate," I say, "how the people you love are the ones who oppose you in everything, and if they were dying of thirst and you gave them water, they wouldn't drink the water because it was you?"

"Yeah, I wouldn't know, I never loved anyone."

"But that's exactly the kind of thing I <u>mean</u>."

"Ha! Paydirt! BOOKS never means fucking BOOKS."

Reaching into his carton, he withdraws a wad of creased handwritten pages.

"Oh, God," I say, sidetracked. "Do you think we really actually?"

He looks at me and time stops. It teeters and yields a brief peaceful Eddie who:

"You know what it is?" He puts his finger to his temple, serious. "It's just weird someone as small as you being so intelligent."

We are struck and exalted by this wonderful non sequitur. I say equally truly:

"I like talking to you."

We grin at each other in congratulation. It's so good. Then Eddie looks down and says,

"Wait. Shit. This is to Mom."

## The 1001 love letters Dad wrote Mom

They're called that, although no one has counted them – 1001 meaning, just, fabulously many. Mom kept them in a suitcase under the bed. Family legend states that, when he was away from home, Dad wrote a page every day. The letters are genial, tending toward anecdote and travelog.

Writing from the Vietnam War, Dad

- calls insects "critters" and warns, "these brutes would laugh at Raid"
- includes a line drawing of his potted orchid mascot "Bud"
- tells "The Sorry Tale of Private Pinching and the Shrinking Trousers"
- loves her on every page; more than ever, like a madman, too damn much
- never hints at any warfare

Therefore the post-Vietnam letters are near-identical. His friends still have military ranks. He carefully avoids place names. Since the envelopes have been discarded, there are no telltale postmarks. It's "hotter than heck" and he doesn't know the "lingo." That rules out Scotland.

The letters are, on average, four pages long. They have dates, but they've gotten out of sequence under Mom's curation. Many pages are embossed with her signature maroon rings, where a tumbler of wine once rested. Some are torn in half and mended sloppily with Scotch tape.

The exemplars in Ralph's belongings are mainly unfinished, unsigned. They have not been folded to fit in an envelope. It seems fair to presume they are rejected "manuscript" letters Dad never sent.

They are among a bundle of letters and postcards which,

on inspection, prove to belong to Denise Cadwallader. The first evidence of which Eddie registered by blurting,

"OH MY JESUS FUCKING CHRIST!"

and holding up a glossy photograph.

"What? What?" I squalled feebly back.

"NO. Just a second!" He was shaking his head at the picture as if actually telling it no. He turned it over and I saw:

*A gawky thirteen-year-old girl in pink dungarees, hugging my father aggressively around the waist. They are in that seedy Chinatown, she is that hound-nosed Denise, beaming with wild love.*

"Listen," Eddie said, suddenly hoarse. "This is on the back." He handed me the snapshot, reciting unsteadily: *"Me with Corporal Channing's daughter. Ate sea cucumber here. Plenty ketchup!"*

I stared at the photo for a minute although I already knew what it looked like and I didn't want to. I read the back. And winced: it was written in the same faded pencil in which Eddie's photos were signed LOVE, DC.

"Funny," I said.

"Okay," said Eddie. "Okay. Don't panic. Right?"

"Well," I half-wailed. "Well, maybe it is Corporal Channing's daughter? And that's why, you know – she looked different when you knew her?"

"NO! Fuck off! That is fucking Denise! Ralph identified her! Ralph identified her!"

"Well, I didn't do it!"

Eddie leapt to his feet, almost slipping on a blazer, and shouted for all the world to hear,

"LYING PRICK! LYING FUCKING PRICK!"

I shouted, "Calm down! WHY are you so angry? Calm down!"

Eddie goggled at me, breathing hard. He rasped: "Don't

you see what this – I mean, the bastard was fucking her. Gotta be."

"That's stupid."

"No. Don't tell me. Cause it's <u>that kind of lie</u>. I mean . . . that picture? That shit? That's what I do. That's exactly the kind of shit that I do, send the fucking picture of my new chick, and say . . ."

"That's stupid. Really."

"Yeah. He wrote that to <u>Mom</u>, okay? Just, shut up and don't talk to me. I'm going to sit down and fucking deal with my head."

He didn't sit down. When I tried to catch his eye, he waved my gaze away with an actual fly-swatting gesture. Forlorn, I lay down amid the interwoven junk.

I wanted to tell him that Dad didn't matter. Mom didn't matter: Eddie was the one I loved. They were just parents, they were bad, dead parents. Eddie was my comrade, who'd been through hell with me and back. We'd been captives together, of the harrowing Mother, who raved and dashed her glass to the floor, and drove off crowing *I should jump off a cliff*, and the Father popped up fleetingly, saying, "Kids, for Mom's sake, you have to be brave."

*I loved you best,* I wanted to tell him. *I always always loved you best.*

Eddie sat down. Kicking for purchase in the slippery mess, he maneuvered himself against the wall and slumped. He groped to find the whiskey bottle, and took it in his lap.

"Could you kind of leave me alone now?" he said, surly. "Cause, no offense, but suddenly I feel like you're contaminating in my space?"

I looked at him, uncomprehending. He said, "Like – now?"

275

"Yes . . . but. Do you want me to help –"

"No, I'll clean it up or not, when I fucking feel like it, thanks."

I got up hurriedly, and went to the door almost scrambling to appease him. I could take a few kicks. It was actually a luxury of being halfway sane, that Eddie could take things out on me. I wanted to tell him: look, just take things out on me. I got outside with the expression on my face that I would have had, if I'd actually said that aloud.

The bright day was strange and lonely. I balked and looked back:

Eddie was crouched low beside the bed. His lips were moving, and as I watched, he grasped that orange *Soul – various* tape. A strange chill came over me, and I froze as if that would make me invisible. He was just holding a cassette. He was just holding a cassette. But lingering on the step with my mouth hanging open, stalled, I had a stirring vision of a strange pale beach. Eddie was standing in the sand, with his back to me, one hand raised as if waving. He was unnaturally still, like a cardboard cut-out.

The sea moved in the background. The moon flowed, too, if you watched it closely – it was only masquerading as a moon – it was something worse. Even the sand gently guttered. Only Eddie was stock still.

It wasn't our beach but I felt certain I had seen it somewhere, it was a real beach somewhere. And it was The End.

My gut kept insisting this was a true and urgent premonition.

I pulled the door shut. It was too much, finally. My premonitions never came true, no matter how they trumpeted themselves as "really true this time." All such tub-thumping from my brain was sheer agenda. This was a thinly veiled excuse to go back and emote.

I turned neatly (while my heart remained at 180 degrees to me, aimed steadfastly at my brother) and walked away, back into my life with Ralph.

## AIRPLANE SECTIONS

### Argument

*Two weeks later,*
*Eddie receives a letter from Denise Cadwallader.*
*Per its instructions, he flees to Malaysia, where he dies*
*for no reason, all alone.*

## 29. Changi International Airport, Singapore

The guy tore off the LAX and SIN tags and stuck on KL. Eddie considered that an actual sign. He'd, like, even got through that whole flight without drinking, and he'd had to swallow his last pills with no water. Then they were duds, so that was massively backbone. He felt like fourteen hours in the trunk of a car.

And it was this next flight, and a cab to the hotel, which, by that time he'd need a whole day in the shower. Like, oriental girls beating him with loofahs, or an actual autoclave was really what would work. Cause, at this moment, Denise even seeing him was like, he lost his whole fear of jumping under trucks.

As he crab-stepped down the aisle of the plane, he just let his fucking briefcase bang people, he felt that shitty. God just don't let the other person talk to him. And he was totally shutting the window and sleeping, none of that view crap. He was 24A, he had absolute window reign, no kowtowing to the scenery fascists.

It was a frumpy middle-aged woman in 24B. She was stooped over a book, oblivious to the baggage and potbellies grazing her ear. Eddie addressed her, curt:

"I'm the window. Excuse me?"

She looked up and smiled. She said, "Hi, Jack."

## 27. Rotterdam, the Netherlands

### (three weeks earlier)

1    Recently, Denise had realized she was going to die.

1.1   From nowhere, from a clear blue sky, she felt certain she could not live a year more.

1.2   She went to play as usual, the croupiers greeted her. The same faces and the same rote cries, like the opening credits of a dull-beyond-belief TV show, the gaming employees introduced another day.

1.3   As usual, she lunched alone. It was a workers' café with plasticized check tablecloths and empty vases on the tables. She looked up from her sandwich, awed and curious:

1.4   she was going to die.

2    Then the pains and vomiting, the nagging greed for air. She could not get clean, she could not eat certain foods anymore. She faltered, close to tears, on the steps.

2.1   In her grueling, super-real insomnias, she traced the pain to her bones and traced her bones to moon, a xenophobic stone, too solitary gladly to wear living flesh: too cold-loving.

2.2   In pain, she fancied these things, and unevenly laughed.

3    She saw a doctor, just, to cross all the t's. There was a series of hospital wards; chipper nurses explained the machines. In the last act, a specialist sat at the foot of her bed, stumbling over the sad news:

3.1   Her cancer was grave but not inevitably fatal. A range of treatments could be tried. Although complete recovery was rare, her tumor was not too advanced to exclude hope. There was reason for cautious optimism,

3.2 said the old man, and rubbed his veined, alcoholic's nose. She smiled cordially:
"Oh, I won't despair. After all, my mother died of cancer."
He patted her ankle and rose, she put on her old clothes.

3.3 She left the hospital and there was no one who would mourn her left, she had no goodbyes, she could step right out of life – without trifling.

4 The letter from my brother was waiting for her at home.

4.1 "God, whatever you do, just don't not answer this. I won't even briefly survive you not answering."

4.2 "Selling point: I've been practicing blackjack for ten years."

## 30. Singapore – Kuala Lumpur, Malaysia

"Okay, say you <u>didn't</u> do the sitting-together deal, like total coincidence. I'll give you that one just to show I'm a team player. But I'm saying, why you asked me here?"

"There aren't <u>reasons</u>," Denise said, stiff. And scowled down, hiding her reasons, drawing a finger down the spine of her airplane reading, Stanford Wong's *Professional Blackjack*. Then the plane picked up speed, forcing its way into takeoff, and Eddie lay back into the thrust, just frightened: just risking everything for this asshole mistake.

And he remembered benelia, his pretend all-healing grain: he saw a streaming mental banner with REMEMBER BENELIA printed on it in handsome gold. But old hags dragged it, through a wasteland of rotting stalks, it was a funeral march for Eddie's heart. A uniformed monkey led the cortege, cradling a rusty horn. The instrument drooped in the hairy arms, dust ran from its dull bell . . .

Ten years. He'd got to know she'd be older, but not fucking <u>old</u>. Not, not the same <u>shape</u>. And yellow and baggy and the toadskin thing. Could he even get it up, you'd have to drink so much you'd be first principles impotent. And would she still take him gambling, NO, even if he played the homo card, NO. Go back to Ralphie's House of Horrors, NO FUCKING NO. The suicide thing loomed, except he never felt like dying in planes, it was totally Murphy's Law.

"At least we can give Kuala Lumpur a miss," she said, with a polite effort, attending to business. "As we've met. I thought of the beach, because I have to teach you blackjack, and it makes no odds where. And, after all, our beach in Egypt."

"FUCK that. Just, <u>why you had that picture of my father in your briefcase?</u>"

# FRENCH SECTIONS

## Argument

*John Moffat secretly a professional blackjack player, also.*

## 6. Café Casino, Avignon, France, 1973

John burst into the café resoundingly, like he'd come to do something about this damn situation. A man's man with the demeanor of a coach, his dyed black hair gross against his ruddy skin, wearing cheap eyeglasses and an unpressed suit, he was also drenched and dirtied with rain. He'd had a run of luck at cards, and beamed with that mania. Among the elegant clientele of the staid café, he was disturbing like a loudmouthed drunk.

He strode through, grinning to the whole room as if they were his favorite people. Some of the diners shot him reproving looks, at which he nodded. Then it was over, he dropped into a chair and neatly out of the mirrors, the draconian French sense of what is seen erased him:

Denise looked up from her reverie, surprised.

"Hey, there, Dees. Look at the drowned rat, it's raining like a Noah's flood." He passed a hand over his wet crewcut. "Oh, boy, I need a coffee."

He made his gesture to the waitress – who, an Austrian, adored him, and knew his usual by heart, and was laughing as she already brought his *café au lait* – then turned to Denise again:

"Your dad's not coming to lunch because I threatened to cut his throat. I said, Peter, in so many words, I will cut your dang throat."

The waitress set down his cup, and he asked her to marry him. She said she would be pleased but her husband would not. He clutched his broken heart as she left and added, to Denise:

"I wouldn't ever really cut his throat."

"I would," she said, taken. "I would, I detest him."

"Whoa. Don't you talk that way about your dad," John

said uncomfortably, and looked at the floor as if something had hurt his feelings.

"But, you wanted to cut his throat?"

"Well, never mind what I want to do. I'm a big fool for telling you." He sat back and crossed his arms, unhappy. "Look, Dees, I gotta ask you a favor. It's a kind of a favor."

"Oh, I actually wanted to ask you something," she said, startled. Then she'd already said it — it just came out. She was frightened again, although of course he wouldn't say yes.

He said, "I think maybe . . ." and interrupted himself; with a thoughtful face, he asked, "I guess you're looking forward to going back to school?"

"Oh, no," she said factually. "I'm not going back to school. I did *tell* Daddy but I guess he never listens."

"Sure, no kid likes school, I got you." He fooled with his napkin, embarrassed. "Yeah, thing is, looks like Peter and me are splitting up for a while. I guess he's tired of my company's, the way it is."

"He's tired of <u>you</u>," Denise said contemptuously.

John laughed, fake and big: "Hey now, you're gonna make me think you like me or something, that's no good." Then he put both hands on the table, squaring up to her, man to man. "Thing is, I was wondering if you might want to team up with me for a wee while. Cause I'm going on to Spain, you know. Try to make some money for a change, but your dad's got his heart set here. I thought you could keep me company, I don't speak any of that Spanish talk."

Offended, she plucked her napkin from her lap and began to fold it with brisk, adult gestures. "Dad asked you."

"Heck, no! I asked him. Honest Injun, that's how the whole riot started, him fussing and puffing. Should have seen him, steam coming out of his ears!"

"Oh, I do believe you," she said, sarcastic. "Daddy would be just miserable to lose me."

"Oh, well, if you're going to be like that," he said, mock-grumpy. "You just give it a good old think, and when you're ready, tell me yes or no."

The waitress brought him his Croque Madame, he told her "Gracias." Pointedly forlorn, Denise turned to the window, to the other, serious world of rain.

Boxed into the pavement, so its mean pen of earth had puddled around its scaly roots, stood an old plane tree. It had fresh boughs low on its trunk, and the shadows of the leaves lay purple on the wet bark. They convulsed like fish in the poking rain: they couldn't stand it:

## Context: Unhappy Childhood

1    In her summer holidays, Denise joined her father

1.1   • in that year's country
- on the cheapest flight, via two third-world airports
- the in-flight meal a hard-boiled egg in a damp napkin
- no one met her, she carried her own bag, directed the cab
- "I thought it was next week," Peter sighed at her mistake. He turned away, he turned the television on.

2    He drank most nights, that was a different ordeal.

2.1   "This is just my daughter, I'm not robbing the cradle," he winked to the barflies.

2.2   To her, *sotto voce*:
- "That girl's a little well-developed for a Chinese."
- "Aren't you old enough to drink yet? Why not?"
- "Oh, you look at me with those cold, judging eyes."
- "I know you must hate me for giving you that face."

2.3   As she grew up, she repaid him with impassioned scorn.

2.4   She stole 10,000 dollars from him and went adventuring in the Himalayas. She came back haughty as ever. At Peter's demands for the cash, she sighed: "It's gone, it's gone, you'd best forget it."

3    Peter told her John Moffat was:
- "An old friend of your mother."
- "He said he gave you a lobster once and you might remember it, I don't know what that's all about."
- "I taught him all the cards he knows. He looks up to me – don't look as though that's so incredible."
- "Maybe she was having an affair with him," he concluded with the air of a man philosophically inured to life's blows: "He has a good physique."

4    She remembered Mr. Moffat holding the lobster by its waist, Mum wheedling, "Don't cry, Deesey-beast, it can't bite." She remembered him singing to her on a carousel, sidesaddle on a static kangaroo. At some point in her childhood he had kneeled to hand her a square of pink frosted cake on a napkin. He'd taught her "See ya later, alligator," at some point.

4.1    "I remember him," she said, stunned: "They played tennis."

"Well," Peter ended the topic: "He'll be in France."

## 5. Casino Avignon, France, 1973

5    John was 2,000 up when Peter tapped on his shoulder. He turned from his stack of chips, smiling his habitual hello – and saw the suitcase.

"I'm clearing out. You know I still owed you 500 when we last divvied up: I'm here to settle that." Peter put his suitcase down and scowled as he counted the money out of his pocket. The other players stilled to watch; the croupier frowned, waiting.

"Well, I know we had our differences, Peter, but I'm sorry. And I'll sure miss your Denise." John put his hand out to be shaken.

"No need," Peter said, as he pressed the notes into John's hand. "She's staying here."

John cocked his head at Peter. The memory of a previous conversation passed through his eyes, narrowing them.

Peter said tartly, "I told you, I'd had enough."

John stood up. "Well, if I didn't know you're just blowing steam."

"I don't think she'll starve," Peter said, and picked up his case. "She's got ten thousand dollars of my money."

## 6. Café Casino (cont.)

"So, yes or no?" John said, wiping his mouth. "I was going to give you some time, but you just broke my secret rules."

"Your secret rules?" she said, ridiculing him—although she didn't want to ridicule him and she instantly looked her fear, to show – she didn't want to ridicule him.

He said, "I'd be beholden to you. If you came."

"You wouldn't make me go back to school?"

He said, "Plenty of time to lock horns over that. Worst happens, you could end up a bitter old gambler like us." He put out his hand: "Shake on it?"

When she took his hand, it was damp with sweat: a mysterious, adult anxiety passed through his eyes. Then it was blotted out in his usual corny grin. She let go his hand, and she'd been tricked, it was something – Daddy was up to something. They were ganging up.

John cleared his throat: he had his fork up for attention. "Now, you, I recall, were going to ask me a question?"

"Yes," she said listlessly, "I was going to ask you the same thing. So I can be honest, at least, if no one else can."

He laughed loudly, looking away at the waitress as if he might repeat the whole thing to her, for her appreciation. Skewering the last corner of his sandwich, he said, "Well, partner. Touché."

1   John looked after Denise until his death, four years later.
1.1   They ran into Peter once, at the tables.
1.2   The three stopped to chat but no one suggested lunch.

2   The first year, she did nothing, she was in the hotel.
2.1   She studied French, she studied Dutch, she studied Spanish, from books.
2.2   She walked the streets sometimes, but disdained sightseeing.

3   Then she was in the casino, working-playing. She proved to be a dogged, gifted player:
3.1   she was lucky.

# In Depth: Denise Cadwallader's Luck

The first, iron-clad rule of professional blackjack is, there's no such thing as luck. Mathematical rules govern the game. Your play is determined by those rules. Any straying results in the gradual loss of all your money.

In some ways, it's a solid training for life. You proceed on the knowledge that you have, though that knowledge is slight. If you know, from your count, that there are many high cards remaining to be dealt, you place a large bet. You cannot know whether you will get any of those high cards. You may feel deeply, in your gut, that you are not going to get a single one of those high cards. But you place the large bet.

No intuition, no high or low spirits can change your actions. Every move is born of your imperfect knowledge.

Denise, too, played a disciplined, textbook game: as if her knowledge was of the same kind and degree as John's. She counted cards, and placed bets based on the count. But when she had good luck, she won much more than he did. When she had bad luck, far less. And, worst of transgressions: she knew ahead of time.

Since it fluctuated, and consisted not of stunning, but at best 11% wins, a normal player might never notice the phenomenon. 11% was well within the bounds of an average "run of luck," and would only be plain after hundreds of consecutive hands. Her bad luck was even less marked, tending towards 7–8%.

Because she and John monitored their wins, they were constantly reminded of her luck. Still both treated it frivolously, as an oddity which sooner or later would "work itself out." Sometimes Denise even lied, predicting that she would lose when she knew she would win. And when she did have bad luck, she played on obdurately, and John encouraged her, cheerily describing it as "grace under fire." In such small ways they conspired to dismiss it, as not <u>really</u> real. Over years, they ungrudgingly threw away thousands of dollars in gaming losses on this mental luxury.

The only time her luck became outrageous, and defied them, was in the final period before John's death. Denise felt the difference in her own mind: she was manic and more than usually compulsive. The lucky streak was also accompanied by a rash of coincidences: stories in the newspaper about a Denise Cadwallader who had won the lottery; a croupier dressed in the same clothes John was wearing; chance meetings; freak accidents.

She and John both remarked on it, unnerved. Coincidental events seemed weighty, insistently significant. The urge to interpret them became irresistible. "This means God wants me to –" sprang perennially to mind.

There was a sense that anything could happen, that <u>you could not predict</u>, and –

4    In Casino Atlantic, Ecuador, she won every hand.
4.1   Ten thousand, twenty thousand, only Denise laughed.
4.2   An hour passed and the mood grew threatening.
4.3   When they left, three "security guards" left too:

# Emotional Digression: Before It's Too Late
## *"The only good thing anyone has ever done"*

★ ★ ★

1 He took her in place of any woman or friend;

1.1 down to Perth and up to Rotterdam, holding her cold hand;

1.2 where the four winds blew, bearing passenger aircraft;

1.3 he took her wherever blackjack was played.

2 This is her myth, what Denise held sacred in her life; the unreflective goodness of Jonathan Moffat. When she was ugly and uncouth and could not be loved, he loved and rescued her. He never wanted anything in return.

3 It wasn't one good deed, it was four years;

3.1 when people thought he was a pedophile,

3.2 Denise got ever crazier, took all his time, and cost him real bucks.

3.3 He never had a day's peace after that.

4 Well, there were certainly some folks who needed an easy life, but he was Texan. You did what you had to do. He wasn't breaking his neck to be liked, and he personally never had a day's regret for doing a human being a good turn. Most folks would do the same, in his shoes: he was just that kind of a man.

4.1 – he would explain, genuinely naive.

5 When he died, that kind of a man died out. The world became a lightless sewer, as he closed his door behind him.

5.1 "I've mourned him, that's all it is. That's what I've done with the rest of my life."

## 8. Casino Atlantic, Quito, 1978

When she recognized the danger, the parking lot suddenly became beautiful and strange, an arena for great events. One of the men threw down a cigarette as she and John approached. John said: "Don't look now."

They'd tied their shirts around their faces, but she recognized the fat one. They spoke in Spanish, barking as if rushed. She should have translated for John.

And she had already seen in her mind, how he would empty his pockets for them and the men would search him roughly for concealed cash. How they would search her and make obscene jokes. She would remain stiff until it was over. She and John would have to walk to their hotel, and make excuses at reception for the lost key. "*Ladrones, ladrones,*" she would explain, to general tuts and sympathy.

John swung at the gun. The man fired. It was bright and then much darker. Blinded, she lunged for John, as the man fired three more times. Then it was hitting a loud wall. It spun her onto her back.

She still didn't believe it had happened. It was all right, she could see John's leg kicking, his shoe's gleam on and off. She was thinking of what might have actually happened, one hand feeling the dry asphalt curiously, as the pain hit and she blacked out.

# 31. Airplane Sections (cont.) / Waiting for permission to land

"So that was how the plastic surgery began. Because my jaw was shattered, I'd lost five teeth. And I was back with Peter, I had nowhere else. He paid for all that, and he wanted a beautiful girl. It really was that simple."

Eddie stared inconsolably at his tray table. Suddenly the stewardess reached in and snapped it shut, latched it, and was off, saying "Excuse me!" brightly.

"Oh, God," said Eddie. He tried to shift his weight of self-pity, which possibly Denise didn't see the humor of. His Eeyore schtick.

She said, low and apologetic, "I've gone too far, of course. Really forgive me. Ah, I think we're slanting. I get nervous now. Should I distract you with the story about my plane crash?"

He said, "But, like, you're saying he was totally this gambler? You know, cause we grew up, he was supposed to be some fucking CIA guy."

"Oh, that's so not important. He wasn't an <u>agent</u>. He just worked with them, after Vietnam."

"But – not an agent? What did he work with them <u>on</u>?" Eddie caught his breath, thinking *biological weapons*, and she said, lightly,

"Biological weapons."

And smiled. He stopped with her face stopping him. A brick wall. He muttered, hateful, "I guess that doesn't matter?"

"No," she confirmed. "It absolutely doesn't."

"Well, I don't know how you figure that."

"Oh, don't be stupid: because he was good. <u>I'm</u> a bad

person, just to give an example. It doesn't matter if I do good things, it makes no difference, people see straight away. They don't <u>love</u> me, if you know what I mean."

Eddie took a deep breath, seized by an enormity. He said in a weighty, careful voice, aiming it, to break the evil spell:

"<u>I love you</u>."

"No," she said, untouched, "you don't."

"I've loved you for ten damn years," he swore, and felt a prideful ache in his chest: *No matter what. No matter what she looked like.*

She sighed: "Anyhow, the people who love me, die, so I have to discourage you from thinking along those lines."

So she broke him again, and her eyes changed focus, passing his profile to see Kuala Lumpur rising in the window, the tiny neighborhoods, near-geometrically aligned, like electronic circuitry only here and there bashed, coasting in, at the speed of wind, and Eddie croaked,

"Why did you want me here? Why?"

There was a long pause where he couldn't read her expression at all.

Then she said, "Look, as I get older, you can see the scar when I smile."

She smiled, and traced one finger down an S-shaped dimple, corrugated and deep in her soft cheek. Then unsmiled, as the plane touched down. "Oh," she said, in pleased surprise. "We're alive."

300

# *The Main Dread Secret*

## My Father's Involvement in the CIA's Secret Biological Weapons Program

★ ★ ★

1 John Moffat was still a university student, when he began his career in biological warfare.

1.1 The Naval Biological Laboratory was then based at UC Berkeley: John did his PhD there, on virulence in *psittacosis*.

1.2 In the wake of the student protests, his experiment, among others, was moved to the premises of a nearby pharmaceutical company, Bulwer-Sutton Industries.

2 *Psittacosis* is more commonly known as parrot fever. It is classed as an incapacitating, not a lethal, weapon. Its mortality rate is close to zero: only young children and the elderly are at risk of death. It's only mildly contagious: its only practical use is to disable enemy soldiers, in time of war.

2.1 John told Denise: "We used to kid the guys who worked with the plague."

3 Vietnam came along, he did the honorable thing.

3.1 He lasted his two years, then, what do you know, the bigwigs are crying for biologists.

3.2 "They made me an offer I couldn't refuse, two more years risking my life for peanuts."

3.3 His new job was studying the efficacy of defoliants. He took aerial photographs, he collected botanical samples. He had a little lab in Saigon he called Rat Central Station.

3.4 In this new post, he worked for the CIA.

4    In the spring of 1971, John Moffat was going home.

4.1  He was looking forward: his wife was nuts how she was looking forward.

4.2  Hot baths, real steak – a list of things he'd do first.

4.3  He'd hardly set eyes on his two-year-old son.

4.4  Then his CIA boss came to him with an offer.

5    The first test of biological weapons in real conditions was due to take place in Guatemala that year.

5.1  There were rebels in the hills: infection would disable them, allowing their arrest by local forces with reduced violence. If successful, the strategy could be invaluable in dealing with Communist insurgents, worldwide.

5.2  The US planes could fly in and out of Panama, never touching down on Guatemalan soil. The CIA man called it "a zipperless fuck."

5.3  "I thought of you right off. I know you did that work with parrot fever. That's what they're using, my man said to give him a call."

5.4  "Well, I couldn't let it go, you know. That was my baby. Worked so hard on that thing, six years of my life. You'll make fun of me, but I thought it was going to end war. No lie, the dreams I had back then. All the bombs in the world were going on the scrap heap, worst ever you'd fear would be a bad stomach bug."

6    He was in Guatemala nine months, waiting for the drop.

6.1  The day after the bacteria was spread, however, he flew home, deserting his post without warning or leave.

6.2  He never carried out his studies. He would not consult with his replacement, and he had nothing to say at his debriefing.

6.3  The CIA offered to send him to an in-house psychiatrist.

7    John left both science and the military behind.

8    He took up blackjack:
- just, to buy time, while he figured what he'd do
- ran into Peter Cadwallader, John always had a soft spot for Karen and
- you know guys get to talking.

8.1  He played for six years. Secretly, and died.

8.2  In the Casino Atlantic, Ecuador, he told Denise:

8.3  "You know, I put myself between a rock and a hard place. Never could tell my wife, it'd break her heart, she ever thought I was . . . I never meant it, you know that. Always thought I'd have plenty of time, this was supposed to be a part-time job! Well, I sure hate leaving you, is the only thing. But I guess I better face, I'm not a young man. Children growing up!

"No! I guess if nothing else, we certainly learned to trust each other. You, Dees, no question, I would trust you with my very life."

# Facts for Tourists: Pullau Pangkor

An island off the coast of Peninsular Malaysia, Pullau Pangkor is distinguished by its clean white sand beaches. The ocean is warm in its many coves, and late-night swimmers may witness the unearthly gleam of phosphorescent plankton in the waves. Tasty local dishes, featuring fresh-catch seafood, are offered in the friendly restaurants. Palms and wild orchids complete the idyllic scene.

The island is not without its disadvantages. Though snorkel trips are available, the coral has perished, and most fish fled, from heavy industrial pollution: only the wormy, black forms of sea cucumber stand out on the grim bottom. The jungle interior is picturesque, but harbors cobras. The sea snake is likewise fatally toxic: pangolins and bats may attack if startled. The many insects, venomous and huge, make sturdy footwear a must.

For those intending an overnight stay, the Pangkor Inn comes highly recommended. Run by a Scotsman, Ian Johnston, its simple rooms are clean and each features a framed photograph of a famous cricketer. Towels are available with payment of a small deposit.

Redheaded Johnston first came to Southeast Asia on a package holiday with friends. Wooed by a Malay girl, he sold his janitorial supplies store in Aberdeen to marry her and move to her native Penang. The further move to the remote island was prompted by his desire to practice his hobby, the trumpet, without harassment from touchy neighbors.

In his island isolation (his wife is now in London, and seeking a divorce) he is free to wander the beaches after dark, playing Dorsey standards. The inn's modest restaurant affords him a chance to indulge a new enthusiasm, Indian cookery. Sometimes, when he thinks no one can see him, he will stoop to stroke a drowsy massive beetle on its shell with a careful fingertip.

"Hello there, little fella," says Ian Johnston.

## "You Can't Go Home Again Because You Are Poisonous"

### Returning from the burial of Ralph the cat

It's our walk the way we used to do it, when we were new; down by the clearing with the pale tossing grasses; into the shadows and looping gnats. We meander, and our pity for the cat makes us gentle. How we tucked the swaddled corpse carefully into its rough hole. How we filled the grave in and secured it with big, practical stones. We stood for a long time and left without speaking.

Under the climbing oak, just before we come back out within sight of the house, Ralph stops and we hold each other for a long time. Our silence is like a long release of breath. We don't kiss, we don't kiss anymore. We just stand together in this chilly shade, clinging, smelling the damp earth. Together, we fear one thing and then another thing, and don't want to return and are going to return.

Then Ralph says, "I was thinking . . . I've decided to announce that I've attained Buddhahood."

The way he says it is so square and weird. It puts a stop to us.

"Oh, no, you're kidding me," I say uncertainly. I stand away, ready to laugh.

He shrugs, "Might as well be hung for a sheep as a lamb."

We still hold each other's elbows, but we're enemies. I can't stand him. I can't stand him so much I flag and think of other things. But at last I say, in a lethargic, inattentive voice:

"Well, if you do that, I'll just leave."

# The Origin of My Concept of God

1    When I was a child, there was a series of television ads for Star Kist tuna fish.

1.1  It featured an ambitious tuna, Charlie, who longed to be accepted by the Star Kist brand.

1.2  Realizing that Star Kist had high standards, Charlie spared no effort to improve himself.

2    In one ad, he busied himself with literary classics.

2.1  In another, he learned to play the violin.

2.2  Week after week, Charlie slaved away, acquiring new refinements.

3    At the end of each ad, Charlie would present his most recent skill to the Star Kist quality controller, who was represented only by a godlike voiceover.

3.1  Eyes shining with hope, the tuna would loft his violin/golf club/copy of *Moby-Dick*.

3.2  The verdict of the Star Kist God was always the same:

4    "SORRY, CHARLIE!
STAR KIST DOESN'T WANT TUNA WITH GOOD TASTE:
STAR KIST WANTS TUNA THAT <u>TASTES GOOD</u>!"

5    As a child, this ad disturbed me deeply.

5.1  I feared for the selfless tuna, clamoring to be tinned as food.

5.2  Why didn't Charlie taste good? What about Charlie wasn't good?

6    A superficial reading yields an anti–intellectual agenda.

6.1  Going more deeply, one might posit "tasting good" as a Zen no-mind state.

6.2 Or: tainted by original sin, we can be saved by Grace alone.

7 Pondering it now, I shoved away the vile Star Kist God and defied him:

## So Much for the Cat and Mouse

"No, you can't even say that, you a Buddha – you're so fucking cruel. All this time, we're all crazy with fear. You stamp people out, you hate us so much. Why do you hate us so much?" Then I gulped and hugged myself against the chill, he was standing there with his red face.

"Oh, thanks." He made a fragile sneer. "That's so helpful."

"It's not supposed to be helpful. Some things aren't for you."

"Right. Right. I'll try to keep that in mind."

"And you saw God?" I screamed, "Was that a lie, too?"

"No," he said, and his whole face squinted against what I had said. I glared, self-righteous and myself disgusting. I was suddenly aware of the dusk coming, the darkening showing that time had run out. Our race was run, we'd wasted our three wishes, and we stood wrong and polluted and without means.

Ralph said: "That's it, then."

And walked away from me, so it seemed then, forever.

I watched him going, and hated him. His shape faltered in the changing shadows. I stood paralyzed and evil. As good as dead.

But at last a brief sweet spangle of love woke in me and I woke –

I chased after him. Hearing me coming, he began to run.

As he came out on the back lawn, he was pelting along like a boy, I had no chance of catching him. Me and my stubby legs, damn! But then he stopped short.

I thought he'd been stunned by my same love blow. This is the reconciliation, I knew. I love you! Don't suffer! The rest is all shit! (I would say that: "The rest is all shit! Come to bed!")

I walked the last few steps and caught his arm.

He shook me off with a grimace of distaste. He looked away and I saw what had really stopped him.

A little cluster of smokers was staring at us from the back door of the Land of the Lost. Secure at that distance, they brazenly gawped, leaning one to the other to comment on the spectacle. They made and unmade fireflies, sucking on their cigarettes. Then there were real fireflies in the shrubs, more yellowy.

I said, "I don't care. Forgive me."

Ralph said, deaf to me and all else, "I've fucked everything up."

"No kidding," I laughed. "But let's please start over?"

He winced and hated me, clenching his shoulders. Then he threw it off: with a whole, liberated rage, he roared at the smokers:

"I DON'T KNOW ANYTHING! I'M A FRAUD!"

They all shifted as if slapped.

Ralph was trembling and I daren't touch his arm. I felt futile and tiny in the face of what would happen next.

Then, weakly through the seemingly clouded twilight, a ragged call came from the smokers:

"I don't know anything!" they echoed. "I'm a fraud!" And again: "I don't know anything! I'm a fraud!" They stood up straighter, anticipating praise.

Ralph and I grimaced at each other for a moment, like parents recalled from a quarrel by a demand from their children. Then he just walked away.

I let him go this time, having failed to understand the

events. I crossed the lawn hoping that the smokers would give me a cigarette. We would discuss what this latest exercise meant, and smoke, and when I went up to my room, Ralph would be there, watching Wimbledon like normal on ESPN.

# Endgame

In the morning, Ralph has taken up his post by the swimming pool. He sits on a Hooters beach towel, in dirty red swim trunks. His bare feet dangle in the water. Beside him on the concrete poolside lies a shopping bag full of dope. He's smoking and smoking. I can smell it from upstairs. He throws the spent roaches in the pool.

If anyone tries to talk to him, he ducks his head and seethes. The anger comes off him in palpable waves, it's frightening. He won't talk/look up/move. Left alone, he is absolutely still, but when someone approaches, he trembles with rage. Gradually, unconsciously, his hands form taut fists. His bloodshot eyes narrow.

I give myself an hour's rest time between tries. I go out to him with glasses of water and juice. I place them beside him carefully, to rub in my patient goodness. Then:

– "You realize this was all I had, and you're just destroying it? But I guess that's hardly important to anyone."

– "I loved you, anyway. I loved you so much, once."

– "Are you okay, Ralph? I'm only worried that you're not okay. Though you treat me as a ridiculous patsy."

– "I'm so sorry. I don't mean anything I say. I don't know anything. I'm so sorry."

When he drinks the water, I feel vindictive glee. It's all I can do not to jeer at his capitulation. Once, I bring him a cheese sandwich, diagonally halved on a folded napkin, hinting at the one he brought me, when it was me crazy. He knocks it into the pool, seeing through my feeble ploy.

Finally I see myself as a buzzard, greedily pecking at the dying man. Then I make myself stop trying. I send Kate Higgins out with two cartons of orange juice. The fact that it's Kate is my parting shot, and I'm left with a lingering, toxic craving to apologize because it was Kate.

Sometime toward evening of the first day, Ralph empties the bag of dope into the water. Then he just sits. The dry grass floats out and looks like leaf-fall, it gives the pool the incongruous look of a pond in late autumn. From time to time, Ralph raises a foot from the water, and inspects the clinging shreds there. He gets up, from time to time, and shambles to the bathroom, graceless as he never was, and seeming much shorter.

The second day, it rains on him for hours.

The guests gather in tense huddles, they slink from place to place. No one showers, and the cooking rota has failed. The men wear three-day beards. They have a shifty-eyed look, like ambivalent mourners, who have wished Papa dead too many times. But even more, they are hungry: their meal has abandoned them. They are hollow-eyed and restless with the need of their cruel meal. Shrinking from them, I'm unhappily reminded of the cannibal starving children I once tried to hallucinate. I tried too hard, and now I have been punished by my dream made flesh.

When I pass, they whisper: then they send a representative. "Is Ralph okay? What's going on? Is this a teaching?"

I say I don't know. I'm perilously tempted to hint that Ralph, like Shakyamuni Buddha, has sat down for forty days to garner enlightenment. My voice quavers, saying I don't know.

In solitary fantasies, I explain to them how the School really came about, Eddie's cockamamie scheme, the slippery stages to the false reality. I say, "It's all really a macrocosmic projection of Ralph's personality disorder." I promise to sell the house and return all donations. I confess in self-defense that I, too, was duped. I explain it all again to Jackson Pollock, who would understand.

Another day passes, taking several years to pass. We have all aged: Ralph is wet and gnarled like vegetation. Looking in the mirror, I notice that my sense of humor is entirely gone. Getting myself a Coke, I watch myself in curiosity: here she is, getting a Coke as if drinking matters. I walk past *the-pool-and-Ralph* like it's an oil painting of my lover's brutal death. Then I'm angry again, wondering how he can possibly blame me for this disaster.

## Day Four, as I begin to wake

The sun shines brightly from early morning. Lying in bed, half-awake, I am already with Ralph by the pool, feeling the harsh sun that will become a problem. The rain of the last two inclement days is drying from my swim trunks, leaving them stiff with dirt. My back is killing me, but I won't admit I want to leave.

Finally I open my eyes to the pretty ceiling, sighing because it's me. I sigh again, grateful that I'm clean and indoors. I sigh a third time, grateful that I'm not underneath the bed, and Ralph is the sick one, not me now, and I'm going to have breakfast.

I'm hungry for the first time in three days. Excited, I sit up buoyantly and leap out, I throw clothes on. Rattling down the stairs, I prepare myself not to look at Ralph and go out the door with paranoid haste.

He's sitting there. His hair has dried in strange tufts. He's sitting there.

My appetite gone, I change my mind and walk stiff-legged to Eddie's door. Still seeing Ralph's figure, which has lodged in my mind as a half-man blot, which becomes more unfinished even in those few steps, until its defects suggest a decomposing zombie, and oppress me −

I don't realize Eddie's door is open
until I'm standing in the open door.

The room is bare. I stagger in, drawn by the vacuum of it, the stillness. All his junk is gone. The bed is stripped to the stained mattress. The floor is cleared but hasn't been vacuumed; shreds of lint, foil, paper lie exposed.

When I open a drawer, it's cavernously empty, nothing nothing but the wood bottom. I open more drawers, I begin to sweat.

There are no clothes and his briefcase isn't there. His diary isn't there. His <u>ashtray</u>.

I call, foolishly: "Eddie? Eddie?"

Then I spot the snail, on the floor beside a lone tack. It's an ordinary garden snail with a brown shell. As I stoop, it flares its neck like a brontosaurus. Like a circus brontosaurus, about to curvet, and its phlegm-like stalks gesture.

Plucking it loose blindly, I head out to the flowerbeds (again <u>not looking</u> at Ralph, dammit, not now) and drop the snail under a shrub.

Then I hear the voices. They're coming from the kitchen's screen window, just above my bent head. Guests, assembling, as they have every right to, in my kitchen.

Now I can't use my kitchen. Instantly I realize I'm desperately thirsty, and I freeze, anguished by this new-minted dilemma. I watch the snail struggle to right itself, its shell heaving with the effort, and I hear:

*"It was cruel, you just tried and tried, and it was, you were never good enough."*

*"I never wanted to say, but I actually went back to therapy as a direct result of Ralph."*

*"But there was no room with him, for our needs. It had to be all one way."*

*"It's cause, I don't think he realized our value. Cause I gotta believe, I know you have value, so maybe I do too?"*

*"He was just like my father."*

They all laugh then, and I'm released, I go, tonguing my dry sticky mouth, toward the dining room, with a hysterical certainty that Eddie will be there (but also knowing there's a mini-fridge, with cold sodas)

(Ralph passing in my peripheral vision)

(I open the front door just enough to slip through sideways, as if that's safer)

(the living room with its long curve of marble stairs where Eddie once successfully completed the self-imposed task of pissing on every single stair in one mad run, God don't let him be gone)

(the dining room is lit)

There are people there. I halt in the doorway, and Kate Higgins waves.

It's her and Anna Rossi and Jo Minty. Assembling as they have every right.

Anna's doing Ralph.

"Stay in your center. You aren't in your center." She strides, haughty and ponderous, along the dining room table, pausing to frown at a shoved-out chair. "Come back to your center. Fool." She shoves the chair in.

Kate and Jo are in stitches. They turn away from me, but I see Kate peeking, her eyes meet mine with sensuous hate.

Jo says to everyone but me, "You guys know what? I got a stash of beer under my bed. Only it's not cold."

"Oh, I usually don't," Kate simpers, "but today."

Anna puts a hand on her hip, and says, "Since we don't have dope to smoke."

"Oh, let's just call the cops on him, that would settle this." Jo dusts her hands together, settling it.

"No, I still couldn't do that to him," Kate sighs. "He was my teacher, I could never raise my hand to harm him."

I say something, some moan of farewell, and stagger back, cursing the impossibility of getting a drink in this place, heading to the john where there are faucets after all, but there the GUESTS are, in the hallway, in my path.

It's Arthur Clough and Mat who commutes from Sacramento. They straighten up, but studiously pretend they haven't seen me.

Sacramento Mat is saying, "No, I get he wants us to go, but I don't get why."

Arthur Clough holds up his hand. He says confidentially, "What I'm saying, I had an idea he's trying to weed us out? You know, the ones who stay are real seekers, and then the . . . secret teaching could start."

"Wow. Right. So, this is a test."

"That's what I think. I'm just telling you this cause you've become a good friend."

They pause, just managing not to turn to me hopefully.

Mat says, trying to laugh, "But it could be not –"

"Yeah, that's it. That's why you've got to use your own perceptions."

I walk towards them mechanically, say,

"It's not a test,"

and walk away mechanically. My eyes water a little but when I wipe them, I don't cry after all. I go outside.

Of course, my saying it's not a test could be another test. If Ralph and I publicly fucked at poolside, that would make a splendid test. We could hold guns on them and scream "Fuck off, you revolting ass-lickers!" That would be an advanced test.

We are forced to shoot them. They become instantly enlightened, having passed all the tests, and their souls fly away to nirvana, cleansed. We bury the corpses underneath the tower.

I head toward Ralph. He has turned bright red already in the sun. I call gaily, stronger than him, in my desperation: "I'm just going to get you some sun block, okay? Back in a second!"

To my pained empathy, he flinches. Oh, God! He's real! I think, running for the sun block. I slip on the stairs and crawl the last several steps. Then I make myself get up on my hind legs again, walking sensibly to the bathroom. I drink from the faucet, the water splashes down my chin. Then I grab the sun block, spilling everything else out of the cabinet, and laugh and almost pause to trample the skin products underfoot. But no: Ralph is waiting. I run laughingly out, and wave the fat tube over my head as he doesn't look.

"Okay, hold still." I squat down beside him, and squeeze cream onto my palm. It's old and a crumb of congealed goo comes first. I wipe it off on my jeans, not wanting to squish it on Ralph, who's clearly feeling sensitive.

I get a fresh globule and reach to his shoulder.

"Get the fuck off me," barks Ralph.

My mind instantly flies back to the night he punched Eddie. It's that voice. I say, loving him, "You can die of sunburn. Ralph?"

He doesn't move. I love him. I pity how he's made dirty fingermarks on his cheek. He doesn't move.

"At least you're talking," I comment. He turns his head away. Frustrated in my friendly intent, I squeeze fat rings of sun block on my hand, puckishly meaning to absolutely smother him, and reach for his forehead.

He swats my hand away hard. It stings and a glob of cream flies in the water. Ralph's muttering:

"Rip your fucking head off, you shove your hands in my face."

I squeal, "I'll just keep trying, though! I'll sit here with the sun block all day, we'll both be burnt!"

He says nothing, vehemently. I falter away and we sit, mutually staring into the fouled water. The sun block drifts into crumbs, not dissolving. I rub my sticky hand on the concrete.

With time to kill, I ponder dismally the possible derivation of the zombie myth from people like my boyfriend. I picture Ralph blackened, semi-fingered, with bright bone peeking through his flesh. The odd small worm clings, festively wiggling. In my image, Ralph's really upset about decaying, and I feel for him sorrowfully. I want to tell him I

320

would still love him, if he were decomposed. Of course in practice there is no predicting what I'd feel, and besides which, it's a wild associative leap.

I ponder dismally how I've alienated people, all my life, with my bizarre associative leaps.

I look at him then for real.

He's a middle-aged man with dirty skin, slumped in a "penniless" attitude. In this sedentary year, his body has lost tone, and the trunks' elastic cinches up a fold of sweaty flab. His face is set in a sullen resentment. He could have known better than to trust anyone. He could have known better than to think he was any good. People just fuck you over.

I can be trusted. I love him right now. I want to touch his shoulder –

Then I remember, shocked, and say, "Eddie's gone."

I look at Ralph and he doesn't look at me.

I say, "I think Eddie's gone. All his stuff is cleared out. It's scary."

I pause to consider that I can't be trusted in particular. I have already lost an entire family. Although of course Eddie is probably just in San Francisco, buying coke. Then again, he's buried all his things (putting two and two together), which sure looks grim.

And I add, doomily:

"I found a snail."

Then Ralph starts to laugh. It's such a normal laugh, I laugh too, to encourage him, and then just because I can't stand it.

"Oh, God," I say. "Why are you laughing?"

He puts his hand over his eyes. Then he isn't laughing.

"Ralph?" I say, falsetto with suspense.

He takes his hand away and looks at the grimy palm.

He says, "Okay."

"Okay?"

"This is a farce."

"Yes, yes . . . are you . . . talking, now?"

He looks around him for the first time in days, grimacing ruefully when he comes to me. He stretches his arms out in front of him. "Let's see how it goes."

I watch him examine his sunburned arms, pick shreds of dope from his waterlogged feet. From time to time he gives me a look: the half-shamed triumph of a child recovering from a tantrum. I stop myself from mentioning how shitty he's been, although I sneakily promise myself I'll get to that later. Now I say, nice:

"Would you like to go inside and have something to eat?"

He winces, I've gone too far. But then he thinks: "We could . . . is there anyone in the kitchen?"

"There was. I could check, if you want me to."

"Yeah. I'm just . . . I was hoping they'd all have left."

"Oh, no," I say, jumping to my feet. "Not they."

## The last kitchen scene

I went into the kitchen and they were there. I said, "You'll have to get out now, I'm afraid, because Ralph wants to use the kitchen and he doesn't want you here."

"Oh!" they said, affronted, and "His Lordship! Excuse <u>us</u>!"

But the cunts left. (I wasn't feeling very generous.)

When they were really gone, I leaned out the door and called to Ralph.

He came shambling, clumsy. He kept stretching out his legs, mid-walk. In the doorway, he balked, unhappily frowning at the Oscar Person chairs.

I looked at them too, the horrible shitty awful chairs that hurt you. Ralph was exhausted! I wanted to kill the chairs!

Yet he just sat down.

I brooded over him, worried. "Are you okay? I guess you can't be . . ."

"No. I need . . ."

"I'll get you some juice?"

"No, I'll get some in a minute. Thanks."

I sat down, useless. Then he reached out and I reached out and we held hands.

He said, "Really thanks."

I said, "Thank God it's over."

Then, just as I looked up and saw the pale blue envelope, gaudy with foreign stamps, addressed in near-invisible pencil, propped between two corn muffins on the microwave:

my chair began to play "Pop Goes the Weasel."

*round and round the mulberry bush* It had a bleepy timbre: my first thought
*the monkey chased the weasel* was that a guest had planted a bomb in

*round and round the mulberry bush* the chair, which mocked its victim with this
*the monkey chased the weasel* infantile tune before blowing him/her to
*round and round the mulberry bush* smithereens. I sprang to my feet, and saw:

Deep within the punctured seat, an odd plastic gleam showed. I bent and plunged my hand into the chair's guts, extracting Eddie's mobile phone. I shook it free of cornflake debris, and waved it at Ralph, squealing:

"Oh, shit, we'd better really answer it?"

"You," he said, alarmed. "I can't. I —"

"Oh, shit."

I backed away, stalling, and went to peer at the blue envelope. It had no return address, but it was addressed to Jack Moffat, and somehow I knew, and when I finally pressed the right button and held the tiny phone to my comparatively colossal head, still frowning at the awful tune and reluctant to press the thing which made that noise to my ear, and more absorbed by the envelope, which I'd plucked from its nest and was opening with one hand,

the phone call was from Denise Cadwallader too.

"Hello?" I said, and for the first time heard her cool, self-conscious voice.

"Hello. May I speak to Chrysalis Moffat, please?"

"This is . . . Chrysalis."

"I'm sorry. I'm afraid I have bad news."

# MALAYSIA SECTIONS

## Argument

### "You Can't Go Home Again
### Until Your Whole Family Is Dead"

# Context

★ ★ ★

Having scrawled a suicide note on a paper placemat,
over its depiction of "Fruits of Malaysia,"
and recorded his goodbyes on an audio cassette,
Woolworth's brand with orange stickers, labeled:
*Soul – various,*

my brother Eddie died in the course of a massive
epileptic seizure.

He was on a small island off the coast of Peninsular
Malaysia. He was thirty at the time, although he looked much
older. No one was with him.

His body lay on the white sand beach, with the sea
approaching and retreating, making a fringe of white bubbles
and absorbing it into the dark water again, as if thoughtfully.

Eddie had made a mark like a snow angel, flailing,
before he suffocated. Then a damp stain of urine and dilute
feces. Found by an early swimmer, an Australian who reported
that the sand was bright yellow like dyed hair at sunrise and
my brother was like a few stones in his dark suit and it was,
like, a spooky postcard. Closer, you could see the insects, so
many they made a heat shimmer. You were aware of your bare
feet suddenly and saw what that was and then you stopped as
if hurt.

"And I just thought, you know, shit, that's a dead guy.
You know. That's a corpse. Cause they were all crawling
round in his eyes."

There was sand in the briefcase the tape was in. Not much, but I could feel it when I handled things. The placemat smelled of food. At first I thought that meant he was alive although I already knew and I don't know why really. Then I put the tape on and listened to his voice.

Dear Jack Moffat,

In response to your recent letter, after a brief hiatus I am returning to professional gambling, and need a partner urgently. Having recalled your once eagerness to learn, I thought this might be of interest, and so invite you cordially to meet me in my first port of call. I will be in Kuala Lumpur the 8th–14th of this month, and can be contacted via the Awana Hotel, whose card I enclose. Naturally, all travel expenses will be reimbursed.

Yours sincerely,

Denise Cadwallader

1    Ralph and I flew
     LA – London
     London – Singapore
     Singapore – Kuala Lumpur.
1.1  In Singapore, we spent the night in the airport hotel.
1.2  The room was windowless, and smelled of concrete.
1.3  We smoked until our eyes burned. Showering made us feel better.
1.4  I lay on the chilly carpet, and wept. When Ralph stroked my back, I got annoyed.

2    The 30-minute hop to KL, then we caught a bus.
2.1  All day through the jungles and the windy plantations. Children waved, they demonstrated their yo-yos.
2.2  At every stop we bought a liter of water, parking lots smelled of rotting fruit.
2.3  All the Malays smiled. I wanted to shut my eyes.

3    We had lunch in Ipoh: a whole extended Chinese family cooked, stir-frying noodles as they talked.
3.1  Ralph made me eat and I was starving. Those wonderful noodles made me cry again: how happy people must be here.
3.2  And walked down to the pier. I cried mechanically and sweated. The sun made the view hurt. My brother was dead.

4    Just fucking sorrow. The ferry had backless pews. It was cool on the water, the little boat hurdled the waves, making breeze. Sea-birds followed in circles overhead, looking down at us.
4.1  "It's the Indian Ocean," said Ralph, and I wondered if he was right.

4.2 Once I had wondered, I felt better. I leaned my chin on the side of the boat.

4.3 "That's my favorite ocean," I said, remembering childhood. And added:

4.4 "It was Eddie's favorite, too," and we both laughed at the fact that even that made me cry. Ralph pressed my hand, he pressed my head to his chilly, sweat-damp chest.

5 Denise was waiting at the dock.

5.1 Long dark hair, blue dress, as she'd described herself. She looked summery, among the chatting fishermen.

5.2 She held a black urn in one hand.

5.3 Greeting us, she asked if I wanted to carry Eddie.

## 32. Pullau Pangkor, Malaysia:

## at a picnic table on the beach, the sun setting

## and the sea reminding us, in waves

"No, your brother was still in good spirits, when we arrived. Of course he was drinking heavily, as I've said, I take it he was something of an alcoholic. It was only when he wanted to sleep with me, and I said no. Then he changed. I don't think I've left anything out. Of course I'm willing to tell you as many times as you like, but there's nothing else. He just, called me names." She smiled, remembering. "Old walrus. That was one."

I said, "Oh, Eddie says anything that might be painful to hear. He can't help himself, it means nothing, though."

"No, I don't care," Denise said, looking away at the violet, indistinct ocean. "The point is only that he went, and when he didn't come back."

"Oh," I said. "Well, that's really all right."

We all then looked at the beach where Eddie had died three days before. The moon had come out and it was bright there. It looked like a place people went to die.

We'd been sitting at the picnic table for some hours, drinking beer from plastic wine glasses, watching the (under the circumstances) baleful ocean. I'd made Denise tell the story of Eddie's death three times: in between, she'd volunteered her stories about her gambling years with my father, until I was punch-drunk and couldn't ask questions, and couldn't stop her. Then I would ask to hear about Eddie again.

Now the sunset had spread its layers of violet low, tinting the mussed sand. The flowers had changed to their evening smell. The spaced line of coconut palms behind us that marked the road were sable now, and seemed taller.

Their broad leaves rose and fell, revealing the shadowy nuts underneath, like stallions arching lush tails to show their ample testicles (I thought, inappositely).

Ralph sat too quietly. It was (he later told me) a daze, in which he couldn't imagine giving 10,000 dollars away to pauper children, or what it would be like, directly to experience God. He didn't have that sweet, victorious heart left.

Denise did (thought Ralph)

– and while I saw her as a callous neurotic whom my brother had fetishized because of her (still evident to me, despite the walrus thing) remarkable beauty, and who'd known my dad too well for my liking, and I wanted her to be full of shit about the aliens, out of puerile jealousy,

Ralph saw her as a magical being. His silence was a childlike, struggling awe.

Of course, men who are incapable of intimate relationships are prone to fall under the sway of charismatic figures who can allay their fear of choice. Hence the rise of fascism. Later that night, however, when Denise had unexpectedly been sucked into the bright maw of an alien spaceship, never to return, Ralph's view was semi-vindicated, although I must coolheadedly observe that we, too, are aliens, to those aliens, and there may not be anything magical about them.

At the time, Ralph's silence just seemed rude.

On the warm picnic table, between my hands, stood the morbid urn. It was larger than my mother's urn: this I attributed to crude Malaysian manufacture, knowing, as I did, that Mom and Eddie were the same size. I kept addressing it telepathically, though I didn't honestly believe it was Eddie. I was just, unwilling that nothing should be Eddie.

At first I had been saying, how lonesome I was, and would he come to me in a dream, please. Then I began to make the urn answer back, as if playing dolls. Now, as Denise's long tale faded from our minds, and we all waned away from the moment of recognizing Eddie's ultimate beach, I said to the urn, sadly, *I could scatter your ashes there. If you don't mind sandcastles, et cetera.*

*I'm holding out for toilet,* the urn said. *Seriously, final wish.*

Then I looked at Denise, considering her ideal profile as something people could love. Feeling my look, she clenched her jaw. Her face settled into a different intensity, drawing back from the seriousness of privacy.

And she said, quietly, into the sea's receptive space: "But of course I knew your brother was going to die."

I had to clear my throat. Then I said, "How?"

She shook her head. And didn't answer, just shrank kind of miserably, burdened with her terrible knowing. Ralph caught his breath.

Then we all sat around, we were supposed to be awed. I was brattishly unawed. In rebellion, I thought about the way my mother said, every time she got a phone call, "I was just about to call you! It's mental telepathy!" – although, to be fair, Mom knew it wasn't true. Of course, if Ralph had been skeptical, I might have played the credulous role, and been disdainful of his closed mind: there's never any telling what you genuinely think, once you enter into group dynamics.

This is why we should avoid each other, carefully (I'd got around to thinking – we'd been awed for some time). Then Denise said, shattering my cozy inner monologue:

"Actually, he said he was going to kill himself. Eddie, when he left –"

I blurted, "Oh, of course!"

Ralph put his hand on my shoulder as if I needed comforting.

I said, "He was certain to . . . I don't mean anything. That is, he probably said that to anyone who wouldn't sleep with him, although it was harmless, actually." Then I frowned and had to think exactly how this was harmless. Ralph was bugging me, rubbing my shoulder.

Then he said, carefully, "But Denise didn't mean . . . you said you knew?"

"Oh, yes," she said reluctantly, "I meant a presentiment. But I wouldn't place too much importance on it. I only – you know, I should have chased after him. And I thought, oh, no, he's going to die, and I went to sleep. In actuality. So that's my guilty conscience, which, I'm sorry to burden you."

"You let him go?" I said, suddenly giddy.

"I think I must have been ill." She frowned, checking her memory. And added, absently, "I have pancreatic cancer. I'm dying as we speak."

I looked at the table defensively, I didn't want other people to die. There was sand in the grain of the wood.

She amended, in a wry tone, "Not exactly, as we speak."

Ralph caught his breath again and I listened to him let it out while I picked at the grain in the wood. I told Eddie, *everyone's dying, this sucks.* When Ralph said he was sorry I looked up: Denise was smiling again, at Ralph her old childhood pal. She announced:

"I can understand <u>you</u> wanting to think . . ." and stopped herself, with a grimace of suppressed mirth.

"What?" Ralph said, absolutely nakedly afraid.

"Oh, our strange experience together. You know."

"Yes . . ." Ralph said carefully, giving her an eliciting look.

"You saw God," she reminded him, grinning.

"Did I?" said Ralph. He looked at me, I had to touch his arm, he looked so awful. But he just looked at my hand, stunned.

Denise said wearily, "I didn't see anything, you said you saw God."

335

"Let's take that as given," I said hastily. "Is that all right?"

"I just wanted to say," Denise resumed, "as an example. There were those strange events, with the cat and so forth. And then it began again before John's death. So I expected him to see God, I thought I was a conduit. But in fact, it's just more events, one after another, at random. So I really try not to make sense of things, nowadays."

"But your luck," Ralph objected.

"I was a teenager," she said flatly, and lifted her plastic glass of beer. She put it to her lips, but then grimaced and put it down again, crabby.

Ralph and I exchanged glances, on the same wavelength again, meeting a common threat.

Then Denise butted in from her different, upsetting wavelength:

"Oh, I've just told you, haven't I? That I was lucky, but you know, I tell it different ways. I gave you the naughty version."

We looked at her unwillingly, not going to ask. Ralph noticed my hand on his and grasped it suddenly, making me jump.

"Of course," she said, with an air of confronting an old enemy, "Admittedly, I think I'm the touch of death, and my life is a series of bizarre coincidences, and it's all very laden with meaning."

"But it's not?" I said courageously.

"No," she said. "It's not. There's a famous man who's been struck by lightning four times, you know. I imagine he thinks it's to do with him. People like to make things into stories." She gave her mental adversary one last defiant, withering look, and subsided.

*Good! You shut up now!* I thought out of nowhere. Then

336

I wanted to burrow into the sand and think. I wanted <u>Eddie</u> to bury me in the sand. I needed that.

Nonetheless, I thought on without it, pell-mell, how I lacked any sense of fate; to me, coincidences were pure coincidence. Even my own life had not been about me.

Immediately I perceived this as a shortcoming. Even now, I was all about Eddie, having barely shed being all about Ralph. Narcissism, I thought, wistful. Why can <u>they</u> all do it? And, steeling myself for a last-ditch effort, I faced the grim, gloriously selfish Denise:

"You've left me out on purpose," I said, boldly. Immediately I was alarmed Denise would now reveal I didn't exist.

"What?" she said, squinting, as if startled from sleep.

"I mean," I pressed on, "that is, my father finding me? Or whatever . . . if . . . he always said he found me in Peru?"

"Guatemala," she said, flatly. "I'm tired. You know, I don't feel well."

Ralph cleared his throat and said, in a muted, respectful tone that made me personally queasy:

"Do you want to go to bed? Are you going to be all right?"

Denise shook her head: "No, no. I'll rally." She folded her hands and squeezed them as if to generate energy. Then she smiled at me, personally. To my alarm, I warmly responded and immediately wanted to do something nice for her.

She said, "It's all right, I'm honestly not stalling. I think I should get up and walk, though. That often helps."

We all looked around as if there might be good places to walk, hidden cunningly. Then all looked right at Eddie's beach.

## moonlit Eddie, going out

stopped at the totally monster bug-laden restaurant, hoping to shit they'd have a knife, but of course the assholes locked up, like who was out here to steal anything (he fumed, frustrated in his fucking stealing mission), so he took a pen cause that was all there was to steal and scribbled a stupid suicide note to disgrace himself for all time, then realized he was fucking drowning himself, so the note in the pocket deal was out, he had to go back to the goddamn room again, and Denise probably awake.

Only weirdly when he got there, his briefcase was outside, like she had put his stuff outside in total heartless assumption he was just walking out and not killing himself like he'd specifically said, only she still had his shoes. Like, where was he going to go barefoot. He whispered to the door, "Thanks, bitch."

Then whispered to the door, "I love you."

He bent and opened the briefcase. He put the suicide note in the empty briefcase and then got the tape from his pocket and put that in too. Like trusting and hoping nobody stole the briefcase while he was dying, cause you never knew, in a place like this, the fucking backpack fraternity.

At last (he thought in total frustration, like you kill yourself and it's all this same annoying shit that goes wrong, just thank Christ it didn't involve a bus ride, he'd be stuck on a fucking bus all night) he headed to the beach

watching his feet the whole way, shit scared of stepping on a bug when he was about to

Christ, he needed to die now

Christ, he couldn't fucking take it

he scratched his face in the frenzy of, you fucking piece of shit man, disappear and drown yourself, you fucking, something people used to know how to do, he didn't even know, could he do it. Breathe water, which, why they had to be there, at the beach like he was in some fun beach mood

then a sick joy hit him, as if summoned by the thought of fun.

He stopped in his tracks. Everything became yellow and interesting. It passed.

and back down into hell. His skull felt wrong, there was some bad drug thing. And couldn't think. Christ, he needed to die now, and

there was the beach, shiny white between the trees. He didn't run but he thought about running. He realized no one would ever know he'd died, it would be like he'd never existed, he felt reassured and noble.

He strode through the last trees.

The sand was cool. For a second he wasn't going to kill himself, he was just going to sit on the beach all night, and fuck them. He threw the pen into the sea. Stare at the moon all night though it was only a half-moon, and kind of beige.

He took a step into the water, and noticed the lambent sparkle.

He thought of germs. The whole joke of it washed over him and he began to stagger into the waves, but something enormous came into his head that wasn't a thought, that was like a physical object entering his head, he screamed. He tried to stop it with his hands.

## on the beach, with the sparkling waves done and undone, in black and white, Guatemala:

### *"John Moffat: A Hero in the Lists of Cain"*

★ ★ ★

1    You could only get burgers or fried chicken. The bars weren't to his taste, the music all sounded the same. He gave up trying to learn Spanish.

He spent a lot of time wasting time at the office. The boys had got Space Invaders on the computer; he played that, sometimes they all played Monopoly.

In the evenings, he sat in his hotel room, writing letters.

*I miss you like all tarnation,* he wrote. *It's hotter than Hades, the mosquitoes sweat. I can't wait to get back to my own bed and my best girl.*

2    By day, they talked, they had meetings and drafted plans. They distributed schedules and approved alterations. They had to find a new translator, the air conditioning needed work. Everything went through Washington.

With the Guatemalans, it was always, walking on eggshells. They came to meetings armed, they met every American proposal with outrage. If the General stormed out, the whole next week was down the drain.

They demanded:

- a deadly, not an incapacitating weapon
- vaccines for their troops, and the means to make more
- technology to breed the bacteria itself

They displayed an unsettling predilection for the word "plague."

2.1 "It's just yank, yank, yank – yank our damn chain," said the Head, despondent. "No way they'll get thing one of that stuff. All's they really want is payoffs, and they had their thirty pieces of silver, it won't fly."

3 The Guatemalans pulled out.

3.1 Washington decided to go ahead.

3.2 The Guatemalans were back.

3.3 And again.

3.4 Time stood still. Whatever you tried to do, there was some Guatemalan hell-bent to stop you. In the morning, you put on a shirt ruined by the Guatemalan maid; the Guatemalan cab driver took you miles out of your way, to a meeting where a Guatemalan colonel would rattle on irrelevantly for an hour about trade concessions.

4 John would not allow the word "Spic" to be spoken in his presence. Where he was from, half of everyone was Mexican, and some real nice people. Just as bad as the f word, and he was raised Baptist.

But it came a point, the boys complaining and cracking jokes, and the old hands egging them on 101%, until John spent a week honestly believing what some guy told him, that the Spanish word for "lie" was the same as the word for "talk" –

The word "local" got to be like a swearword itself. He would not have called a man Guatemalan, to his face.

And it was just a darn fool South American war, cowboys and Indians. He wouldn't give you two cents for the Spanish, if that was the best they could do in three hundred years. Be another three hundred years before he saw the end of this job. Well, had he known.

One day, he was shooting the breeze with the Head, and the bug just bit him. "Vietnam, we were fighting the

Communists. All fine and dandy. Now, who in Sam Hill are we fighting here?"

The Head just looked away, dismal. He said: "Yep."

5     It got worse. Time on his hands, he got hooked on thinking.

5.1   He'd make simple things real complicated. Then he'd take a break to over-generalize.

5.2   He started writing letters home just to tear up. To chew things over.

5.3   It was as simple as pie. He just didn't understand.

6     It was a war of the rich against the poor.

6.1   The poor were Indians in bright cotton clothes, ever bearing loads on their backs and heads.

6.2   The rich

- exterminated them en masse and stole their land
- enslaved them, man, woman and child, to work the cotton fields
- hunted those who resisted down and tortured them to death

6.3   In the bloodier acts of this old American drama, the poor were now "guerrillas."

6.4   But, in plain English: his was an evil cause.

7     You could count on John Moffat like death and taxes.

7.1   What he had undertaken, he would surely do.

7.2   He would soldier on. Under torture, John wouldn't talk; in a prisoner-of-war camp, John, clean and buoyant, would rally the men's spirits.

7.3   His honor crippled him: he could not shirk his task.

8     Then the details were finalized. Suddenly it was done.

8.1   The raid was dubbed Operation Pretty Boy. A reconnaissance plane and three dusters: *psittacosis*; from and to

Panama; just as it had been envisaged from day one. It was set for 10:00 P.M., on the 4th of July.

8.2 The date's feeble irony thrilled the Americans. They brayed and made jokes about fireworks and independence. They laughed boastfully, eyeing the deadpan Guatemalans.

It was a thing John never could stomach – disrespect. He stood and waited for the boys to hush up. Then he turned to the Guatemalans' head honcho, a man he never spoke to if he could help, fellow looked like an honest-to-Betsy Gila Monster, but.

"Señor," John said, "I'd like to apologize for my colleagues. I think we're all a little bit crazy today. I sure hope our antics haven't caused offense."

The Guatemalans stiffened: mortally insulted. John had pointed out their cowardly submission to dishonor.

9   But then one Guatemalan – one of what the boys called Juan Does, who had no rank and no apparent role in the project, a hothead who'd been a keen advocate of anthrax at the fractious meetings, one Victor Caceres – stood up, crisp.

He said that in the light of Mr. Moffat's apology, his countrymen would overlook the slight to their nation.

The Guatemalan higher-ups bristled, usurped.

Caceres walked away from the table with the confident ease of a good-looking man.

John followed him. They reached the door at the same time, and Victor held it open for John to pass. The door shut on the silent room.

In the corridor, John said to him cheerfully, "Whew! Do we get away with that?"

Caceres snarled, "They are pig cunts! Whores!"

and when John laughed, the mad Guatemalan nodded, as if that entered neatly into his plans.

They crossed the parking lot together, and John admired Caceres's Mercedes sports car. It was a clear March day, like a June day in Texas, the moist heat good in the air, like a food. Parting, the men shook hands, and John got into his own car feeling fresh and excited, as if Victor had offered him a way out of his dilemma.

## Segue: to the point

1    Then John had a friend: or he had Victor Caceres.

1.1  They used to play poker. Neither man drank, John Moffat was relieved to meet another teetotaler. There was something in Victor's rabid spiel –

"I am a sadist, but this is a good thing in me."

"I am a great saint in my childhood."

"I am the only real man in this army, but I am a coward."

– that leavened John's anomie.

1.2  Victor was anti-American, anti-left, just plain contrary.

1.3  The Indians were racially underdeveloped. The *ladinos* of his own class were Indians in suits. Guatemalan women were whores without exception.

1.4  "But I am a patriot of this disgusting country."

2    Over cards, Victor peppered John with tales of massacre and torture: the women with their breasts sheared off; the children mutilated; all the men shot in front of their wives. Though some horror stories were the doing of Victor's "friends," and some disturbingly like the accounts of an eyewitness, Caceres would study John accusingly, wronged.

"Who began this shit?" he would ritually demand.

John would chirp to order: "The CIA."

And both men laughed, cheered by the frivolous sound of the catechism.

3    Once and only once, he met Caceres drunk. John was walking down the street, he heard a man screaming at him. Next thing he knew, it's Victor spitting in his face. Shouting: America was shitting on his country, on the Madonna, John was a man of shit. Caceres pulled a gun, and had to be restrained by embarrassed friends.

345

3.1 The next day he sent John an expensive watch and a note of apology.

3.2 John thought that was real style.

# Beside the point: all tarnation

His wife used to take his face in both hands and shut her eyes. She would run downstairs to meet him, whimpering like a pup. Sometimes when she was sleeping, he would finger-comb the pale blond hair between her legs. It turned dun when it was wet.

He'd stopped drinking once and for all, after his last visit home. Little Ed had woken him at 6:00 A.M., they went down together to find Mom. She was lying on the couch with a bottle. Tipping it down like that was some escapade. "I just never do this," she'd sworn, in a voice no one could believe. When the little boy tried to tug the bottle from her hands, she giggled and slapped his wrist, calling him jealous.

He wrote: *I would walk through fire for you, Elaine. I would lay down my life to spare you one solitary tear. Just you keep your spirits up, and I'll be back to take good care of you and Ed before you know it. Cross my lonesome heart!*

– and put down his pen, and rubbed his eyes until he saw stars. The air conditioner chugged on, it had some thing, you couldn't turn it off, he was getting pneumonia. He saw Lannie, twenty years old, at that Tex-Mex place on the coast. She wore a straw hat that made her look like she had long hair underneath. After lunch, they walked in the sand, and she threw the hat at him, saying, "Catch!" But it fell in the water and before you knew it

# 1. July 4, 1971: Operation Pretty Boy

**7:00 P.M.**

You heard Caceres's car radio coming from, about a mile away. It would come up until you thought it couldn't get louder. Then it got louder.

And he could sure as heck hammer on a door.

John opened up to him and that was his mistake. The fellow was drunk as a skunk.

Caceres told John he was coming out for a ride.

"I don't think so, Vic," said John. "I'm kinda pooped. Plus I gotta get back to the office. The big night, I'm manning the phones."

"No," Caceres said, and put his hand inside his jacket. "Hurry up." He produced the pistol idly, and looked back over his shoulder at the empty hallway.

"Are you threatening to shoot me, Victor?" John said, as if that was the most remarkable thing.

"I will shoot you here, I will shoot you there. Come for a ride." He waggled the gun in John's face to demonstrate. "Bang bang," said Victor Caceres. "I threaten you."

**7:15**

Well, why he ever got in the car in the first place, mad dog Victor and the way he drove alone enough to kill you with a heart attack, the colonel calling at eight-ish from Panama to say when the planes went, he had an hour, supposed to be on call, the big night, but now the fool was heading God knew where, clean out of town.

The mountains stood warding off the huge gleam of sunset. Behind, the city dissolved in its brown pollution.

"Well, any time you feel like saying where we're going, I'm listening."

"You don't like my car?"

"Any time."

"You don't like my company?"

"Any time."

## 7:30

In the swooping pasturelands, pale and tilted till they hiked up into a horizon: John smoked and bided his time. Looked ahead at the darker jungle slopes. Too near for his liking.

So sudden it flashed, they came up on a line of jeeps pulled up on the side of the road. They idled, the wind bore a streamer of gray exhaust. Victor hit the brakes, and my dad's heart started going, he could hardly think what to do for his heart. All Victor's stories ran through his head: the ride out of town, the men waiting. It was always the genitals cut off. The soles of the feet.

He braced back into his seat. His head went ten to the dozen. No cover: too many guns.

Victor honked the horn in passing, picked up speed again. Jeeps full of little Indian soldiers, all crammed together. Like boy scout troops. Somebody honked back, there was an arm waving.

Craning back, John saw the jeeps pull, laboring, into the road. They all fell into line behind.

My dad tried: "Look, now, I sure wish you would tell me what all this is about."

"Indians in uniforms," Victor said, waving dismissively. That sent my dad wild.

"This may seem like a joke to you, Victor, but I won't stand for it! You hear me? I want to know! And I want you to turn this car around before —"

Victor pulled out his gun and pointed it at my dad without looking.

Neither of them said anything for a long time. Finally Victor put the gun back in his holster.

Victor said, "Momostenago."

## 7:45

And he continued, "You will enjoy this town very much. It is pure Guatemala, but a very important mistress lives there, so we have all the comforts of your home, of course my home is not comfortable. My car is not comfortable enough for you, I am ashamed of my car in American eyes. But you will see, we have a paved road all the way for Momostenago. Electric light, everywhere. The water from the sink."

Momostenago was the target for Pretty Boy. John had guessed they were going there, but then he hadn't liked that guess. He said slowly, "Okay."

Victor said, "We go to see the mistress." And he pronounced, in a careful, altered tone, as if it were the Latin name of a disease:

"Fernanda."

Then he asked my father to pass him his bottle, and my father obliged. It was tequila with a worm. The worm jiggled with the bumps in the road.

"Well, you tell me what she's still doing there," my father said, hearty.

Victor secured the bottle between his thighs. My dad was already saying *Whoa* when Victor'd got his gun out.

And the bumps in the road. The muzzle wavering. Finally finally Victor put it back. But John went on waiting for the shot, he couldn't put it out of his mind. He couldn't look away.

He didn't know how you asked a man, was he really planning to kill you.

## 8:30

The jeeps had long since fallen behind, John had lost sight of the dust their tires raised. Then they hit the brink of jungle, a change of light like a dive into deep water. They lost the radio station and sometimes Caceres sang himself.

Sometimes Caceres talked, beguiling the time.

He told my father the jeeps were there to contain the people, to prevent them from fleeing in the wake of the alarming planes. "We keep them together, under the plane," he said, raising his bottle to the sky. "We tell them to breathe deeply in. It is bad for your theory of warfare, but the Guatemalan people are not allowed to escape. One escapes, the good mood of the General is ruined."

Then he looked at John and raised his eyebrows as if they were sharing a joke. John laughed like a stupid toady.

"Yeah, it's not so good for the point of the exercise," John said. "Supposed to be too dangerous for the Army, your guerrillas, right?"

"No one escapes," Victor said. "So we send our Army without telling our wonderful American allies. But now you are here." He nodded to himself as if this was the key to the matter.

They had rolled up the windows against the insects. There was still sunlight in sparks overhead, but the road was dark. The road was deeply pitted, and the expensive car bounded deftly like an animal. Then the trees thinned to show the gathering night and then cleared to cultivated land as

## 9:00

they drove into a Guatemalan village like every Guatemalan village was: thatched huts, spindly crops, half-naked children who stared and then ran. A burro hefting its head to bray. Weeds flowering in the dirt road.

But smack in the middle stood a tidy white clapboard

house. It had red shutters and screen windows, a tarred and shingled roof. It was like any house from a suburban development in Iowa. Caceres drove right up to it, until the headlight beams shrank and focused on the pale siding.

"We are here," he said, suddenly animated and glad. He punched my dad in the shoulder as if congratulating him. He pointed at the house and introduced it: "Fernanda."

My dad got out of the car just like, people get out of cars. Mostly that house was too normal. And Caceres strode ahead, like he was late for a party, excited. He pressed the bell and laughed, singing: "Ding dong!" He beckoned John impatiently and John tried to smile.

The important mistress opened the door.

She was not a mistress. She was the farthest possible cry from a Latin mistress. A somber dark woman in a tank top and slacks, she held a hardcover book half-closed on her thumb. She had a broken nose, concave and skewed, and one of her eyebrows stopped at a deep scar. Overlooking Victor, she introduced herself to my father, with a measured courtesy, testing the waters.

He said, "John Moffat," beaming to reassure her. She checked his clothes again and decided, apparently, there was no knowing. Then she turned to deal with Victor Caceres.

She gave him a wry, affectionate sigh: *you washed up at my door again!* Her eyes found the tequila bottle and she shook her head.

My father realized how long it had been since he had seen an intelligent, fearless woman. He realized the "important mistress" was Victor's, and that Victor was a complex man, and my father had been vindicated in his trust of him. They would all three get in the car. Plenty of time to get clear of this doomed place.

Victor shoved the woman in the chest. She staggered

back still smiling, and stepped to one side to let Victor come shouting into her house.

## 9:10

He swore in Spanish, for her ears: and she laughed and applauded him. He stamped into the dark room and back to the entryway, his boots clopping undramatically on the heavy tiles. He called suddenly to my dad, "Electric light!" and hit a switch. When nothing happened, he berated Fernanda again, and she laughed as if he was telling jokes, pressing the book to her stomach.

"Light, light, you see?" Victor said, pointing to a light bulb hanging from the ceiling. He shrugged as if he was deeply sorry to disappoint my dad in any way. He explained, "Electricity sometimes cuts. A short time only."

At last Fernanda went and fetched a lit candle. She used it to light more candles, one here, one there. My father followed her spotlit, musing face as the room came to light in flickering pieces. A bookcase, two unmatched chairs, a table with aluminum legs and a cracked formica top. The walls had been painted inexpertly, a clouded orange.

Caceres rapped the table with his fist, watching it rock on uneven legs. A candle toppled and he looked at Fernanda triumphantly, not catching it.

She said something arch, and my father interrupted:

"Look, Victor, we really got to be getting on."

Victor turned to him with the crazed glee of a master of ceremonies, raising his arms. "I am a man of fate!" Victor trumpeted. "What will I do?"

My father tried: "You'll tell your friend what's going on, and we'll get out of here, it's nine-fifteen. It's nine-fifteen."

Victor pulled his gun. This time my father groaned, rolling his eyes at the waste of time. But Victor fired.

There was the moment when everyone jumped, then the plaster dust and everyone unharmed. Fernanda sneezed and Victor giggled, delighted.

Now Fernanda swore. She called in a high, furious voice, called a word three times that sounded like:

"Kreesa-lees! Kreesa-lees! Kreesa-lees!"

A door banged open. Out marched the children.

First a little pint-sized girl, no more than three years old. She didn't call hello to anyone, she just hurried, she knew her business, which was to vanish fast as she knew how. The thing that held her up was her big brother.

The boy had something wrong with him. Big, like those people are, somehow. And he had a hunch – how retarded people often do, just messed-up top to bottom. One of his wrists was tied to his little sister's waist with a stout rope.

He was twice the girl's size, but he minded her. Never looked at his mother, at the strange men, the gun; just feasted his eyes on his sister, with a docile grin. She muttered to him, in a low efficient voice. Not Spanish: some Quechi-what-have-you Indian tongue. As they went outside, she shoved him in the back, and he barked like a seal and clutched his rope with a kind of fond respect.

Caceres stared after them and his whole face gathered into nausea. He glanced at Fernanda as if she had wronged him. Her face too was bleak, brooding on some memory.

Then she looked up clearly at John and asked him if he understood Spanish.

He said he knew a little. She told him to go outside.

Victor crowed and waved bye-bye at my father. "Go! Go! Everyone go!" he cried and with one step he had his gun in Fernanda's face. He grabbed her by the hair. Then he was wielding her head like a gun, pointing it at John Moffat as he caroled on.

The woman continued to tell John to go, though her voice was strained and her mouth had set into a non-smile of fear.

My father stood like a stupid rock. He would have loved to go. He said,

"Victor. Look at me. You know at ten o'clock —"

Victor howled and

## An Essay on the Futility of Earthly Love

My real parents, Victor Caceres and Fernanda Espuelas, met as university students. Fernanda was the only child of a doctor, a member of the sparse Guatemalan middle class. Victor's family came from the ruling elite: but were disgraced and dispossessed by their support for the left-wing leader Arbenz, who was toppled by a CIA-sponsored coup in 1954.

Though reduced in fortune, Victor's family still enjoyed the fierce loyalty the very wealthy extend to the members of their class. The sons obtained sinecures: the daughters married well. Their radical sympathies diminished neither their cachet nor their own snobbery.

The closest Victor came to a political conviction was a burning resentment that his father could not afford to send him to college in the US.

Fernanda, on the other hand, embraced Marxism with the fury of the very young.

Yet Fernanda and Victor met and fell in love unwisely: with the disregard native to just-nineteen. He paid lip service to her beliefs, she flattered herself she had convinced him. When he explained that his family's position meant he couldn't actively participate, she argued with him, earnest and foolish. Their pillow talk was of disguised priests, forbidden books, battles in the mountains kept secret by the ruling class. There was real work to be done – she whispered, hot against his neck – lives to be saved.

And with time, with the easy valor of inaction, Victor began to see himself as a future Che, a warrior, redeemer to his bitter family.

But when she became pregnant, his family's position meant he could not marry her.

The love story ended there. They parted, he drank to his satisfying guilt.

She was arrested. The other story began.

Victor fought and bribed and lied indefatigably to secure his jilted lover's release. He pounded on doors, he pushed his way past secretaries. He got away with it and that became his motive, *just to fuck them just to fuck them* feverish in his head. He discovered his forte, the role of loose cannon. Greasing palms, he made powerful friends.

By the time he was called to collect Fernanda from prison, Victor was manic with pride. Greeting him, the duty officer was shifty-eyed, monosyllabic – afraid of <u>him</u>! Asked to wait, Victor put his feet up on a chair and smoked. He blustered at the long delay, laughing inside.

He was still blustering when she came into the room, supported by a nurse. Although he didn't recognize her, he fell silent. Then the duty officer had his revenge. "There's your girlfriend," he said, and cackled.

She had been beaten so she was fat with swelling, beaten out of human shape. Her eyes were crusted with blood, she had no teeth. Her arms were broken and some of her ribs were broken: her painful gait came from burns on her genitals. He would later come to know well the strange, starfish scars where her nipples had been sliced away: through two pregnancies the milk trapped there would make her sweat and clench with pain.

She moved her head, ungainly, to acknowledge him. But she couldn't speak; he didn't know if she knew who he was. So he cursed with helpless rage, alone with his rage, as he drove her, speeding, to her father, the doctor.

The people in that house met him with shifty eyes and monosyllables. The mother spoke to him as if she were not weeping. They were cravenly grateful, but they wouldn't let

357

Victor Caceres in their house, thank you, and the door shut in his face, the sound of locks, a bolt drawn and checked.

The other story came into its own. Victor Caceres had decided he was a good man. He devoted his life to the cause of rescuing Fernanda.

When his son was born, Victor sent Fernanda every article a new mother might want. It was then, too, that the queer clapboard house was built, in an area reassuringly far from power. He begged and borrowed. He sold his car for her, he sold his clothes. His parents refused to give him money, flattered him with their anger. His friends called him crazy, admiringly, and Victor Caceres grew into the part.

Fernanda refused to see him, but he was gratified to learn the boy had been christened Victor. And when the child was eight months old, and she at last was healed from one thing and the other, Fernanda consented to be taken to her new home.

Victor stayed with her there for a year. They were lovers again, after the fashion of harmed people, bonded by distrust of others. For that brief span, the house became a mystery to its humble neighbors; children whispered ghost stories, passing that house.

Slowly, in exhausting stages, the baby son turned into a thing; a staring, awful reminder; the personification of blight. Fernanda cosseted him still with the impervious love of mothers. He was just her stupid child, her silly child, her child.

Victor suffered agonies of detestation at the sight of the dazed, incurious face, the asymmetrical mouth ever open.

When Victor left finally for Guatemala City, I had already been conceived. He never acknowledged me: for him, the canceled son had canceled the possibility of children. He even regarded me as something done to spite him, a gratuitous salt in his wound. I was born nevertheless, and grew to be a normal child. Without him, we became a contented family.

Without him, Fernanda resumed, too, her own life; the life of forbidden books and meetings, the life of real work to be done. She came to know the local people: through them and through her old contacts, she came to know the guerrillas of that district. Her odd house became a haven. Arms could be hidden there; the wounded could die or be healed in peace. Through her father, Fernanda obtained basic medicines; through Victor Caceres, she had a generous flow of cash.

The money this time was not begged or borrowed: Caceres had at last begun his glorious career. He fought and bribed and lied his way into his chosen sinecure: a commission in the Army was secured by a helpful cousin.

He embraced the diversions of his class. He drank away his monstrous son, he whored away his monstrous son. The political killings he used to relate to my father with such relish were a part and parcel of that life: another communal shame of whose excess young men boasted. But also, for Victor: he disappeared and disappeared thoroughly his monstrous son.

When he drank alone, he drank too much. It was then that he would drive out to Momostenago.

That became a routine. He arrived in a fury, cursing and raving. The children would be sent next door. She learned how to answer him, the path of least resistance. Sometimes he waved his pistol and threatened to shoot her, but he never struck Fernanda, he never touched her. He treated her in all ways as if she were a ghost of his own imagination, an incarnate doubt he fought to conquer.

He would pass out suddenly and wake with no recollection of having driven there. He would be sick, horrified, he would drive back to the city in a blind panic. That afternoon, after no conscious thought on the matter, he would arrange to send Fernanda a sum of cash.

He came to regard her superstitiously. She spirited him back to her, against his will. In his mind, she took on the toxic powers of a nemesis.

When he suggested Momostenago as the target for Pretty Boy, Victor did not have any clear plan. And through the following months of negotiation, when he fostered the idea of it as a hotbed of revolutionary activity, when he even lied and fabricated to secure his aim, he did it with no firm intention. There were images only, which came and went: stories in which he conquered her by saving her at the last moment; stories in which he let her know he had decreed her death.

He fought bitterly for a lethal plague, no mere fever but incurable death. He liked to think of Fernanda dying prettily, judiciously, among hushed American nurses. He imagined himself with flowers at her bedside; placing flowers on her grave. Her father the doctor would shake Victor's hand. The children too, the children too, and a final stone would be placed on his old shame.

The agreement which enshrined *psittacosis* as the agent employed in Operation Pretty Boy included the provision that, after medical tests were complete, surviving prisoners should be yielded into the custody of the Guatemalan police. Then the Yankees would pack their bags and depart, seeing no evil. The standard process of interrogation would begin.

Fernanda would be tortured again, to death.

Perhaps she would not betray him, but someone would. His donations would be revealed, his lies about the village. Victor would be tortured, too, and killed.

For three months Victor played poker with my adopted

father, Jonathan Moffat. He didn't dare take a drink, he feared waking in Momostenago as he feared hell. He had no plans because his life had already ended.

He told himself the story of the woman and the man who must be tortured to death, as if it had already occurred many times. He loved Fernanda. He hated Fernanda. There were many stories in his mind, but they ended all the same.

Then, at the last moment, the loose cannon jerked from its rut and wheeled:

# 1. Momostenago, Guatemala (continued)

**9:20**

and howled at my father to leave, and Fernanda said to leave, to leave.

They became one person suddenly to my father. One vile, crazy person who had been threatening his life for so long, for hours, for months. And he was sick and tired.

He nodded, curt, and did just as they said.

He shut the door behind him. In the clean spaciousness of outdoors, he balked and almost went down on his knees. Behind him, he heard Fernanda's voice again, raised in mockery. He took a few steps around the corner of the house, where he'd see Caceres coming before Caceres could see him. Then he leaned against the clapboard siding and gave himself a short breather.

Some yards away, by a slanting thatched hut, he saw the children. They were pulling up grass to feed to a skinny tethered donkey. The donkey curled his lip daintily, craned his neck to nip at their offerings. The girl coached her brother, pointing out rich tufts of weed.

Then she peeked over her shoulder at my father. He grinned by force of habit, that was what he did with children. She beamed, flattered, and stretched her handful of grass out toward him. He mimed putting something to his mouth and munching it down. He rubbed his belly to show how tasty.

The little girl waved her arm and laughed, delighted. She stretched the grass out, insistently, again.

My father thought suddenly, miserably, of *psittacosis*. Only young children and the elderly at risk of death.

He had half a mind to grab her, spirit her away and put her in some boarding school. *He who saves one life, saves the whole world.* Who said that?

As he slumped against the house, staring at the child who had now gone shy and turned her neat back, he delved into the fantasy. How he would get her back to the city; the reaction of his superiors; the reaction of his wife. And untying the girl from that brother, his loving-kindness didn't stretch to the weird boy.

But then the child wouldn't want to leave. He could picture her carrying on, shrieking, breathless with tears, arms stretched out to her ogling brother. That would bring Victor and all the demons of hell down on his head. And Mama none too pleased. What that writer didn't take into account, whoever he was. Most times, you couldn't save just one life. They all stuck together in impossible bundles.

Then he heard low voices and the unmistakable sound of bedsprings, and realized he was leaning right beside the bedroom window. He glanced back in a kind of real Baptist boy's disgust, and almost laughed when he saw a tidy red shutter. That must be his cue to go. If Victor had time for that, John Moffat sure as heck did not.

With a last look back at the little girl he wasn't going to save, he started walking briskly, back the way he had come.

Soon mosquitoes covered his face and arms. He began to jog, dashing them with his palms, reckoning how far away he'd get in forty minutes. More Victor he was fleeing than the damn disease, a big guy like him would hardly –

the shots began. By force of Vietnam habit, he dashed for cover, running and clinging to a tree. Then he knew his foolishness. When the next shot came, he heard shattering glass, and pictured in a flash the little girl flung into the dirt, her blood.

And he cringed in frantic unhappiness, knowing what he was going to do.

And he was going to save one life, and he was going to

be too late, and there was something anomalous in the way he ran, easily as if there was no emergency. There was the village again, the huts that now seemed familiar: the weird clapboard house. The donkey alone, rolling wild eyes and fighting his tether.

He spotted the little girl right off, crouched beneath that bedroom window. Her brother was lying beside her, in the loose, expressive posture of a fainting woman. Both glittered with broken glass.

John stopped running and came up stealthily.

Just as he came back to where he'd slumped before, watching that bedroom window like a hawk:

The lights came on in the house, blindingly. All the lights in the house. My father staggered, reaching out.

In the window, Victor Caceres was neatly framed. He was stripped to the waist, and he had his trousers down to his knees, fucking Fernanda.

Dead, the woman was again calm. My father was standing so close, he could see the vermilion stain on her temple, and the dark puncture in her shirt where the bullet had gone in. Against the jolly orange walls, the dribbles of blood looked drab. My father crouched down and untied the rope from my wrist.

I bore it patiently, staring at my dead brother. When my father picked a shard of glass from my cheek, I kept still, solemnly watching his big hand. He whispered, although he knew I wouldn't understand, but he couldn't think of any Spanish, and he just thought a quiet voice would calm me:

"You wanna come along with me?"

I put my arms up to be lifted. He carried me away.

Mosquitoes covered his face and arms. Carrying me, he couldn't brush them away and he couldn't run. When he heard the jeeps, he was still within sight of that awful electric light.

He staggered out of the road. Of course there wasn't a bush any higher than his knee here, he finally just slid to the ground and lay flat. He mashed me down flat beside him, crooning *no tengo miedo, hija, no tengo miedo* because he couldn't remember the right words.

The nightmare got worse. He had a long time to reflect, and all he could think was, how awful this night was. He kept stroking my head, more to comfort himself.

There was rifle fire. There were screams that just went on. After a while, he could swear it was just repeating itself, it was a broken record playing the same horror noises over and over. *They're killing them all*, he thought. He knew he should wonder why, but he didn't, he just had to go and stop them, stop it, and he couldn't do a damn thing. Too many guns.

Finally there were only men's voices, distant and inconsequential. An engine started up, then another. He tried to count the jeeps as they passed. The last was the different, genteel drone of the Mercedes. That made John raise his head, incredulous that any man could survive what Victor Caceres had done.

Then he lay with his ear against his watch for a long time, listening to it tick.

"Well, kid," he said at last. "Let's just try our best to get out of here."

And he'd just got to his feet, and got me to my feet, when he heard the planes.

He stood there yelling, "That tears it! Goddamn it! Goddamn it!"

I started crying for the first time, staring at the angry man. He had to calm himself and crouch down to me, mumbling some kind of comforting nonsense. He had to get me to come into his lap, and hold me still while he opened his shirt and pulled it over my face as if that would protect me.

Of course they flew with no lights. There was nothing to see. Still he looked up, and for a moment mistook the Milky Way, powdery and bright, unencumbered by the lights of cities, for a luminous spray of germs.

He smelled germs, he tasted them salty in the back of his throat. That shirt was no use. No use. You just had to try. No use. His mind gave up and he began to sing, under his breath:

*one little, two little, three little Indians,*
*four little, five little, six little Indians,*
*seven little, eight little, nine little Indians,*
*ten little Indian boys.*
*one little two little three*

He couldn't remember the verses, he just sang the refrain over and over as the planes groaned and banked and finally vanished like everything else. I was squirming and he had to use his strength on me. Getting to his feet like that, with the kid fighting him all the way, it would have been funny any other time. That night it was the unfunniest thing that ever probably happened.

Then the walk ahead of him.

He walked and walked. I struggled and butted my head at the constraining shirt. The mosquitoes came and went, his face grew stiff. He let one leg kick at the bushes as he walked, making noise to ward off the jungle predators.

After a while I had fallen asleep.

A while after that he tugged the shirt away from my face, cautious as if taking off a bandage. He rested then, and stared at my sleeping baby features in the moonlight. When the mosquitoes settled on my cheeks, he flapped at them carefully, his mouth forming the word *shoo*. I turned in my sleep, reaching out, my hand clutching in the air, and he gave me his fingers to grasp. I pulled them to my chin, greedily, and eased.

366

He was near to tears as he'd ever been, then. He tried to think, what if it was his own son, but he hardly knew his son. That moment, the little girl in his arms was the only person in the world. The one life.

## Why you can't go home again

1    My father and I never developed any symptoms of *psittacosis*.

1.1  Eddie nearly died of it two weeks after Dad's return from Guatemala.

1.2  In the course of his high fevers, he suffered his first epileptic episode.

2    So I, the

T    tiny
U    ultra-
V    vulnerable
W    waif
X    X-ed out my father,
he gave his place up
to me/for the wild

superior yonders            Y
on
Z    beyond

## 33. Pullau Pangkor, Malaysia: Deus Ex Machina

– Denise concluded, and got to her feet. A ghost of sand slipped from her hand but vanished before it hit the beach. Her affectation seemed to have failed; she looked simply weary.

I said, "Thank you."

"Well, that's finished," she said, with a quick ferocity. She looked at Ralph and changed again, became sad and ashamed. "Don't look at me that way, would you? I don't know what . . ."

He said, "Are you all right?"

It was such a sensible question. In the midst of all the high drama, it seemed actually rude. I frowned at him, but Denise answered straightforwardly, "I'm all right. But I'm sad from all this. It's strange being here on the beach. I do feel very strange." She looked up at the sky, and then back at us, and then up at the sky. She said, abstracted, "Does anyone else feel strange?"

I felt <u>really fucking</u> strange but I didn't say. Ralph just came to me and took my hand. He was looking at the sky, too. It was shot through with cloud, the moon a russet blot. It seemed to tremble under its load of light.

And Denise walked down to the sea where my brother had walked down to the sea, she moved fluidly as if singing. At the labile hem of water, she stopped and tensed. She whispered something, then said aloud, "Oh, my God."

The brilliant lozenge appeared, superimposed on an ashen cloud.

It slipped to and fro as if frisking.

The insects' tweeting switched off. The sea alone moved.

Then the beam grew explosively: into our faces. Boomed. It filled the world and it was gone.

Denise Cadwallader was gone.

She really just wasn't there. The sea came and went as before, the sand made the same fuzzy drawings in the dark. The sky was shot through with the same clouds, and the inanimate moon stood where it had been, as if feigning innocence.

Her footprints were clear where she had crossed the wet beach. You could see where at the end she had gone up on tiptoe. Then the next wave filled them.

1    DENISE I TOTALLY ACTUALLY LOVED YOU [BUT YOU JUST FUCKING USED crossed out] IT KILLS ME I COULDN'T EVEN FACE THAT SO IT'S NOT YOUR FAULT.

CHRYSA I'M SORRY

I CAN'T DO ANY MORE HOPELESS SHIT FOR NO REASON. I'M GOING TO DROWN MYSELF SO THAT'S WHERE TO LOOK IF I CAN EVEN MANAGE THAT.

2    "Yeah, I had a lot of shit on this tape I won't mention. So this is like my thirtieth try to do this, and I'm almost, like, running gag territory."

(A long space of silence. Then a match struck. A few seconds later:)

"I guess I only wanted to say I love you, Chrysalis. I mean, totally I pray I don't get hit by a car and you listen to this while I'm still alive. But I always loved you more than anyone else, not like that's saying much. I just kind of, I mean, this is not like every time I did this this is what I said, I'm maybe just wasted.

"Oh, fuck. I'm going to have to tape this fucking thing again.

"Oh, fuck."

(A long space of silence. The tape breaks into the middle of "Stayin' Alive" by the BeeGees.)

3    When I was packing Eddie's ashes into our bag, wrapped in a shirt for safe-keeping:
3.1    The urn rattled. I shook it and it rattled again. Because I'd already broken the wax seal the day before, when I'd

had to peer in at the fine grit which meant nothing, the stopper came out easily. I carried it to the lamp.

3.2 The ashes were gone, and in their place was a stone; smooth, egg-shaped, white quartz. It had a crevice that glittered when you held the urn's opening to the light, and could be made out to represent a rounded E.

3.3 The stone was too large to have fit through the slender neck of the urn. It was a ship-in-a-bottle puzzle.

3.4 Now that it was in, it looked completely ordinary. It didn't look like a miraculous stone.

3.5 The whole was conveniently portable: unsettlingly like a souvenir.

We sit in the boarding lounge, waiting for our connecting flight. We've been talking all night, on the flight from Singapore, and our eyes feel like felt from wakefulness and dry air. We're not tired, though: we both keep mentioning that we're not tired. We just look very pale, and we're oddly clumsy.

They call to board disabled people and mothers with small children, and a flood of able-bodied adults streams past us. We watch them curiously, as if they're our first people.

Then Ralph says:

"Going back."

I wince. We both look at the crowded gate as if we'll see California. It strikes me that our lives might not change. Then I realize Eddie won't be there, and I look away.

"We could just stay here," I say. "After all, you are British."

He smiles nervously. "Actually, I've been putting off telling you this, but they may not let me back into the U.S. I overstayed my last visa by twelve years."

"Oh. That's pretty bad."

We laugh irresponsibly. Ralph won't be let in! Ha ha! Life down the drain! I say, laughing:

"Well, I'll come back to England with you. We'll get married! Obviously!"

"Obviously," he says, not laughing.

I continue, improvising: "We'll get married and go back to California. We'll sell the mansion and use the money to open a pottery shop. Then we'll have two children."

He says, "I couldn't have a pottery shop. It seems like going backwards."

"A furniture shop, then. We'll sell top-quality tables at a fair price."

I think of the furniture shop as salvation. From now on, things will be ordinary and good. Then Ralph says,

"You seem to have my whole life mapped out for me."

"Oh," I whine, wronged: "But I was trying to map it out in the way you would map it out, so that's actually ungrateful. Anyway, I don't know what we're going to do in the next ten minutes, as you're well aware."

They call to board first class. A few first-class people lurch to their feet. They don't even look rich, and I glare at them sulkily. They should make an effort, I think, forgetting that I'm rich.

Then Ralph says, anxious: "Well, let's try to stay together."

"Sure," I say, thinking, *Oh, of course we won't stay together, what garbage.*

They call to board rows 65 to 45. We stumble to our feet, noticing again our absurd tired demeanor in the absence of any tiredness. We join the unmoving queue. Ralph drops our only bag heavily and I stop myself from dropping to the floor and embracing my hurt brother. We move forward a little bit.

Then over the tannoy, they call: "Would Miss Moffat please come to the Assembly Point. Miss Moffat, please come to the Assembly Point."

A man behind us says, "Where your spider is waiting," and his friends all laugh.

"It's not me," I whisper to Ralph. "I don't −"

"No, of course," Ralph says, hoarse. "It's a coincidence."

We look at each other with a bleak superstition. We both smile although we're not tickled.

"I hope that was the last gasp," Ralph says, tense.

"Of coincidences?" I clarify unnecessarily. We stand

thinking. We move forward a little bit. I bring the bag along with a loving, herding motion of my foot, and consider that although the sudden appearance of a spaceship <u>seems</u> to prove a sly coherence in events, it is in fact just another odd event. Perhaps at random. Then my mind quits suddenly before I understand anything.

"Oh, well," I sigh. "We made it from Singapore, after all."

Ralph shrugs and turns away. Then he thinks again and takes my hand.

We move forward a little bit. I remember dressing for a Halloween party as Miss Moffat, with a large googly-eyed stuffed spider. My date stood me up and I sat all night on the couch with my spider, eating Orville Redenbacher popcorn and watching *Carrie*.

Then Ralph squeezes my hand. He says, "All right."

"All right?" I bend and pick up the bag with my free hand. "I don't like Eddie on the floor," I say kind of reproachfully.

He bends way way down and kisses my forehead. He says, "I want to marry you and open a furniture store."

"Oh, right," I say stupidly. "I hope we survive, then."

Then we're at the front and hand over our passports and get them back. We start down the bouncy tunnel. We go boing boing along. It's a happy-couple walk: I think officiously that this is what they should show in love montages in films, instead of people eating Chinese food and riding bicycles. Perhaps at the register of the furniture store, I could write screenplays. They would be innovative and thoughtful without sacrificing dramatic interest.

It's then, as we hand our tickets to the stewardess, that I first think of writing an account of our experiences, in the hope that others might learn from our mistakes. It would be highly fictionalized, of course, to save time on fact-checking.

The idea grows, and I already feel successful. Busily inventing a cool name for myself, I forget our worries. As I edge into my seat, with my fiancé's hand tender between my shoulderblades, I'm euphoric. The glee mounts and I can hardly sit, I press my hand to the scratched window.

Then, alongside the plane, in the sickly, wind-beset grass, I see a jogging white towel. I start, nonplussed, but when it stops, it's a cat. It crouches, looking up at the mammoth plane, inspecting it left to right, its tail alert. As it meets my eye, I guess, I am already looking up in the sky for God. Then a loathed thing drops behind me, I'm unsheathed:

The city courses on the deeps of the earth. Trees reach and fountain. The clouds and their mother lakes enter the powerful stone, the grass drinks them with its frail heels. This knowing is participation in its seamless play. It's a gladdened, headlong, adamantine life.

The cat pounces up into the misted undersky. I pounce along, maddeningly clean and aware. Somewhere Ralph cries out, frightened.

The clouds peel away from the blue to let me go

My name is Rosa Espuelas. I was born in Guatemala. When I was three years old, my life was saved by a stranger. He took me home with him and gave me a new name. I have no memory of my former life.

# APPENDICES

## Appendix A: Pro Blackjack

### Basic strategy

The following table shows what total you should achieve in your hand before you stop drawing to it:

**DEALER SHOWS**

|  | 2 | 3 | 4 | 5 | 6 | 7 | 8 | 9 | 10 | A |
|---|---|---|---|---|---|---|---|---|---|---|
| STAND ON | 13 | 13 | 13 | 12 | 12 | 17 | 17 | 17 | 17 | 17 |

If your hand includes an ace, the figures change as follows:

**DEALER SHOWS**

|  | 2 | 3 | 4 | 5 | 6 | 7 | 8 | 9 | 10 | A |
|---|---|---|---|---|---|---|---|---|---|---|
| STAND ON | 18 | 18 | 18 | 18 | 18 | 18 | 18 | 19 | 19 | 18 |

Those hands on which the player can "double down" should be doubled when the dealer shows:

| YOU HAVE | DOUBLE AGAINST |
|---|---|
| A, 7 | 3–6 |
| A, 6 | any card |
| A, 5 | 4–6 |
| A, 4 | 4–6 |
| A, 3 | 4–6 |
| A, 2 | 4–6 |

| YOU HAVE | DOUBLE AGAINST |
| :---: | :---: |
| A, A | 5, 6 (unless aces can be split) |
| 11 | any card |
| 10 | 2–9 |
| 9 | 2–6 |

Pairs should be split when the dealer shows the following:

| | |
| :---: | :---: |
| A, A | any card |
| 10, 10 | never |
| 9, 9 | 2–6 or 8, 9 |
| 8, 8 | any card |
| 7, 7 | 2–8 |
| 6, 6 | 2–7 |
| 5, 5 | never |
| 4, 4 | 5 |
| 3, 3 | 2–7 |
| 2, 2 | 2–7 |

## Card counting

Although pro players have devised an array of complex counting systems, the basic high-low count will pay as well as most. Likewise, while it is possible to alter your strategy according to the count, this pays so little, percentage-wise, that it would take hundreds of years of play for it to be felt.

When this is taken into account, card counting is insultingly easy. The principle is simple: because of the rules casino dealers play to, high cards give an advantage to the player and low cards give an advantage to the casino. By keeping track of how many high/low cards have already been dealt, we can know how rich in high/low cards the remaining decks are. Then, when there are many high cards remaining to be dealt, we place a very large bet. At all other times, we place the minimum bet. Because all these low- or no-count minimum bets are (statistically) losing hands, the "spread," or difference between the minimum and maximum allowable bets, is key in judging the value of a game. A large spread (e.g. 1–100) will pay much more than a small spread (e.g. 10–100). One counts as follows:

The cards 2, 3, 4, 5, 6 are counted as +1.
The cards 10, J, Q, K, A are counted as −1.
The cards 7, 8, 9 are not counted.

For example, the dealer deals:
J, 2, 6, A, 5, 7, 9, 2
The running count is now +2.

The running count, however, must be changed into a true count. One does this by dividing the running count by the number of <u>half-decks</u> remaining to be played. The game of blackjack is usually dealt from a 6-deck or 8-deck shoe: however, it will take some time for a significant running count to develop. Therefore, one is typically dividing by 5 or 2 rather than 12.

For every single point of true count, one may bet 1% of one's bankroll. No more. This is why a large bankroll is crucial: it is not worth beginning a counting game with less than (roughly) 20,000 dollars.

## Shuffle tracking

Basic shuffle tracking involves keeping track of areas of the deck which have very negative running counts (i.e. are rich in aces and tens). Then, when the cards are shuffled, one watches where those sections go. One can then bet for them as they are dealt.

Shuffle tracking is practiced by many but with little success, as it is nearly impossible to perform with accuracy.

## Ace tracking

Ace tracking depends on the fact that, if the player's first card is an ace, he/she immediately has a 52% advantage. That is, for every dollar the player bets, he/she will earn 52 cents. A player, therefore, who can predict when he will be dealt an ace, can earn money at a rate far in excess of a mere card counter.

In casinos, dealers pick up cards at the end of a hand in a predictable fashion: they sweep them up in a sort of reverse-domino effect, from right to left, each card sliding underneath its neighbor. Then they are put into a box, awaiting the shuffle when all 6 decks (for example) have been dealt.

The trick of ace tracking is to memorize the sequence of the last two cards which are slid underneath each ace. That is, if the two cards lying to the right of an ace are the Queen of Hearts and the four of Diamonds, one can memorize this and when, in the next deal, a Queen of Hearts is dealt, closely followed by a four of Diamonds, one knows an ace is likely to follow. Since the shuffle separates the cards out, and sometimes (but not very often, depending on how many times the cards are split and shuffled) entirely breaks up a sequence, the game is not exact. However, it is a higher percentage game than any counting game, and can be played with a smaller bankroll (say 10,000 dollars) for that reason.

It is generally easier to memorize sequences by assigning code names to all of the cards. For instance:

| | |
|---|---|
| Four of Diamonds: | FORD |
| Four of Clubs: | FUCK |
| Three of Hearts: | MOM |
| Three of Clubs: | MICK |
| Queen of Clubs: | QUACK |
| et cetera. | |

# Appendix B:

# What Happens To You After You Die

*Withheld.*